The
Last Days
of
Summer

Sophie Pembroke

ONE PLACE. MANY STORIES

HQ
An imprint of HarperCollins*Publishers* Ltd.
1 London Bridge Street
London SE1 9GF

This paperback edition 2017

1
First published in Great Britain by
HQ, an imprint of HarperCollinsPublishers Ltd. 2016

ISBN: 978-0-00-821149-3

Printed and bound by
CPI Group (UK) Ltd, Croydon, CR0 4YY

Sophie Pembroke write~~s~~ ~~very~~ ~~British~~

~~Romance, Avon and HQ~~ turn or

been dreaming, reading and writing romance ever si~~nce~~
she read her first Mills & Boon as part of her English
Literature degree at Lancaster University, so getting to
write romantic fiction for a living really is a dream come
true!

Born in Abu Dhabi, Sophie grew up in Wales and
now lives in a little Hertfordshire market town with her
scientist husband, her incredibly imaginative eight-year-
old daughter, and her adventurous, adorable toddler son.
In Sophie's world, happy is for ever after, everything
stops for tea, and there's always time for one more page…

Website: www.SophiePembroke.com

In memory of my own grandparents,
Elfed and Olwen Whitley.

For everything you gave me that helped make me
who I am today.

I miss you, every second.

Prologue

*"Home isn't a place, Grace. It's a feeling.
An overwhelming emotion that, once you've
felt it, you can't live without."*

"A bit like love, then?" Grace asked.

*I nodded. "Sometimes, I think they might be
one and the same thing."*

Going Home, by Nathaniel Drury (1980)

I like to think that there's a book for any feeling, any emotion, any problem. In my world, the cure for what ails you is always a new story, or, sometimes even better, an old one. Some might say it's a distraction, a diversion from whatever is wrong with your reality. But for me, I often find the answers I'm seeking within the pages of a book – or at least by the time I've followed a story from beginning to end, I have a new perspective on my own problems.

I think I read more books in the two years after I left Rosewood than ever before in my life. Or since.

Sometimes I'd read romances, to remind myself that love *could* end happily. Sometimes I read fantasy novels, for the joy of a high quest and magical solutions. Sometimes I read literary fiction, to experience the world through another's kaleidoscope. Sometimes I read children's books, to escape to a simpler time.

And whenever I felt homesick, I read my grandfather's books, and imagined I could hear him speaking the words to me.

I was homesick that Saturday morning in May, when the first phone call came.

Dressed in my pyjamas and dressing gown, I'd decided to laze around my tiny flat in Perth, Scotland, drinking too-strong black coffee and nibbling on endless pieces of toast, until I felt better. But instead, I found myself moving around the flat restlessly, a copy of *Going Home* in my hand, absorbing a page or two at a time before my own memories overtook me.

Nathaniel always claimed that the house in the story wasn't Rosewood, the same way that *Biding Time* wasn't about him and my grandmother, Isabelle. But as with all his books, every time I reread them, I found another hint, another clue, that led me towards the truth. Like a treasure hunt Nathaniel had laid out for me, he hid patches of his own history, his own life, in his fiction, waiting for me to find them.

Like the house. However much he denied it, the description of Honeysuckle House in *Going Home* matched Rosewood to the letter. Not just the honey-coloured brick, symmetrical Georgian design, or the twelve chimneys, or even the white-marble steps leading up to the front door. There was something about the feel of the place – the way he described the sun on the terrace when the gin and tonics were being poured, or the coolness of the middle room when the rain came down outside – that made it feel like home to me.

I flipped a few pages through the book again, pausing at a description of Honeysuckle House:

When the afternoon sun alighted on the windows, the whole house lit up, as if it were night and every light

*inside had been left on. Inside, the house could be cold –
Grace's mother had decorated it in the latest styles, with
lots of white and sharp edges. But she couldn't cool the
natural warmth of the house as I looked upon it, or
sharpen the corners of the worn golden brick exterior.
And when the house filled with people... Ah, that was
when Honeysuckle House came alive. And so did Grace.*

I put the book aside. I didn't need Agnes's descriptions
of Grace's house – not when I had my own memories
of Rosewood. Of the Rose Garden, the Orangery, the
sweeping staircase that dominated the main hallway.
Of Nathaniel's study, every inch crammed with books
and papers.

And of Nathaniel, most of all. The way his voice
boomed and echoed around Rosewood, or how he
poured his drinks too strong, or how every meal became
story time, somehow. How every little event of his day
became a hysterical monologue by the time he'd finished
telling it. And how he knew to listen, sometimes, and
just be there – a warm, comforting, reassuring presence
I'd relied on my whole life.

I'd always have my memories. It was just hard to
imagine not knowing when I'd next be there in person.
When I'd see my family again.

The phone rang, and I put my book aside, reaching
past my empty coffee cup to answer it.

"Saskia? It's your grandfather." As if I couldn't tell
from his voice. "Now, tell me, did you see the ridiculous
invitations your grandmother picked out for this Golden
Wedding thing? You *have* to come home and help me
through it."

I frowned. "Golden Wedding?"

"Fifty years of wedded bliss and she wants another
damned party." Nathaniel's voice dropped low, as if he

were afraid someone might be listening. "Don't worry, I've got something in mind to fire up the festivities. You really don't want to miss it, Kia."

It wasn't as if I didn't *want* to go home for my grandparents' Golden Wedding anniversary. Isabelle and Nathaniel Drury knew how to throw a party, after all, and this was sure to be a big one. The sort of shindig people talked about for decades to come. In fact, people still told stories about the first ever party they held at Rosewood, back in 1966. There were reports in the society pages. Couples met at Isabelle's parties, or got engaged – or even pregnant. But they weren't the sort of parties I imagined when I thought of the sixties – I'd seen photos. Isabelle's parties required full evening wear, champagne, important people – and enough drama to keep people gossiping for weeks afterwards.

There hadn't been a party at Rosewood since Ellie's wedding, as far as I knew. I didn't want to miss it – and I *really* didn't want to be the person at the hypothetical future dinner table saying, "I don't know, I wasn't there," when someone asked, "And do you remember the bit when…"

I just didn't know how welcome I'd be when I got to Rosewood.

"I didn't get an invitation," I said, as lightly as I could manage. "But I take your word for it that they're awful."

"Hideous," Nathaniel said, with an audible shudder. He paused, then asked, "Did you really not get one?"

"Nope." I ran my hand over the cover of *Going Home*. Apparently, I wasn't. Isabelle knew every tiny detail of party etiquette, and obeyed it all, when it suited her. If she'd wanted me there, I'd have received an invitation. The fact that I hadn't – or even any notice that the party was happening at all – told me exactly how welcome I'd be.

"Well, that's stupid," Nathaniel said. "You should have done. Consider this call your invite."

I gave a small laugh. "I'm not sure that's quite how it works."

"It is now. It's my party too, isn't it?"

"Not really." I was pretty sure that, in Isabelle's head, the man she married was entirely incidental to the party she was throwing to celebrate that aforementioned marriage.

"Then I'm reclaiming it. And you're invited." There was a rustle of paper on the other end of the line, and I leapt on the noise as a way to change the subject.

"What are you working on?" I asked, trying to be interested in his answer. It had to be better than thinking about how my own grandmother didn't want me there for a family party.

"I've been thinking about the nature of truth in fiction," he replied, instantly distracted, as I'd known he would be.

"Truth in fiction?" I echoed, topping up my coffee. That sounded like a fairly epic procrastination exercise. I wondered what Nathaniel was supposed to be writing that required such distraction; he never liked to talk much about his works in progress until they were shiny and published and winning awards.

"Are all stories just reflections of ourselves? Are even the fictions we write based on the truths of our own lives?" I tried and failed to come up with a satisfactory response to what I hoped was a rhetorical question. "Take your work at the paper," Nathaniel went on, apparently not noticing that I hadn't responded. "How much do your own life and your life experiences colour the reports you write?"

Since most of what I wrote for the *Perth Herald* was based entirely on press releases, and my main concern was getting them all in on time, probably not a lot. But, on the other hand, I didn't want Nathaniel thinking that I wasn't properly investing in my artistic side, so I said, "Probably more than I know," in what I hoped was a thoughtful voice.

"Exactly my point! So, the conclusion I've reached is that it is only through knowing ourselves, understanding our true selves, that we can hope to create anything meaningful in fiction."

"That's... interesting." Did I have any more bread left for toast, I wondered? Not getting invited to a family party definitely deserved self-pity toast.

"So, you agree, then?"

"Absolutely." Maybe even chocolate spread.

"Perfect! We can discuss it more when you visit this summer. For the Golden Wedding party."

I froze, halfway through putting more bread in the toaster. "I can't come, Nathaniel. Not if I'm not wanted there."

"*I* want you there," he said. "And I'm sure the others do too, even if they don't know it yet. You wouldn't let an old man down now, would you? Leave him to face *all* his wife's acquaintances while wearing white tails and a bow tie? I'll probably even have to make a speech..."

"I'm fairly sure you can cope with a party with your friends without me," I said drily. "Besides, you love making speeches. You'll survive."

"Oh, I don't know. You haven't heard what I've got to say in this one, yet. Really, Kia. You don't want to miss it. Trust me."

There was something in his voice, a hint of mischief and possible magic, something I'd missed so much over the last two years, that it tugged at my heart to hear it again, trying to lead me home.

I wanted to be there. I wanted to go home, more than anything.

And so I said, "Okay. I'll come." Even though my brain was screaming that it was a terrible idea. Sometimes you have to let your heart win.

Nathaniel whooped. "Fantastic! Send me your train times. It's August twenty-fourth. See you there!"

And with that, he hung up, leaving me wondering what on earth I might have to wear to a garden party thrown by Isabelle, not to mention the rest of the weekend.

After all, Rosewood was another world, a throwback to a time that had passed before Nathaniel and Isabelle even bought the house. We always dressed for dinner at Rosewood, and had pre-dinner drinks on the terrace if the sun shone. Rosewood didn't have Wi-Fi, or video games, and Isabelle had even hidden the telly in the middle room, down the darkest downstairs corridor. Rosewood had stories, and mystery, and ghosts, and champagne… and my family, who hadn't invited me home for the Golden Wedding.

Maybe, if I could find the right costume, the right clothes to blend in, no one would think to ask what I was doing there in the first place.

Chapter One

*"We'll take it," I said, making Bella laugh as
she looked up at the imposing house.*

*"You can't just buy it! We haven't even
stepped inside yet."*

*I pulled her close against my side.
"I don't need to. This is it. This is home."*

Biding Time, by Nathaniel Drury (1967)

Two long years away, and the first person I saw upon
my return to Rosewood was the ghost. Even if I didn't
quite realise it at the time.

I'll admit, I was preoccupied. I hadn't planned on
going home so soon, not until Nathaniel called and
insisted, and the temptation was too great to resist.
Oh, I'd assumed I'd go back eventually, for a visit,
at least. But two years away didn't seem like enough.
Two Christmases, two birthdays, two anniversaries –
Ellie couldn't possibly have forgiven me so soon.

This was a mistake. Which is why I was loitering in
the Rose Garden instead of going inside.

The walled Rose Garden is one of my favourite
spots at Rosewood, especially at midsummer, when it's
overflowing with flowers. As children, Ellie and I would
mix up buckets of perfume from the petals: pungent

flower water we'd sell to charitable passers-by at the end of the driveway. This year, however, it seemed that someone else had got there first.

Almost all the yellow rose bushes had been decapitated, leaving only stalks, leaves and thorns. As I blinked at the empty spaces where the flowers should be, I thought for a moment that I saw someone standing across the flower bed – a girl, younger than me, with long dark hair and pale features. The summer sun shone through her skin, lighting her up from the inside, like a creature from one of my grandfather's more fantastical stories, only existing between one second and the next. Because when I opened my eyes, I was alone again, standing outside the house that was supposed to be my home, wondering if I'd be welcomed or dismissed.

Wasn't that Rosewood all over? A place out of time, more fiction than real it seemed sometimes. Like Nathaniel had pulled the house itself from the pages of one of his books, complete with secrets and mysteries – even the paranormal.

Before I could fully process what I'd seen, my grandmother's voice echoed out from the terrace, imperious and impatient, just as I remembered. Isabelle Drury was the mistress of Rosewood, and she never forgot it, not for a moment. It was more than a home to her; it was her kingdom, and she ruled it – and us, her willing subjects.

"We'll need more of the eucalyptus. You can go and tell her."

There was no response, and I found myself waiting, breath stuck in my chest, all thoughts of the strange girl forgotten. I wanted to hear another familiar voice, there, in the buzzing summer air, with its insects and pollen and freshly cut grass, rather than over a too-clear phone line. I wanted to feel like I was really home again.

I hadn't intended to come back to Rosewood so soon. But now that I was here, I couldn't imagine how I'd stayed away so long.

"And don't forget the etched vase," my grandmother's voice rang out again. I smoothed down my hopelessly creased pale linen skirt and stepped out of the Rose Garden. Time to face the music.

Isabelle had moved back inside, and whichever family member she'd been ordering about had obviously rushed off to fulfil her demands; haste was always a good idea when dealing with my grandmother's requests. The terrace was deserted again.

"In and out," I muttered to myself as I retrieved my suitcase. "Minimum casualties." That was the plan. This was a tester weekend. If it wasn't dreadful beyond all measure, maybe I could come back for Christmas. Start finding a place here again. Maybe even find forgiveness, eventually.

But first I had to make it through the weekend.

I climbed the few steps to the glass-panelled doors that led from the terrace into the house, pushing down the hope beating in my chest. It was all so familiar, as if at any moment Ellie, aged seven and a half, could come running out carrying dolls for a tea party, Isabelle following with the second-best china tea set. At least, until I passed through the empty drawing room and reached the cool shade of the hallway.

The tiled floor of the wide entrance hall was covered in buckets, vases, stands, and what appeared to be chicken wire. Bright yellow roses and dark green foliage were stuffed and stacked into any and all containers; loose leaves and petals littered the ground. And in the middle of it all sat Isabelle, head bent over a small crystal vase filled with two blooms and a few sprigs of lavender, sunlight from the windows either side of the front door shining silver on her hair.

I leant my overfilled suitcase against the wall, and asked, "Can I help?"

Isabelle jerked her head up to look at me, and she lost her grip on the vase in her hand. It tumbled to the floor, spilling water across the floor tiles and crushing one of the rose's stems. I darted forward and righted the vase, miraculously still intact. For one, brief moment, I saw the depth of the shock she must be feeling flash across her face, before she recovered her composure.

She really hadn't expected me to come. As much as I knew the lack of an invitation wasn't a mistake, I realised a small part of me had been hoping against hope that it was. That I hadn't been forgotten, cut out.

Except I had.

"Hi," I said, trying to look less nervous than I felt.

"Kia, darling, really!" Isabelle smiled, but she still looked a little shaken. Older, too, I realised. Faded. Frail. "You should have told us you were coming. You can't just show up, scare people half to death."

I reached my arms around my grandmother's body, feeling bones and skin. "I did tell you. Well, I told Nathaniel I'd be here, when he rang to invite me. I even gave him my train times when he called last week."

He'd wanted to check I was still coming. I wasn't sure that it was a good sign that Nathaniel was so desperate to have me there to witness whatever he had planned to add excitement to Isabelle's party. It almost made me an accessory.

Not to mention the fact he hadn't told anyone else he'd invited me. What did that say about the welcome I should expect?

Isabelle wriggled out of the embrace and, regaining her natural poise, set about choosing a new rose for her vase. "And isn't it just like him not to mention it."

"Perhaps he wanted it to be a surprise?" I suggested, feeling even more uneasy. I'd honestly assumed he'd have at least told them I was coming. I should have known better. This all had the stink of one of Nathaniel's Plans – and they seldom ended well.

"I'm sorry, Isabelle. I really thought Nathaniel would have told you." Isabelle sniffed, but looked faintly mollified, so I went on: "Where's everyone else?"

Isabelle checked her watch and ticked them off on her fingers. "Your parents have taken Caroline to buy a dress for the party, as the one I picked for her was apparently unacceptable to her. Your grandfather has the DO NOT ENTER sign up on his door, so I choose to believe that he is writing. Therese is probably still wandering the woods aimlessly, and has forgotten she's supposed to be collecting foliage for me. Edward's here, though. He can help you with your bag."

No mention of the two people I wanted to know about most, I noticed. Had it been Ellie Isabelle sent for vases? I wanted to ask a thousand questions. About how Ellie was, how she'd been, since I left. Whether she still hated me as much as I imagined she must. And, most urgently, what had Ellie told our grandmother about why I left? From Isabelle's reaction, I suspected that she knew more of my secrets than I'd like. When I'd left, while Ellie and Greg were on their honeymoon, what happened had been a secret between the three of us. I couldn't imagine that Ellie would want anyone else to know, any more than I did. But it was clear that Isabelle knew *something*.

God, what if everybody knew? My hands started to tremble at the very idea, a horrible sense of dread seeping through my veins. What if my secret was out, and I was walking into a house full of people who utterly – and rightly – despised me?

It was enough to send me running back to the train station, and the safety of my flat, hundreds of miles away in Scotland. But then, something curious about her list struck me.

"Edward?" I asked, trying to shift my focus away from my fear. I was pretty up to date on family members, despite my absence, and I was sure that there hadn't been an Edward when I'd left.

"Yes." Isabelle moved to the stairs and called, in as genteel a manner as possible, "Edward!"

I went and picked up my suitcase. If my grandmother had started hallucinating household help, I'd probably better get used to carrying things around myself.

To my relief, when I turned back a tall, slim stranger was leaning on the banister at the top of the stairs, looking utterly at home. "You hollered, Isabelle?" The man raised a sandy eyebrow. "I don't suppose that you were just missing my company?"

"Always, dear," Isabelle said, absently. "I thought that you might like to help Saskia with her bags, while I call Sally and Tony and inform them that their prodigal daughter has returned."

"Might like to?" Edward asked, taking the stairs at a lazy jog, long legs making easy work of the wide steps.

"Would if I asked you to," Isabelle clarified.

"Of course." Edward hopped over the last few stairs and landed on one foot on the hall tiles. "And I assume that this is Saskia," he said, turning on his heel to face me. He looked a little older than my twenty-six, with the start of tiny laugh lines around his eyes. He wasn't smiling now, though, and he didn't seem in any way pleased to meet me. In fact the coldness I felt from him suggested exactly the opposite.

"I've heard a lot about you from Ellie," he said, which explained the chill. Even if she hadn't spilled the whole story to this stranger, I was under no illusion that she'd have spoken about me in anything approaching glowing terms.

"Oh good. Listen, I'm fine carrying my own case, honestly." I had four whole days stretching ahead to spend time with people who disapproved of me. I didn't really feel up to starting off with someone I'd never even met before.

Edward took two long strides across the hallway and snatched up my bag. "Not a problem." He gave me a short, tight smile, then swung round to face Isabelle, suitcase swaying in his hand. "Which room is she in?"

"My room," I said, as if that should be obvious, at the same time as Isabelle said, "You'd better put her in the Yellow Room."

"Right-ho." Edward hefted the case up the first few stairs.

"Hang on. What's wrong with my room?" It was, after all, my room. I snatched the case out of Edward's hands.

"Caroline's sleeping in it." Isabelle looked vaguely regretful for a moment, but it didn't last. "But really, Kia, it is a little girl's room, and Caro's too big for the box room, now. She's almost ten. She needs her own space."

Caroline – our last-minute-accident baby sister, and the shocking evidence that our parents were still having sex into my secondary-school years. How could she be ten already? How much had she changed in the last two years? How much had I missed?

"It's my room," I said again, even as my brain acknowledged the ridiculousness of this statement.

"Your room is the candy-stripe confection in the attic?" Edward reached out and retrieved the case from my hands again, his long slim fingers brushing against mine as he took the handle. I gritted my teeth against the slight shiver his touch gave me, even in the warm summer air.

"My grandfather helped me decorate that room." One long summer when my parents were abroad and Ellie and I had stayed at Rosewood for six glorious weeks, instead of sweating it out in our semi in the suburbs of Manchester. It had taken an age, because Nathaniel had been working on *Rebecca's Daughters* at the time and would regularly disappear into his study for hours in the middle of painting the walls.

Edward grinned. "Strange. Nathaniel never struck me as a candyfloss kind of guy."

"Who are you, anyway?" It didn't seem fair. I'd been home mere minutes, and I was already being mocked by strangers.

"I'm your grandfather's assistant," Edward said, making his way up the stairs, lugging the case alongside him.

I looked to Isabelle for confirmation. "I know," she said. "We were surprised too. But he's been here over a year, now." And no one had mentioned him to me – not even Nathaniel. Which said more about how far I'd run away than the seven hours it had taken me to get back by train that day.

Edward reached the top of the stairs and paused, obviously waiting for me to follow. I looked at him with a new appreciation. The last assistant Nathaniel had hired, six months before I left for the wilds of

Scotland, had lasted approximately a fortnight before falling down those very stairs in his hurry to get away from Rosewood. Granddad did not work well with assistants.

"Well, okay then." Picking up my handbag, I turned back to Isabelle. "Do I really have to sleep in the Yellow Room?"

"It has a lovely view of the Rose Garden, darling."

"But all the roses are in here!" I waved an arm at the overflowing buckets of blooms.

"Don't be melodramatic, dear. There are plenty of roses left. We're only using the yellow ones, anyway." She plucked a few leaves from the bottom of a rose stem and added the flower to the bucket. "Besides, these are just for the house displays. The florist is doing the stands and centrepieces outside."

That sounded like an awful lot of flowers. "But the Yellow Room's all... yellow." There was a muffled snort of laughter from the top of the stairs, and I mentally glared at Edward, wondering what it was about Rosewood that made me thirteen again. "Never mind. I'll go get freshened up, and maybe by the time I get back my parents will have found their way home."

"Perhaps. Kia..." Isabelle paused, as if trying to decide whether to speak again or not. Finally, she said, "Did your grandfather say particularly why he wanted you to come back?"

I blinked in surprise. "It's a family occasion. I assume he wanted us all here."

Isabelle gave a sharp nod, and turned back to her buckets of roses. "Of course."

Confused, I turned to follow Edward. But I couldn't help wondering what Isabelle thought Nathaniel was up to this time.

"There you go, then," Edward said, placing my bags on the window-seat. "I'll leave you to settle in."

I nodded, gazing around at the sunshine walls and golden blankets, wondering how many guests had visited twice, after being put to stay in the Yellow Room.

Probably all of them – at least any that had been invited back. A weekend at Rosewood had been a highly sought-after ticket, back in the day. Well, according to Isabelle, anyway.

"Actually," I said, trying to sound decisive, rather than just unsettled, "I think I might go and find Great-Aunt Therese. It must be almost time for her afternoon tea." Never mind that I'd spent seven hours on various trains and really could do with a shower; first, I needed to feel *home* again. And after that very lacklustre welcome from Isabelle, I knew I wasn't going to find that feeling in the Yellow Room. At least Great-Aunt Therese might be pleased to see me.

Assam tea and a Victoria Sandwich in Therese's cottage garden were more familiar to me than even my attic bedroom. Nathaniel had moved his younger sister into the cottage on the edge of Rosewood's gardens as soon as her husband died, the year I was born, when she was only forty-one. Almost every afternoon that I had spent at Rosewood since had always paused for tea with Therese at half past three, first with my mum and Ellie, and later just the two of us.

Edward shrugged indifferently. "I'll come with you, then. May as well see if she's finished collecting leaves for your grandmother. Pre-empt being sent."

"If you're Granddad's assistant, why aren't you assisting him rather than Grandma?" I asked, as we trotted out into the sunlight. It felt odd to be at Rosewood with a stranger – especially one who seemed far more at home than I did.

"He's having one of his Great British Writer days. Doesn't like anyone hovering, in case it disturbs his flow." Which might explain why Edward had lasted longer than the other assistants. A keen sense of when to get lost.

"So you're just making yourself useful until he needs you again?"

"Got to earn my keep somehow." Edward gave me a quick smile as he turned off the drive and onto the long, rambling path that led, eventually, to Therese's cottage.

He didn't seem inclined to any further conversation, and I found my attention drawn instead to the familiar sights along the way – the huge magnolia that overhung the path, the strange fountain statue that Isabelle had found on holiday in France one year and had shipped back, the wild flower patch my mother planted which, over the course of a few summers, overtook almost a whole lawn.

As we reached the bend in the main path that led down to the abandoned ruin of the old stables and Therese's tiny cottage, my great-aunt appeared in the distance. Therese was unmistakable with her 1950s silhouette of full skirt and tight cardigan even when, as now, her arms were full of eucalyptus leaves.

Edward squinted up into the sun, the light bleaching his sandy hair even paler. "This looks like another of those 'earn my keep' moments," he said. "Isabelle will only send me back for them later, anyway." He jogged away down the path to relieve Therese of her leafy burden. He had a point; Isabelle never came down to Therese's cottage if she could send someone else. In fact, I didn't think I'd *ever* seen her there. "I'll take these up to the house for you, Mrs Williams," I heard Edward say. "Save you the trouble, since I'm heading back anyway. Besides, you've got a visitor."

Therese's pale blue eyes widened and her red lips pursed as I came close, and I wondered what changes she saw in me. But then she smiled, and I was eighteen again, home from university as a surprise one weekend, folded into her expensively perfumed embrace and thoroughly kissed, leaving lipstick marks on my cheeks. Therese was an anachronism, a throwback to a decade she'd only just been born for, with her fifties costumes and curled and pinned hair. But she was a part of Rosewood for me, every bit as much as Isabelle's cocktails before dinner and Nathaniel's stories.

"It's so good to have you home," she said, leading me inside, and I blinked away unexpected tears as I realised just how much I had missed her. At least someone was pleased to see me.

Therese's cottage was as I had left it, filled with knick-knacks and jugs full of sweet peas and dishes laden with glass bead necklaces. The only difference, as far as I could see, was the vast collection of clothes that hung from every hook and corner and ledge in the lounge. And the hallway. And running up the stairs. Dresses and skirts and blouses and coats and handbags, with gloves and scarves and tops and shoes spilling out from old steamer trunks, stacked carelessly against the walls.

Therese had always been a bit of a clothes horse, but this was taking things to extremes, even for her.

I peered into the lounge from the hallway, and saw that in amongst all the accessories, my favourite photo of her still sat on the mantelpiece. Therese, aged nineteen, pale and pouting in black-and-white with crisply waving hair surrounding challenging pale eyes. It must have been taken in the tail end of the sixties, I'd worked out once, but Therese looked like a screen siren from thirties Hollywood. It was one of a very few photos I'd seen of Therese out of her fifties costume, and even that was out of sync with the rest of the world – but fitted perfectly at Rosewood.

Rosewood existed in a bubble all of its own, out of time, because that was the way Nathaniel liked it. I wondered absently how Edward was coping with the lack of internet at Rosewood. Maybe I'd ask him later.

Picking up the picture frame, I studied the photo, finding familiar lines in the much younger face. She kept it up as a reminder, Therese always said. A reminder that she'd been beautiful once. Before life happened.

Turning to watch her potter around the tiny kitchen, filling the kettle and warming the pot, I knew that she was still beautiful. Why had she never remarried? "Once was enough," she always said, but she'd only been forty-one when Great-Uncle George had died. Therese would have been quite a catch, with her perfectly pinned hair, slim waist, beautiful outfits, and her pale blue eyes. She and Isabelle together as young women must have been a formidable sight.

Great-Uncle George had always been a little bit of a mystery. He'd died before I was born, so all I really had to go on were occasional snatches of parental conversation, when the adults thought I wasn't listening. I'd asked, once, but hadn't really received any satisfactory answers.

As far as Ellie and I had been able to piece together, George had been some hotshot trader in the city when he met Therese and they'd fallen instantly in love. They'd married shortly after and gone to live in London, where he showered his new bride with lavish gifts of jewels and dresses. Isabelle, it seemed, was always a little sore on this point.

Still, and this was the part that didn't make any sense, when George had suffered a fatal heart attack at the age of only forty-seven, creditors had swooped in and taken the house, the furniture, the cars, and most of the jewels. Therese had showed up at Rosewood with a suitcase of evening gowns, planning to stay only until she was back on her feet, and she had never left.

Isabelle mentioned that part often, pointedly, usually when Nathaniel and Therese had their heads together, laughing over some private, shared joke the way only siblings could. The way Ellie and I used to.

In fifteen years' time, would I be back at Rosewood, begging asylum again? And if so, would Ellie resent my presence as obviously as Isabelle had always resented Therese's? Probably.

"We'll take tea in the garden," Therese said decisively, smoothing a lace cloth over a plain silver tray, and laying out the china cups, sugar bowl, milk jug, and a plate of chocolate-covered ginger biscuits. "Will you bring the pot, Kia?"

Wrapping the handle of the delicate teapot with a clean tea towel, I did as I was told, and followed Therese out through the back door into her tiny, hedged garden.

Therese's flower beds were tended and nurtured daily, and carefully trained to appear as a hodgepodge cottage garden. Lupins and delphiniums and foxgloves loomed over fuchsias and snapdragons; sweet peas clambered up canes set against the cottage wall, sending their familiar scent past me on the breeze.

In the middle was a small, circular patio, occupied by a wrought-iron bistro table and two chairs, glowing warm in the late afternoon sun.

Therese settled her tray down on the table, took the pot from me and motioned for me to sit down.

"So," she said, pouring the first cup, "you've come home." The 'at last' went unsaid.

I nodded, picking up a biscuit to nibble. "Nathaniel called and asked me to. Said he had plans for the Golden Wedding."

"God save us from my brother's plans." Therese settled into her seat. "I'm glad he did, anyway. I was worried that your invitation might go mysteriously astray if it was left to Isabelle."

I winced. "I never did actually receive an invitation." Isabelle was always meticulous about sending invitations. I remember being made to handwrite invites for my eighth birthday party, not only to all my classmates, but also my own sister, even though she was sitting next to me as I wrote it. If Isabelle had wanted me there, I'd have been sent an invitation. And the fact I hadn't... Well, it stung like a needle pressed up against my heart.

"Typical Isabelle," Therese said, selecting the biscuit with the most chocolate coating. "They were hideous, anyway."

"So Nathaniel said." I sighed. "I can't believe he didn't tell anyone I was coming."

"I imagine that you're part of Nathaniel's plan. You know how he likes surprising people," Therese said. "More fun that way. Besides..." she laid a hand on mine "...this is your home. You have as much right to be here as anyone else." Maybe I could just stay in Therese's cottage for the duration, I thought.

Therese polished off the cookie and reached for her teacup. "Now, tell me about Scotland."

So I did. I told her about my flat on the edge of Perth, and how it wasn't much to look at from the outside, but I'd finally got the inside the way I wanted it – cosy and bright. I told her about the newspaper, about my job, and when she said, "But what are the prospects like? When are we going to read you in the *Guardian*?" I distracted her with a story about a police press conference on an operation to confiscate alcohol from teens in the local park that had to be curtailed when half the cans and bottles went missing.

Therese laughed in the right places, but somehow I still got the impression that she was just humouring me. And, as I finished my last story and my cup of tea, she pounced.

"So, tell me about your young man," she said, picking up the pot and refilling my cup. "Because I can't believe you haven't got one, pretty girl like you."

"Just one?" I laughed, hoping vainly to throw her off the scent. Yes, there was a man, of sorts. But Duncan and I were casual, fun… and just a little bit too complicated to explain to an elderly relative. Still, it might not be a bad idea to let everyone know that I'd moved on, that I had a new life, a new romance in Perth. Even if that wasn't quite the truth.

"Only one that means something, I'm sure." Her voice was placid and immovable. "So, tell me about him."

"Well, his name's Duncan," I said, sifting through my mind for what could be considered safe to talk about, and how to say it without using the words 'friends with benefits'. "He works with me – he's our new editor, actually. Brought in from Edinburgh earlier this year."

"Ah, so it's all quite new, then?" Therese leant forward. "I understand. Still all flowers and romance and sex all day on Sundays. Still in that private, special world where there's only the two of you."

Quite aside from the fact that hearing my great-aunt talking about all-day sex sessions had rendered me incapable of speech, there was just no way I was going to explain to her that, actually, it was less flowers and romance and more the second part, so I just smiled weakly and nodded.

Therese patted my hand and said, "I understand," again.

"Anyway," I said, regaining my voice, just in time to change the subject. "I meant to ask – what's with the clothes shop inside?"

Her face lit up with an excitement I'd only ever seen on her before at the Harrods sale. "So you noticed my little enterprise! Caro helped me set it up."

I wasn't quite sure when my baby sister had become an established business guru, but then, I still wasn't entirely sure what the business was. "Really."

"Oh yes. She figured out with me how to get an account on eBay, and PayPal, and how to list things and set prices. Turned out that there was quite the market for some of my old evening dresses and such." Therese smiled a little ruefully. "Only it takes a lot of restraint to only sell, and not be tempted to buy."

"So, all that stuff inside…"

"Waiting to be sold on," Therese said, firmly. "See, it turns out that a lot of people want to get into vintage wear, but don't know where to start, or what size to buy. So that's my USP."

Which sounded more like something you'd use to track ghosts than sell clothes. "USP?"

"Unique selling point. They send me their measurements, and a photo, and a bit of information about them and what they want the clothes for, and I put together a one-of-a-kind vintage outfit, including all accessories, for their specified occasion."

I blinked. That was actually a really good idea. "That's… great."

In a sudden movement, Therese was on her feet, motioning for me to stay where I was. "Actually, I have something that would be perfect for you," she said. "For tonight. Just wait here."

She was back within moments, holding out a navy dress on a satin padded hanger. "To wear for dinner."

I reached out a hand to touch it. The dress was of a style that had been popular in the 1930s, and the cut was exquisite, with fluted cap sleeves and a silky bow at the neckline, above the narrow waist belt. The cotton was soft and worn under my fingertips, but the colours were still crisp and bright. It was only as I looked closer that I realised; this was the dress Therese had worn in the photo on the mantle.

"It should fit, I think," she said, pushing the hanger into my hands. "You've lost weight since you've been away. Hold it up against yourself." I did as I was told, and she looked at me critically.

"It's lovely," I said, swishing the skirt from side to side. "But you don't think it's a little… too much?" Even at Rosewood, dressing for dinner didn't usually require evening gowns, as such. Not that this was – it was just a hundred times nicer than anything I had in my suitcase.

"Nonsense," Therese said. "George always said that a person could never really be overdressed – merely better dressed than everyone else. Now, you'll need the shoes and a bag too, of course. You're a six, yes? Come with me."

She trotted back into the cottage and I followed obediently. Maybe a makeover was just what I needed to get through the rest of the visit. Maybe Ellie wouldn't remember what I'd done if I looked like someone else.

I returned to the main house some time later, laden down with hangers and bags, to find the place deserted.

Assuming that people were getting changed for dinner, I followed suit and sneaked up the stairs to my allotted room, pulling a face at the yellow walls as they glowed in the slowly fading sunlight.

On the other hand, I realised, the one good thing about the Yellow Room was that it had an en suite. I decided to take advantage of it, hoping that a shower might wash away the ache that comes from sitting on trains too long, and the tension that came simply from being home. Besides, tea with my great-aunt had left my head overflowing with thoughts, and some hot and steamy water was the best way I knew to flush them out.

The shower didn't help as much as I'd hoped. In less than an hour I'd be sitting down to dinner with my entire family, something I hadn't done in two years, and I was going in with nothing but a vintage outfit and a vague hope that Nathaniel had a plan.

I didn't even know how much Ellie had told the family, or how much they'd guessed, about what had happened.

And then there was Greg.

Tonight, I'd see Greg for the first time in two years. For the first time since the wedding.

Two years, and I still wasn't ready. I wasn't sure I ever would be.

Part of me wanted to see him, more than anything. To get it over with. To know, for sure, that there was nothing there between us any more. To be certain that my heart wouldn't beat too fast when he was in the room, that I wouldn't find my eyes drawn to him every few moments.

To show that I was no longer in love with my sister's husband.

The rest of me just wanted to put the inevitable off for as long as possible.

The love Greg and I had shared had been childish, irresponsible – and all-encompassing, for a time. The sort of love that makes you abandon caution and sense and morals. The kind of love that causes pain.

I never wanted to feel that sort of love again.

But seeing Greg was nothing compared to my terror at seeing Ellie again. I could take any reaction from Greg – anything from love to hate. It didn't matter; it couldn't change anything now.

But Ellie… the thought of seeing the same hate in her eyes as the day she found out, of knowing for certain that nothing had changed, and never would – that filled me with the same paralysing fear that had kept me away from Rosewood for so long. When I was hundreds of miles away, there was still a chance that she might have forgiven me. Once I saw her again, whatever she felt was the truth, and I couldn't spin it into possibilities any more.

And that idea frightened me more than anything.

I ached across the shoulders, and my eyes still felt gritty, but at least I was clean. Wrapping one towel around my hair and another around my body, I wiped beads of water away from my eyes and opened the bathroom door, letting the burst of steam obscure the alarming yellow of the bedroom walls.

My skin burned, and I knew I'd be bright pink from head to toe. I liked my showers hot – hot enough to leave me gasping for breath when I stepped out.

Pulling the towel from my head I shook my wet hair out across my shoulders, and clutched the towel around my body tighter as I crossed the room to open the balcony door. Fresh air filled my lungs as I stared out over the Rose Garden. Edward was there, I realised, his blonde head moving between the remaining blooms. Isabelle had been right; I did have a magnificent view of the Rose Garden. I felt I could almost reach out and pluck one from its stem.

Suddenly, something else in the garden caught my eye. Another figure, too pale in the sunlight. She seemed to move in a different plane to Edward, as she ran her hands over the decapitated rose bushes, as if to her they still bloomed.

Was it really the Rosewood ghost?

I leant further out across the balcony railing to get a better look, until a rush of cold air told me that my towel hadn't leant with me. I grabbed for it, yanking it back up over my breasts, but not before Edward turned towards the house again.

Even at a distance, I could see the sardonic eyebrow he raised at my state of undress. Then he turned his gaze away and walked slowly towards the other gardens.

Damn.

I was beginning to think that I hadn't made the best ever first impression on my grandfather's new assistant.

Chapter Two

*Family is who you have left when there's
nothing and nobody else. When the wind
blows cold and the waves batter the cliffs,
when night falls and darkness seeps in…
family is still there.*

On A Summer's Night, by Nathaniel Drury (2015)

When Ellie and I were young, we visited Rosewood every weekend. Then, as now, my parents kept a house in Manchester, to be near the university – a small, untidy, cosy terrace house not far from where many of the students lived. Day to day, a perfectly ordinary existence for the daughters of a professor and a secondary-school drama teacher. But at weekends and holidays, we were spirited away to the magical, mysterious grounds of Rosewood, where there was always something new to discover or explore.

Rosewood was a grand old manor house from the Georgian era, hidden away in the Cheshire countryside behind wrought-iron gates and too many trees. It had been crumbling when Nathaniel and Isabelle bought it, back in the sixties, but slowly they'd invested in it. First, just enough to keep it standing and habitable. Then, as Nathaniel's career continued to blossom, enough to make it a proper home.

The house's flat-fronted brick exterior was punctuated by white frame windows betraying the sheer quantity of rooms in the place, and the acres of gardens surrounding it led straight onto the woods. The symmetrical chimneys still puffed smoke, and every room held a new surprise, even now – decorated ceilings, or a hidden door, or a story. Isabelle had redecorated a dozen times since they moved in, but she couldn't paper over the magic and the history of Rosewood.

It was my favourite place in the world.

From my usual attic bedroom over the main staircase, which had long ago been the servants' quarters, I could hear everything that went on down below: the sound of feet stomping up the stairs, the laughter floating up from the terrace as my grandfather mixed cocktails for his friends, a couple arguing on the landing.

The Yellow Room was clearly more suitable for guests – situated to the far right of the building, above the back drawing room (rarely used because of the rotting window frames, and the awful draught that blew through every afternoon), away from anything interesting that was going on. It was disconcerting, I found, to be at Rosewood and not know what was happening elsewhere in the house.

But by the time I'd changed into my costume for the evening – Therese's blue dress and sandals, bright red lipstick and my dark, bobbed hair curled into waves around my face – I felt strangely more like myself again, and almost prepared for the night ahead. Almost.

I wasn't sure I'd ever feel quite ready to see my sister again, or Greg. But neither could I stay away.

As I made my way down the main staircase into the hall, I could hear the strains of jazz music emanating from the kitchen – a sure sign that my father was cooking. I smiled. Whatever he was making smelled like home to me.

Sticking my head around the kitchen door, I checked to make sure I wouldn't be interrupting a moment of culinary magic by stopping in to say hello. And if it put off seeing Ellie for a few more moments, well, I wasn't going to complain.

"That smells good," I said, slipping through the doorway.

Dad dropped his wooden spoon into the pan and turned, beaming, wiping his hands on his apron even as he stepped towards me for a hug.

"Kia! I'd heard you were home." He held me close, then stepped back to inspect me, just as Therese had done. "You know I'm not one for formalities, but I believe an RSVP is usual for one of Isabelle's events…"

"And if I'd received an invitation, I'd have sent one," I said, as brightly as I could.

"Lost in the post, huh?" Dad asked, but I could tell from his tone that he knew full well it hadn't been.

"Something like that." I boosted myself up to sit on the edge of the kitchen table, my feet swinging, as Dad turned back to his bubbling pot. "So, what have I missed around here?"

"The usual. Can you hand me the basil from the windowsill?" Dad held out a hand, and it was as if I'd never been away at all. I smiled to myself for a moment before moving to the window to retrieve the herb. "Nathaniel is writing and won't tell us what; Isabelle is fretting that he's really just up there playing solitaire and avoiding her, which he might be. Mum's latest class musical was *Les Misérables*, so we've been eating garlic and misery for months. Ellie…" He stuttered to a stop. "Well. Ellie and Greg are well. And Caro thinks she's a fairy. Still. Didn't you grow out of that sort of thing by ten?"

"I don't remember," I said, absently, as I handed him the plant. I was more concerned with what he wasn't saying about Ellie. "So, Ellie's okay? I mean, she was?" I didn't imagine that discovering I'd returned home had filled her with any particular joy.

Dad sighed, and started stripping the basil plant of its leaves with unnecessary force. "As far as I know. I haven't seen her since we got back from town, but she was happy enough at breakfast."

I bit my lip. "Do you think—"

"Saskia," Dad interrupted me. "I don't know exactly what happened between you and your sister, and that's fine with me. Because it *is* between you and Ellie, not the rest of us. And if you're hiding in here to avoid seeing her…"

"Can't a girl come and get a 'welcome home' from her father these days?"

Dad turned and flashed me a smile. "Of course she can. And, sweetheart, I am so very glad to have you home. I've missed you."

A warm glow spread through me at his words, one that had been missing ever since I left Rosewood two years earlier. "I missed you too."

"Good. Then maybe you'll visit a bit more often after you go back to Perth."

"I will," I promised, and hoped I wasn't lying.

"And in the meantime…" He pointed towards the door with a wooden spoon dripping with sauce. "Go say hello to the rest of them. Because it won't get any easier the longer you put it off, and dinner is nearly ready."

"Yes, Dad." I gave him a small smile, and headed for the lounge, the heels of Therese's sandals clicking on the wooden floor. I paused at the door, and sucked in a deep breath. Dad was right. Might as well get this over and done with.

My mother was mixing some luridly coloured cocktails at the sideboard under the window, while Isabelle critiqued her bartending capabilities from her cream wing-backed chair. Therese, leaning against the gold and cream sofa, was the first to spot me.

"Oh now, there," Therese said, beaming. "It looks perfect on you. Doesn't it, Sally?"

My mother turned away from the drinks tray, the multicoloured chiffon scarf around her neck clashing with the cocktails. She smiled, but it seemed a little forced. "Kia, darling, there you are! What a wonderful surprise." Glass still in hand, she bustled over and wrapped her free arm around my waist. "If only you'd told us you were coming, we'd have collected you from the station."

"It doesn't matter," I told Mum. "I got a taxi easily enough."

"Yes, so Isabelle said." Mum glanced briefly over at Isabelle, then smiled at me again, more naturally this time, squeezing my waist with her arm. "It *is* lovely to have you home, sweetheart."

"Where's everyone else?" I asked.

Therese patted the sofa beside her and I went to sit as instructed. "Your grandfather is still writing, or so we are given to understand." Isabelle made a small, disbelieving noise that, coming from anyone else, would be termed a snort.

"Edward's gone out to fetch Caroline from the woods," Therese went on, ignoring Isabelle completely, as was her usual technique for dealing with her sister-in-law. "Greg isn't home yet and Ellie is…"

"Here." The voice, soft and familiar, was calm and expressionless, without feeling. But the sound of it made my whole body freeze, just for a moment, waiting for a reaction that never came. I forced myself to turn, to look, to accept whatever truth I found in my sister's eyes.

And there she was, pale and blonde in a pastel blue skirt and camisole, her fringe framing her face. Biting the inside of my cheek, I searched Ellie's face for the answers I'd come home to find, but they weren't there. Her eyes were still as sad as I remembered from the day she left for her honeymoon, but there was nothing else. No hate, no recriminations – but no forgiveness or love either. Nothing.

It was as if I didn't matter to her any more at all.

And that was more painful than any of the scenarios I'd imagined, when I'd thought of this moment.

"Hello, Kia." Ellie swept past me with swift but elegant grace, to the drinks cabinet, where Isabelle handed her something pink with lots of ice. Therese passed me her own gin and tonic, since it appeared Isabelle wasn't about to offer me one, and I gratefully took a gulp. It was stunningly strong.

Two years, and she just said, 'Hello.' Like nothing had happened. Like I was a passing acquaintance, holding no importance in her life.

Maybe I didn't. Maybe I shouldn't.

But she still mattered to me, and the distance in her eyes cut me deep, even through my costume.

"Ellie…" I started to get to my feet, but Mum stepped between us before I could get any further. Isabelle, for her part, had already dragged Ellie over to the window, murmuring something about table favours.

They had to know, right? If not the details, they knew I'd wronged Ellie. Why else would they be running interference between us?

"Now, Kia," Mum said, pulling me back down onto the sofa. "Tell me. What are you wearing for the party? Because I'm sure there are still some of your old clothes up in the attic..."

While I was ignoring the question, in favour of trying to eavesdrop on the conversation at the other end of the room, Therese said, "She's wearing a vintage sage-green frock with silver accents." She turned to look at me directly, and added, "It's very beautiful."

If I'd only known that Therese had such a costume store, I wouldn't have bothered bringing any of my own clothes.

"Will Nathaniel be coming down for dinner, at least?" I took another sip of gin and tonic. "After all, he's the one who demanded I be here." Without him, the house felt disjointed, like a collection of people in a waiting room who didn't quite know each other well enough to make conversation. Once Nathaniel arrived, I hoped we'd feel more like a family again.

Therese shrugged. "Goodness knows. He's been working so hard lately we've barely seen him."

Over by the window, Isabelle's glass slipped from her hand and smashed against the sideboard. Mum rushed over to help Ellie mop up and, content that no one was hurt, I lowered my voice and asked Therese, "What's he working on?" And why was Isabelle freaking out about it so much?

Therese looked away from Isabelle and back to me, her eyes concerned. "Nobody knows. Maybe he'll tell you – and I want you straight down to my cottage spilling the beans if he does. I'm ferociously curious."

Dad appeared in the doorway, and I found myself being thoroughly hugged again. "Because I really did miss you," he whispered, before letting me go and announcing the imminent arrival of food in the dining room.

If it wasn't for the intervention campaign my mother and Isabelle were running between Ellie and me, I might almost have felt welcomed home. As it was, Mum ushered me towards the head of the table, just as Isabelle herded Ellie towards the other end. Or possibly, Ellie was herding Isabelle; our grandmother was leaning on Ellie's arm quite heavily, I noticed.

I found myself sitting beside the empty seat reserved for Nathaniel, with Therese beside me, and I looked up at the doorway at just the wrong moment – just as Greg walked in.

I'd known I wasn't ready for this moment. But I hadn't realised how unprepared Greg would be. His eyes met mine and widened, the shock clear. Had no one called to tell him I was here? Surely Mum or Isabelle would have done, if they'd known the whole story? So perhaps they didn't, after all. Ellie sure as hell wouldn't have called him. And me being here shouldn't've made the damnedest bit of difference to him.

But from the way he looked at me, I knew it did.

He stumbled, grabbing on to the door frame like he'd had too many of Mum's cocktails. I held myself very still, tearing my eyes away to stare down at my empty place mat, focusing on keeping my expression neutral, my shoulders straight. Trusting in the red lipstick and an eighty-year-old dress to keep me safe.

"Kia," Greg said, so I had to look up. His gaze was fixed on me, and I winced. There went any hope of pretending that it was all in the past. That nothing had happened at all. I could feel our whole history in his gaze.

I just hoped the others couldn't see it, too.

"Hello, Greg," I said, as coolly as I could. Then I turned my attention back to my place mat, confused. Surely this should hurt more? As much as I hoped I'd moved on, that I was over Greg, I'd loved him once. I'd expected it to cut deep, seeing him again.

As it was, I felt more jealousy that he still had a place at Rosewood, than pain that our romance was over.

"Greg, you're down here between me and Ellie," Isabelle said, patting the chair beside her as she eyed me with suspicion. Great. Well, if she hadn't known what Ellie and I had fallen out over before, she had a pretty good clue now. "We're sitting boy–girl tonight."

"But, Grandma," Caroline said, peeking around Greg, where he was still stalled in the doorway, "there aren't enough men for that. You always said…"

"Never mind what I said, Caroline," Isabelle snapped, and turned her attention back to Ellie and to Greg, who'd finally found his way to his seat.

Caroline huffed as she marched into the dining room dressed in what looked like a vintage cream lace dress, presumably one of Therese's, with a sparkly tiara on top of her light brown hair. The hem of her too-long dress was green with grass stains.

She was followed at a distance by a tired-looking Edward, who slumped into the seat opposite me. Caroline, on the other hand, clambered immediately into the heavy wooden seat on my right: Nathaniel's chair.

"I was wondering where you'd got to," I said, tucking her hair behind her ear.

Caro rolled her eyes. "We had to go and get me a dress for the party, even though I *said* I wanted to wear one from the cottage, and it took *ages*. Then we were late back, because Dad insisted on going to the supermarket, once he knew you were here, and then you'd gone somewhere, and I didn't want to miss the fairy wedding in the wood, so I had to throw on my dress and tiara and run down to the toadstool ring." She pulled a small foot out from under the table to show me her incongruous white trainers. "I didn't even have time to change my shoes," she said, mournfully.

I thought that I'd remembered everything about Rosewood and my family, looking back over long nights in Perth. But I'd either forgotten, or never known, that Caroline had such an imagination. I'd certainly never realised before that she was so like me. A fairy wedding in the woods sounded like just the sort of thing I'd have ruined a vintage dress for.

Dad reappeared from the kitchen, a covered casserole dish in his oven-gloved hands, which he deposited in the centre of the table. "*Ta-da*. Grub's up."

It didn't escape my notice that he'd made Chicken Provençal with thick pasta ribbons and crusty bread – my favourite. Ellie never took to it, mostly because of her irrational fear of olives.

As we all tucked in, conversation was restricted to appreciative noises and requests for condiments. Next to me, Caroline was very carefully removing every single olive from *her* serving and placing them on the edge of her plate. Edward, almost unconsciously it appeared, was helping himself to the abandoned items and popping them in his mouth in between forkfuls of his own food. I wondered if this was an everyday occurrence between them. Perhaps Edward had actually been hired as a babysitter. It certainly made more sense to me than the idea of him as Nathaniel's assistant.

"It's so nice to have all my girls back home together," Dad said, pouring himself another glass of wine. "It's been too long." Ellie didn't think so, given the nervous way her eyes were flicking between me and Greg. "So, Ellie, Kia, what have you got planned for tomorrow?"

Mum glared at him, and I realised that Dad knew exactly what he was doing: trying to forcibly cram a bridge between Ellie and me.

"I've got lots to do for the party," Ellie said, her voice sweet, and achingly familiar. "It's going to be a busy day."

And there, I realised, was my chance to get close to Ellie and start the reconciliation. "I'll help!"

Ellie looked up with unwelcome surprise, but I kept the smile on my face regardless. Across the table, my mother put down her knife and fork and looked up, smiling equally brightly. "So, Kia, tell us about Scotland!"

I toyed with the last bit of pasta on my plate. "Well, it rains even more than it does here. Other than that…"

"What about work?" Mum pressed. "How's the newspaper going?"

"It's fine," I said, shrugging. It *was* fine. Predictable, unchallenging and *fine*. "Busy. You know."

"You've got a new editor," Therese said helpfully. "Let's hear some more about him." She was giving me an opening, I realised. A chance to show everyone – especially Ellie and Greg – that I'd moved on, that I had a new life. But I wasn't sure telling my family I was having sex with my boss on a regular basis was actually the best way to prove I'd grown up.

"Duncan Fields," I supplied. "He just moved up from Edinburgh."

"Brought in from the big city, eh?" Dad said, reaching across Therese for another piece of bread. "Shaking the place up a bit, is he?"

I glanced up at the ceiling. Mostly, Duncan had been shaking cocktails at the bar after work then, later, my bed frame, but I didn't think that was quite what Dad meant. "Something like that."

"Well, that could be good for you, I suppose," Mum said. I resisted the urge to tell Mum that, yes, it was very good for me *indeed*, thank you. "An office shake-up could mean a promotion for you, after all. Next step on the ladder to the nationals."

"Mmm, maybe," I said, in a way I hoped conveyed, 'but probably not,' without adding, 'because Duncan would probably get fired for giving his girlfriend preferential treatment.' Besides, I wasn't entirely certain I wanted that London career any more. Some days I wasn't even sure I wanted to be a reporter.

"Never mind about work," Isabelle said, pouring herself another glass of wine. "I'm much more interested in your social life. Is there anything at all to do in Perth?"

Since Isabelle had spent most of her life living in the middle of nowhere, Cheshire, I'm not quite sure where she got the idea that outside Rosewood, London and possibly Paris, the world was a social wasteland.

"Plenty," I said, racking my brain for an example. Lately, most of my evenings were spent in bed with Duncan. "We go out for drinks with the guys from the office most Thursdays. And Sundays my friend Claire and I tend to meet for lunch." It sounded phenomenally boring, put like that.

"We?" Isabelle asked, suddenly looking a lot more interested in the conversation. "Who's we?"

Across the table, Edward rolled his eyes at me, as if to say, 'Well, really. What did you think she was going to pay most attention to?' I wasn't sure I liked the way that Edward had slotted so easily into my family's life.

"Ah... Duncan and I..." I stopped, unsure as to how to continue. As it happened, I needn't have worried.

"Darling, how lovely!" Mum said, obviously not grasping the implications of 'he's my boss' as quickly as I'd have expected. "I didn't know you were seeing anybody!"

"You should have invited him to the party," Isabelle put in, obviously so annoyed to have been deprived of the opportunity to cross-examine a potential new family member, that she'd forgotten she hadn't actually invited *me*.

"Well, it's all still rather new…" I said, wishing I couldn't feel Greg staring at me. I wanted to explain that it wasn't serious, that nobody needed to buy a hat or anything. But they all seemed so *pleased* that I'd found someone, I just couldn't.

"Does this mean you won't be home for Christmas *again*?" Caroline sounded put out. It was nice to know that someone would miss me this year.

"Of course she won't," Isabelle said, in a definite manner. "She'll want to be with Duncan." Which was a much better reason than, 'She wouldn't dare upset her sister by visiting twice in one year.'

"You'll understand when you have a boyfriend," Mum said to Caro, and sighed. "Which will probably be in about a fortnight, the rate you're growing. It's such a shame they grow up so fast. Christmas isn't the same without little children around." She stared wistfully across the table towards Ellie. "It would be so nice to have a baby at Rosewood for Christmas."

Ellie flinched, and Greg reached for her full wine glass, taking a large gulp. I grabbed my cutlery just a little harder, and was wondering when I'd be able to escape back to the purely aesthetic horrors of the Yellow Room rather than the emotional horror of family dinner, when my grandfather's deep, dark voice rang out through the room.

"Oh, good God, no. I like my Christmas morning lie-ins, thank you." Everyone's attention snapped to the doorway where Nathaniel's broad form was filling the frame, his familiar orange fisherman's jumper clashing with the elegant cream and gold of the dining room.

Nathaniel Drury. Literary legend, imposing intellect, household name and always, always, Granddad.

He'd been twenty-one when he published his first novel, and become a literary sensation almost overnight. There are photos of him as a young man on the wall of every fashionable artists' haunt in London, New York and Paris, and he drank everyone under the table in all of them. He was notorious as a womaniser, and a drunk. Which is why the national presses were so astounded when, a year later, he disappeared from London society for two weeks, only to return with a wife in tow. One Isabelle Yates, local beauty and daughter of the richest man in his home town in North Wales. They bought Rosewood the next year and, well, the rest became our family history.

"What's for tea?" Nathaniel asked, leaning on the back of Edward's chair and smiling at me like no one else in the room mattered.

"If you'd come down to dinner at a reasonable time, and wearing appropriate clothes, like the rest of the family, you'd have been able to find out." Isabelle didn't look at her husband as she spoke, instead apparently choosing to glare at me. I blinked, and tried to figure out how, exactly, this was my fault. Ellie's sad eyes at the dinner table and sulky refusal to talk all evening? Absolutely my fault. Nathaniel's bizarre writerly habits? They'd been around far longer than me.

"We had Chicken Provençal," Caro told him, oblivious to Isabelle's temper. "But we've eaten it all. It's Saskia's favourite, you know."

"I remember," Nathaniel said, grinning at me again.

"There might be some leftovers coincidentally keeping warm in the oven," Dad said, looking up at the ceiling to avoid the moment Isabelle's glare swung his way. "And some bread in the bread bin."

"I'll go and grab it for you," Edward said, presumably more out of a desire to escape the dining room for a while than because he was trying to expand his servant repertoire from carrying cases. "Anyone else want anything? I'll bring more wine." Without waiting for a response, he disappeared through the door and across the hallway to the kitchen.

Watching his long legs stride across the tiled floor, I found myself wondering if his legs really were that long, or if he was just so skinny that he looked taller. *Perhaps more slender, than skinny...* Skinny implied unattractive, which he wasn't. At all. More... graceful, I supposed.

Strange. He was nothing even *close* to my type – I went more for darker, more brooding good looks. Like Duncan. And Greg, come to think of it. Edward was all golds and creams, like Isabelle's decorating scheme. Like sunshine.

And for some reason, I couldn't help but watch him.

"Now, to business," Nathaniel said, leaning on the back of Edward's vacated chair. "If I'm going to eat, I'll need a place to sit. Now, which chair do I normally sit in, I wonder?"

Curled up on the base of Nathaniel's seat, Caroline giggled.

He leant further across the chair back, angling his upper body to stare at Caro. "Well, I'm head of the family, so it makes sense that I'd normally sit... at the head of the table!" He lurched across and grabbed at

Caroline's legs, and she squealed. "But who's this sitting in m-*yyy* chair?"

"It's me, it's me!" Caro squawked, as he started to tickle her. "And I'm not moving!"

"Is that right?" In one deft movement, and surprisingly fast for a man of his age, Nathaniel hefted his youngest granddaughter out of the chair, swung his body round to take the seat, and dumped Caro on his lap. "Hah!" he said, reaching for the unused wine glass above Caroline's plate. "I am victorious. Servants, bring me wine!"

I couldn't not laugh, no matter how hard Isabelle was rolling her eyes. Dad was openly grinning, and even Greg was looking amused.

Therese passed the red wine down the table towards me, and I filled up Nathaniel's glass, just as Edward reappeared and replaced Caroline's plate with a new, heaped one, before reclaiming his seat.

"How was the journey?" my grandfather asked me, ignoring the food and taking a gulp of wine instead.

I shrugged. "Not so bad. I got here about four."

"I'm afraid I was shackled to my desk," he said, with an exaggerated sigh. "Or I would have been here to greet you."

"Since you were the only one who knew she was coming," Isabelle said pointedly, "it was really very rude not to offer to meet her at the station."

"If only she'd received an invitation." Therese sighed and looked innocently around her. "She could have RSVPed and avoided all this confusion."

"What story are you writing?" Caro asked, bouncing enough in Nathaniel's lap to spill a few drops of his wine onto his plate as he lifted his glass. "Is it about people telling lies and secrets and death and stuff? My friend Alicia's mum says that's all you ever write."

Nathaniel muttered something under his breath that I couldn't quite hear, but could probably guess at. Edward obviously heard, though, as he choked on his mouthful of wine.

"My stories," Nathaniel said, loud enough for us all to hear, "are every one of them different and new and utterly unlike anything I have written before. This one more than ever."

Across the table from me, Edward put down his wine glass, too hard, and stared at his empty plate, apparently not even noticing as a few drops of wine sloshed onto his hand.

"But what's it about?" Caro pressed. Nathaniel shook his head. "You'll all just have to wait to read it. You, longer than most," he added, patting Caroline's shoulder, "as not all sections are suitable for such a young lady."

Except for Edward, I realised. Edward, as my grandfather's assistant, would know exactly what he was working on, how it was going and whether he really was writing at all, or just avoiding Isabelle.

Is that why he's looking so nervous? I wondered. If Nathaniel wasn't writing, it might explain why Edward was so keen to make himself invaluable elsewhere in the household. A writer who didn't write wouldn't have much need for an assistant, after all.

"But I want to hear a story," Caroline said, twisting in Nathaniel's lap.

"Ah, but that is a different matter entirely," Nathaniel said. "I may not be able to tell you about the book I'm writing now, but far be it for me to deprive a young girl of a chilling tale of betrayal and murder when she wants to hear one!"

"That's quite enough, Nathaniel," Isabelle said, standing abruptly. "Now, who wants to help me clear the table?"

Caroline shook her head. "Not me, Grandma. I'm listening to the story."

At the end of the table, Ellie got to her feet with her usual grace, before the vein throbbing at Isabelle's temple burst. "I'll help," she said, and began systematically gathering up plates, clanking them together loudly.

Fifty years of marriage had obviously instilled some sense of self-preservation in my grandfather, because he waited until Isabelle had carried the first load of plates out of the room before he began to tell his story. Greg had apparently learned the same in less time – he was already taking the plates from Ellie's arms and whispering something to her. They left the room together, and I couldn't help but watch them go.

"Now," Nathaniel said, his eyes on Isabelle as she disappeared into the kitchen. "This story is a special story."

"Why's it special?" Caro asked, pulling her legs up and wrapping her arms around them.

"Because it's about this house," he explained, "and the people who used to live here." At his words, I knew instantly the tale he would tell. I wasn't entirely sure it was suitable for a nine-year-old, but maybe Nathaniel would edit it for Caro. A consummate storyteller, he always was a great judge of his audience.

As the others disappeared in search of digestifs, I pulled my chair in closer to better hear the story. Across the table, I realised, Edward was doing the same. I raised my eyebrows at him and he shrugged. "I'm a sucker for a good story," he said. "How else do you think I got pulled into this gig?"

"If everyone is quite comfortable," Nathaniel said, feigning considerably more patience than I happened to know he possessed, "then I'll begin.

"This house has stood on this land for hundreds of years." His voice had dropped into a cadence I recognised from childhood – that of a storyteller, rather than a writer. The sound of it, warm and familiar, washed over me and I shivered as I listened to his tale. "There are so many stories in its walls, I could never have time to tell them all. But this is a story of the first family to live here.

"Long ago, a man named John Harrow, a merchant, bought this land and commissioned a fine house to be built. But what is a fine house without gardens? So once the house was finished, Harrow hired a head gardener, a man of impeccable reputation. And that gardener brought with him his apprentice: a boy with incredible talent, a boy who, local people said, could make dead plants bloom."

"Is that possible?" Caro whispered loudly, leaning back towards Edward.

"Absolutely," he replied, straight-faced. "But very rare." I hid my smile.

Nathaniel raised his eyebrows until Caro settled back down, then continued. "Now, Harrow had only one child, a daughter, the apple of his eye. She was young and beautiful and ready for love."

"Did she fall in love with the apprentice?" Caro asked, bouncing slightly. Nathaniel ignored her.

"The moment she set eyes on the apprentice, one summer's day in the new Rose Garden, she fell in love. And he, by return, worshipped her from the moment he saw her."

"I knew it," Caroline whispered, to me this time.

"The young couple knew that John Harrow wouldn't approve," Nathaniel said, raising his voice a little. "So they kept their love a secret, and met only by moonlight, in the Rose Garden where they first fell in love. And as summer turned to winter, the apprentice picked impossible flowers from the dormant rose bushes for his beloved.

"All was wonderful, until the day John Harrow saw roses in his house at a time of year when nothing blooms, and his daughter watching the apprentice from the balcony of what is now the Yellow Room."

"And you complained about sleeping there," Edward murmured across the table to me. He raised his eyebrows and I blushed, remembering exactly what he'd seen on that balcony that afternoon.

"I didn't realise I was part of a literary tradition," I whispered back. I was fairly sure that detail was a new addition to the story. Nathaniel never could tell a story quite the same way twice.

"Suspicious, Harrow lay awake that night, listening for his daughter. When he heard the staircase creak in the darkness, he picked up his gun and silently followed her to the Rose Garden, where he saw her kissing the apprentice."

Nathaniel's voice dropped again, and we all leant in closer to listen. "Harrow went crazy with rage. His beloved daughter, kissing a gardener? It was unthinkable. He called to her to get away from the apprentice, but the young man put himself between his love and her father. Harrow wasted no time. He pulled out his gun and shot the apprentice."

Caroline jumped as Nathaniel's voice rose suddenly at the shot being fired. "Was he okay?" she asked.

Nathaniel shook his head sadly. "The apprentice died that evening, and that same night Harrow's daughter took to her bed and stayed there. She wouldn't eat, would drink nothing but a little water, no matter how much her father begged her."

Caroline's eyes were huge, now, with all her attention on Nathaniel. "What happened next?" she asked in a whisper.

"Nothing happened. Nothing happened for eleven days and eleven nights. She stayed in bed all over Christmas, and refused to move until New Year's Eve came around. Then, that night, she asked to be taken out to the Rose Garden.

"Her father, hoping that she might be ready to forgive him, agreed, and she was carried out in her blankets. There, she asked to be placed on the bench where she'd sat with her love. 'There are no more flowers,' she said, looking around the garden. Her father tried to reassure her that they'd be back with the spring, but the young woman said, 'No. There are no more flowers for me.' Then, with a final breath, she died."

Caroline gulped a sob, and it occurred to me again that this possibly wasn't the most appropriate story for a nine-year-old, just before bedtime. But Nathaniel wasn't finished.

"It's said," he continued, his voice almost inaudible, "that she walks there still, on moonlit nights, looking for her lost love."

"A ghost?" Caro asked, all excitement again. "We have our own ghost? That's brilliant." Slipping off Nathaniel's knee, she skipped towards the door. "I'm going to go see!"

Was that the explanation for the strange girl I'd seen in the Rose Garden that afternoon? Even for Rosewood, it seemed impossible.

Nathaniel stretched his legs out under the table, and pushed back his chair. "Well, now I'm in trouble."

"I think you already were," Edward pointed out, before finishing off the wine in his glass.

From the hallway, we all heard Isabelle saying sharply, "Caroline Ryan, you are not going out in the garden now. It's past your bedtime. You are going to go up those stairs and put on your pyjamas." There was a short pause, before she added, "Now," over whatever objections Caro was trying to raise.

I checked my watch; it was almost eleven – more than past Caro's bedtime, it was very nearly mine. It had, after all, been quite the day. "I think that might be my cue," I said, and got to my feet.

Nathaniel stood, too, and put his arms around me, pulling me in close so I could smell the pipe smoke on his jumper. "It's good to have you home, Kia."

"It's good to be here," I mumbled back, burying my face against the scratchy wool. And, just for a moment, it *was* good. Whatever happened tomorrow, whatever Ellie had told everyone, right then, there was nowhere else in the world I wanted to be but Rosewood.

Upstairs in the Yellow Room, I could just make out the sound of Caroline protesting pyjamas. Switching off the bedroom light, I sat by the balcony, looking out at the darkened garden, Nathaniel's story fresh in my mind.

I didn't see any ghosts, but I watched for a while, just in case, before climbing into bed and dreaming of meadows of flowers in winter.

Chapter Three

"Everyone keeps their ghosts in the attic,
Agnes. It's the only place no one ever wants
to look."

Ghosts in the Attic, by Nathaniel Drury (1973)

I'd left a lot of stuff behind when I escaped to Scotland. I'd been living at Rosewood full time for almost two years when I left, working on a local paper nearby, and I'd accumulated a significant amount of junk that hadn't fitted in my suitcase. If Caroline was sleeping in my attic room, then someone would have had to move my stuff to make space for her.

I woke up the next morning with a desire to rediscover what I had left behind.

It was only just eight, but the day already felt warm. Sorting through the clothes I'd brought with me, I realised that the office wear I'd filled my Perth wardrobe with just didn't fit in at Rosewood. Maybe, if I could find my belongings, there'd be some more suitable clothes there.

Eventually, I settled on a pair of jeans that usually got worn with stilettos, so hung over the ends of my bare feet, and a lace and silk camisole that only normally saw the light of day through a slightly-too-sheer work cardigan I'd somehow neglected to pack. It would do until I found something else, anyway. Fixing my hair back from my face, I set out to investigate the attic.

The obvious place to start was my old room, tucked under the eaves of the house, up in the attic, so I climbed the rickety wooden staircase at the end of the corridor and knocked lightly on Caro's door. There was no response, so I slowly turned the handle and pushed the door open, wincing at the awful creaking it made.

Luckily it didn't matter, since Caroline was already up and out. "Probably ghost-hunting," I muttered, glancing around the room. The walls and the furniture were the same, as was the bright pink radiator I'd insisted on, installed against the only full-height wall. The other walls sloped downwards to the low window and window seat, familiar pink pillows still stacked along the wooden bench.

But there was no sign of anything else that belonged to me. The brush set on the dressing table, the clothes hung over the back of the chair, the books on the bookcases, even the pictures on the wall – none of them were mine. I shut the door behind me.

There was a large storage area just along the hallway, which I remembered as dusty, stuffy and full of rotting cardboard boxes. Of course that was where they'd have stashed my stuff.

The door was unlocked, and as I pulled it towards me a rush of hot, stale air hit my lungs. With one last deep breath, I headed in, leaving the door open behind me in the hope of ventilation.

The attic was much as I remembered, and I tripped over piles of messily rolled rugs and faded cushions on my way through the box maze. On the far side of the space there was a window, and I made my way towards it, hoping it hadn't been painted shut.

It hadn't, and the morning air breezing in over the gardens was cool and fresh. Beating dust out of a large floor cushion, I settled down at the base of the window, and started pulling likely looking boxes towards me. As I pulled out books and pictures, the musty smell of damp paper rose up from the prematurely yellowed and crinkled pages.

Every box I looked in awakened waves of memory I hadn't even been aware I was suppressing. A storybook Nathaniel wrote me for my eighth birthday; a pair of absurdly expensive pink heels I'd bought with my first student loan and never really worn, because they didn't fit with the agreed student uniform of jeans and slobby jumpers; postcards of Devon from Ellie and Greg's first holiday away together; a wire-bound copy of a series of fantastical short stories I'd written for a creative writing course as part of my degree, taking their starting points from my childhood at Rosewood. A hundred wonderful things I'd forgotten all about.

And, shoved down the side of a box of musty paperbacks, a stack of unopened letters, addressed to Ellie, in my handwriting. Still bruised from my awkward welcome home, I couldn't quite bring myself to open them yet. I had a horrible feeling the letters somehow wouldn't say what I knew I'd been trying to articulate. Instead, I turned to my stories.

In the warmth of the attic, with dusty cushions at my back, I settled in and lost myself in my own tales – wincing at jarring turns of phrase, but smiling when I found something I'd forgotten, something true and real from my childhood.

I hadn't fully remembered, for example, that each tale took a turn for the imaginary, somewhere around the second page. Forgotten that my own life hadn't been exciting enough for me, even then. That I'd needed to pretend there was something more.

I was so engrossed in the pieces of my past, I failed to notice that my hiding place had been discovered until Nathaniel's voice interrupted me from the doorway. "What are you reading?"

Smiling up at him, I waved the poorly printed manuscript. "Stories from a lifetime ago," I explained, as he came closer, settling himself on a cushion opposite me. "Just some stuff I wrote for a writing class, once."

"And here was me thinking you might be hiding," he said, his smile a little too knowing. "Anything else worth reading in there?"

I shoved my letters to Ellie further down inside the box, and pulled out one of the birthday storybooks. The golden inked lettering on the front read *The Garden Ghost*. "You wrote this for me for my eighteenth, I think." I glanced through the pages before handing it over. "The story's a little different from the one you told Caroline last night."

In my book, the daughter had fallen pregnant, shaming the family, but refusing to speak the name of her lover. She died in childbirth, and it was only once the child made dead flowers bloom, several years later, that John Harrow discovered the truth about his daughter and the apprentice. Which was the real story? Or were they both just figments of Nathaniel's imagination? I knew better than to ask. To my grandfather, truth and fiction were almost the same thing, there to be intertwined to make the best story.

I worried, sometimes, that I'd inherited that trait, only without using it to write the kind of books that won awards.

Nathaniel flicked through the book with a chuckle. "Caro's still a little young for some stories."

Watching him reread his own words, I remembered something that had been bothering me. "Why didn't you tell me that you had a new assistant?"

Nathaniel looked up. "Edward? Didn't I?" He shrugged. "No idea. I suppose that I was always more interested in what you were up to, whenever you called."

Which was very unlike my grandfather. Nathaniel always wanted to talk about the trials and tribulations of life at Rosewood; a new assistant would normally be prime fodder.

Suddenly, I wondered what other secrets he'd been keeping, what else I'd missed. Staying in touch with Rosewood only by phone or the odd email with Dad, I'd been left out of all the day-to-day events, the little things that tied the family together – and excluded me. I'd called home, once a week on a Sunday, and spoken with Mum and Dad, with Caro, and Therese, sometimes, if she was there. Occasionally I'd shared a few words with Isabelle, too, but not often. That, at least, made more sense now. Whatever Ellie had told her about what happened, it had been enough to dig a rift between me and my grandmother that couldn't be crossed by phone.

I'd never spoken to Ellie, of course.

Nathaniel had tended to call me, erratically, as he thought of it. Sometimes we'd talk for hours, others just for a few moments. But I'd never felt that gulf between us that I'd felt with Isabelle, or even the slight distance that had grown between me and my parents, by virtue of the miles separating us, if nothing else. I'd thought my relationship with Nathaniel was unchanging and unchangeable.

But he hadn't told me about Edward. Why? What else had he kept from me? What else had I been left out of, by being away?

And would I ever be able to catch up?

Nathaniel reached out and selected another of the storybooks he'd written for me – the one he'd presented to me on my tenth birthday, whispering in my ear that the Forest Maiden of the title was really me. I'd held that secret close to my heart all year, I remembered, waiting for my next story. They were all about me, really, I came to realise, much later.

"How many of these did I write for you?" he asked, flicking through the pages.

"One a year until my twenty-first birthday." Just five years ago. At the bottom of the pile was the board book he'd created for my first birthday, full of brightly coloured pictures of things you might find around Rosewood, each with a little rhyme after them.

"I always hoped you'd start writing your own," he said, still staring at the words on the page. "You had such an imagination... I always thought you'd be a writer."

"I am," I said, amazed. Even when I'd signed up for my creative writing course, he'd never said that it was a good idea, never asked to see my coursework.

"I suppose," he said, putting down the book and picking up the next one in the pile. "But it's not really using your imagination, is it."

"You never said anything." My throat was suddenly tight at the idea that I hadn't lived up to my grandfather's dreams for me, even if I hadn't known what they were. "I never thought..."

He looked up at me then, and smiled, his pale blue eyes soft. "Well, you had to choose your own path, after all." He dropped the book back onto the pile. "I always told myself that there was time. Plenty of time for you to find your own way."

Creaking to his feet, he bent down and kissed the top of my head. "You'll get there," he whispered, before turning and leaving, pulling the door shut behind him as I sat and blinked away my tears.

I emerged from the attic at mid-morning, by which time the rest of the house was busy running errands for Isabelle. I, however, had more important things to attend to.

If I wanted to belong at Rosewood again, to be a part of family life once more, there was only one place for me to start: with my sister. I needed to know who knew our secrets, and who might forgive me, even if Ellie couldn't. I needed to know if I really *could* come home again. Even if that answer hurt.

"Have you seen Ellie?" I asked Mum, when I stumbled across her tying ribbons on menus in the kitchen. She was dressed in a long, tie-dye skirt and bright pink T-shirt that contrasted starkly with the elegant cream and gold menus.

Mum looked up sharply. She might look the woo-woo hippy part, but when it mattered her edge was knife-keen. "I'm not sure now's the right time, sweetheart. Your sister's very busy today."

"I just want to talk to her about something," I said, wondering again how much everyone at Rosewood knew about the situation.

Mum sighed, a proper world-weary parental sigh. "Why don't you and I have some tea, eh?" And, without waiting for a reply, she stood and crossed the kitchen, flicking the kettle switch and reaching for the cups and saucers. Resigned, I took a seat at the kitchen table and examined the menus.

"Kia," she said, as we waited for the kettle to boil. Then she sighed, a sure sign we were getting to the important stuff. "I don't know what happened between you and your sister, and I'm not sure that I really want to. I can make certain assumptions, and one of those is that Greg's involved somehow."

I sat very still, and very quiet, privately hoping that if I didn't say anything, she might forget that I was there and wander off to annoy someone else.

But she went on: "Whatever happened, it was two years ago. And while I do sincerely hope that you and Ellie will make up, of course I do…"

"She's not showing any signs of forgiveness," I finished for her.

Mum sighed again. "Exactly." Picking up a ginger cookie, she placed it on a saucer and put it in front of me. "And perhaps it's not a good idea to force it. You know Ellie; she has to come to her own decisions, when she's ready to make them. I think you have to let this happen in its own time."

"You're saying I just have to wait." Which was pretty much the last thing I wanted to do. I'd let it fester for two years, after all. How much more time could I reasonably spend avoiding it?

The secret my sister and I were hiding had kept me away from my home, my family, for too long already.

"I think so, yes." She leant forward and patted my hand, before pouring a splash of hot water into the pot to warm it. Her voice returned to its normal, bright and bubbly tone, as she said, "But that means you have time to tell me all about this Duncan, instead, doesn't it?"

I mentally revised my list of 'last things I want to do' to include 'discussing my casual lover with my mother.'

"Look, Mum, really, I get what you're saying. But like you said, everyone's very busy today – all hands on deck for the party, and all. And I *did* promise I'd help." I shoved the ginger cookie in my mouth. "Thanks for the biscuit!" I said around it, and hurried back into the hallway and closed the door before she could object again. It was quite obvious that Mum was firmly on Ellie's side – which wasn't a surprise. That was the way it had always been: Mum and Ellie, me and Dad. Caro, on the other hand, was her own, complete, confident, perfect person with the loving support of all of us – the benefit of being the baby of the family.

I didn't blame Mum for siding with Ellie. I just wished she understood that I was trying to make things better, not worse.

After some scouting around, I found Ellie in the Orangery, surrounded by sugared almonds and tiny cardboard handbags and top hats. She wore a dark pink skirt with a paler heart print all over, and a T-shirt in a matching rose shade. Her pale hands moved quickly, with efficient finesse, as she folded the table favours.

"Why don't I help you with that?" I asked from the doorway. Ellie looked up, her heart-shaped face full of surprise that quickly turned to doubt. "It'll be much quicker with two of us, and I'm sure you've got lots of other things to be getting on with."

Before she could object, I dropped into the wicker chair opposite her and prepared to assemble.

"You take handbags," Ellie said pushing a pile towards me. She still looked suspicious, and she wouldn't meet my eyes, letting her hair fall in her face instead. "I'll take top hats."

I waited until we'd reached some sort of a rhythm, until our hands were folding bags and hats on autopilot, and the stick-on ribbons were no longer sticking to everything but the favours, before I broached the subject I wanted to discuss. Even then, I thought it best to come at it from an angle.

"Why on earth does Isabelle want table favours, anyway?" I poured exactly four sugared almonds into my current cardboard handbag, folded the top to seal it, then reached for the tiny gold bow to stick on the top. "She does realise this isn't an actual wedding, right?"

"Maybe she feels she missed out," Ellie said, not looking up from her cream cardboard top hat. "You know, eloping and everything. She never got a proper wedding."

"We didn't have to go through all this for their ruby wedding," I grumbled, as a sugared almond escaped my grasp and fell down the side of the seat cushions. I recovered it, and rubbed it against my jeans to get rid of the fluff, before dropping it into the bag. It wasn't as though anyone actually ate the things, anyway.

"But fifty years, that's really something." Ellie added another perfect top hat to the box, and reached for the next one. "It makes sense that they want to celebrate."

"I bet you and Greg will be doing this in forty-eight years' time," I said, trying to sound excited at the prospect. "The big party, I mean, here at Rosewood, with table favours and fruit cake."

Ellie looked up and caught my eye for the first time since I'd come home. "I hope so," she said very quietly.

Her eyes were huge under her tidy blonde fringe, I realised. Huge and sad. As if just being near me was painful to her.

Maybe I didn't need to search for answers. Maybe that pain was all the answer I needed.

But it was a reaction, at last, even if not one I wanted. At least I knew she felt something about me being there. She hadn't cut me out of her life – out of her heart – completely. I wasn't sure I should feel so relieved to cause my sister to suffer.

My thoughts and words started to run together. "I mean, you and Greg, you've already made it two years, that's more than lots of couples make it, isn't it? So, really, you should…"

"Stop it." Ellie's voice was quiet, but when she looked up, her eyes were blazing. "Just… stop it, Kia."

"I just meant—" I tried to explain, but Ellie cut me off.

"No. You don't get to comment on my marriage. You don't even get to have an *opinion* on my relationship with my husband." Every word was louder than the last, ringing out around the Orangery, battering their way into my head. I froze, hands still wrapped around a stupid cardboard handbag. This wasn't the Ellie I remembered at all. Had I done this to her? Awakened this anger? "Whatever you might have thought two years ago, there is *no place* for you in my marriage, or with my husband. You're not friends, you're not confidants, you're *nothing*. Do you understand that?"

"Of course I do," I whispered. "I know that. And I wouldn't—"

"Don't tell me what you *wouldn't*," Ellie said, bitterness seeping through her voice. "You already did. Remember?"

Shocked silence fell between us. *Of course* I remembered. Even if I'd spent two years trying to forget.

"I'm sorry," I said, for what had to be the thousandth time. More, if you counted the letters she'd never read. "I… I'm not back here to see Greg. Or to cause any trouble. I know I did an unforgivable thing; I get that. I just…"

"Want to be forgiven," Ellie finished for me, her voice hard.

"You forgave Greg." I didn't mean to whine, didn't mean to imply that she was being unfair or that I deserved the same. But still the words came out. And as I said it, I realised I wanted to know why. Why did he get to stay here, to be part of my family, to live the life he'd always wanted, while I was exiled to Perth to do penance?

"Greg told me the truth," Ellie said. "After... it happened. He came to me, practically on his knees, and told me the truth. He told me he couldn't marry me, because he didn't deserve me. Did you know that?" I shook my head. I'd been too preoccupied with my own fate to wonder exactly what happened between Ellie and Greg. "He was ready to walk out, leave his home and his family and his job, his *life*, because of what you two did."

"And yet he's still here."

"Because I *chose* to forgive him." Ellie leant across the table between us, hammering her point home. "I *chose* to go through with the wedding, even knowing that he'd slept with my sister just two days before, because I loved him. I still love him. I knew he truly regretted what he'd done, and I knew that together, we'd be able to move past it." She leant back, her gaze fixed on mine. "It's taken a lot of work, a lot of talking, a lot of love, but we have. We've moved on, and our marriage is stronger than ever."

"I'm glad," I said, softly. "I'm so glad that you're happy together."

"We are." Ellie gave a firm nod. "And we will be when you leave again."

And that, I supposed, was my answer. As far as Ellie was concerned, there was no place for me at Rosewood.

"Who else knows?" I asked, looking down at my hands. "When... two years ago, you said you didn't want anyone to know."

"I was ashamed." Ellie gave a short, sharp laugh. The sort that isn't funny at all. "Me. *I* was ashamed of what *you* two did."

"You shouldn't have been. I should. I *am*."

"I know I shouldn't have been," Ellie replied sharply. "And when I realised that... I was able to talk about it, a little."

"Who did you tell?" I asked, desperation leaking out in my voice. I needed to know who already knew my secrets, and who didn't. Who I needed to explain myself to, who I needed to convince I wasn't here to cause trouble. Mum and Dad had both said they didn't know, and I suspected that was more because Ellie had wanted to spare *them* rather than because of me. But what about everyone else?

Did Nathaniel know?

Ellie gave me a long, assessing look. Then she shook her head. "No. It doesn't matter. It was my secret to tell too."

"I know that. I just... I need to know. Please?" I was begging now, and I didn't even care.

But Ellie stayed firm. Standing, she looked down at me, and said, "I'm done talking about this now."

"No, wait!" I grabbed for her wrist and tried to hold her back. "I need to know."

"I said, I'm *done*." Ellie shook me free on the last word, and I grabbed for her again.

"Saskia." Edward's voice wasn't loud, exactly, but still commanding, and it made me jump, releasing Ellie as I did so. How long had he been standing in the doorway behind me? Had Ellie known he was there?

I sprung to my feet and turned to face him. "What? Did you need me for something?" I asked, unsure of what I wanted the answer to be. Part of me wanted to stay, finish the confrontation with Ellie properly. But a larger part of me was grasping for any excuse to leave, to get away from this awful, painful conversation. Even if I still didn't know what I'd come in there for.

Edward nodded, and motioned for me to follow him, back through the hallway into the main house. I glanced back at Ellie, but she had already turned away, and was disappearing through the patio doors into the garden. The conversation was over.

Edward didn't speak again until we were safely ensconced in the dining room, the door firmly shut behind us. He motioned for me to take a seat, and I glanced around at the huge table plan propped up against the dining table, and the stacks of golden cloth napkins and ready-shined silverware, before picking my way through to a spare dining chair. Edward, meanwhile, paced in front of me like an angry headmaster.

Then he stopped, and looked down at me. "This isn't my place, Saskia," he said, his voice still soft. "I know that. I'm not family, I wasn't here two years ago, and I don't really know anything about you, apart from what Ellie has told me." Which was surely damning enough. "But I want you to listen to me anyway, please."

He took a deep breath, then let it out. Shaking his head slightly, he crouched down beside me, looking up into my eyes. "Don't try and do this now, Saskia. She's stressed out about the party tomorrow, and it's hard enough for her that you're here at all. She's trying not to be paranoid, but it's hard, especially when she's run ragged organising things for Isabelle."

All of which I knew, and I wanted to talk to her anyway. I slumped against the hard chair back, gripping on to the wooden arms. "I just want to make up with her. I want to apologise, as long and as hard as necessary, until she forgives me. I want everything to go back to how it was." And I wanted her to tell me who she'd spilled my secrets to.

Edward gave me a sad smile. "You know that's never going to happen; it's never going to be how it was."

I just didn't want to admit it. "Doesn't mean I can't try."

Sighing, Edward got to his feet and shoved his hands in his pockets. "Look at it this way," he said, squinting in the sunlight streaming through the large windows. "You know what you want, and you're going out of your way to get it, with very little success. Maybe it's time to think about what Ellie wants for a change."

The words hit me in the middle of my chest. "That's a very polite way to call me a selfish bitch."

He didn't apologise, which I respected. "All I'm saying is, let's get through the party first."

"Then I'll be on a train back to Perth and Ellie won't have to see me again for another two years." Because I was under no illusion that I'd be welcomed back any sooner, and just knowing that made my heart hurt.

He sighed, and pulled up his own chair. "Listen. This party is making your sister crazy. Please, for all our sakes, don't add to that right now. Okay?"

He was right. Timing, that was the key. There wasn't a chance that Ellie would forgive me when she was so stressed out. But maybe once the party was a success, after a couple of glasses of champagne... maybe that was the time to try again.

Because after being back at Rosewood for only a day, I already knew I couldn't just leave again. Not without knowing I could come back.

Rosewood was home.

"How did Ellie get roped into being organiser-in-chief, anyway?" I asked. Maybe if I understood everything that I'd missed in the last two years, I'd be better able to find my own place there again.

"Self-preservation, mostly." Edward shook his head, a half-smile appearing on his face. "Isabelle was losing it over all the planning. She's adamant that everything has to be utterly perfect. It's just as well Nathaniel convinced her to elope the first time; she'd have been unbearable otherwise."

I clasped my hands in my lap and considered how, in just a year and a half, this man had become close enough to my family to know all their quirks and secrets. And it was pretty clear that he, at least, knew my big secret, too. I hated the thought of someone I barely knew knowing the worst thing I'd ever done. No wonder he'd judged me so harshly when we met.

"Anyway, she was shrieking at your mother one day, something about the importance of centrepieces, when Ellie marched in, dragged Isabelle into the kitchen, sat her down at the table and started making lists." Edward looked faintly nostalgic. "We were in there for three hours. I was in charge of making tea."

"That sounds like Ellie." But even as I said it, I realised that it didn't sound at all like the Ellie I'd seen since I came back. It was the Ellie I remembered from five years ago. Was it only my return that had made her quiet and withdrawn? At least, until she blew up at me that morning.

"Usually, yes." So Edward had noticed the change too.

"You seem to have grown very close to my sister," I observed, trying hard not to sound too jealous. "To all my family, really."

"I think they've all become a little claustrophobic, shut up in that house. Perhaps they just like having someone new to talk to."

And it wasn't like any of them were going to talk to me. But Ellie had clearly been talking to him. Maybe he could answer the questions I still had.

"Ellie told you... well, everything. Didn't she? About me and... well... you know. Don't you?"

Edward nodded, slowly. "I think it helped, having someone who wasn't family to talk to about it."

"But she told family too, some of them, at least." I looked up at him. "Do you know who?"

"That's what you were trying to find out?"

I glanced away. "Yeah. I just... wondered." With an all-encompassing need to know.

Edward sighed. "I don't know who she told what. And I'm not sure it really matters. I mean, the way things are between you... I'm pretty sure they've all guessed."

I covered my face with my hands, wishing I could just disappear. "Of course they have." And that was even worse. If they were just guessing, they were making up their own stories. They didn't know how it was, how I'd felt about Greg, or how he'd felt about me. They didn't know how sorry I was.

I couldn't think about it for too long, or my heart might crack from the pain of it. I needed a distraction. Fortunately, Isabelle's party was the perfect one. Everybody would be so caught up in the party, they'd barely have time to even *think* about me until it was over. And by then, I'd be on a train away from Rosewood again.

Jumping to my feet I paced across the dining room, staring at the giant table plan leaning against the table. "How many people are coming to this thing?"

Edward shrugged. "A hundred or so, I think. Maybe more." A hundred people, the biggest party at Rosewood in years, and I'd not been invited. Why on earth had I thought I needed Ellie to tell me if there was a place for me at Rosewood? The answer was painfully clear already, just staring at the table plan.

"I won't be on here," I said, a little sadly, running a finger across the plan.

Suddenly, Edward was at my shoulder, a pen in his hand. "You can sit with me," he said. And, before I could stop him, he'd inked my name in on Table 3, next to his, in firm, slanted handwriting. "There. You have a place after all."

I smiled, for the first time in what felt like hours. Isabelle was going to *hate* that.

Still rattled by my conversation with Edward, I made my way down to Therese's cottage in time for tea, and found my great-aunt warming the pot. "Oh, good," she said. "I was worried I'd have to come up to the house and find you, and I *really* would like to stay out of Isabelle's way today."

"Why?" I closed the cottage door behind me. "Party craziness?"

"Mostly." She flashed me a quick smile. "Isabelle and I don't have the best track record when it comes to parties."

I perched myself on the edge of her kitchen table, frowning. "Really? How do you mean?"

Therese waved my question away. "Oh, you know. Anyway, I've got your outfit for tomorrow ready."

"Excellent." At least I'd have something beautiful to wear while I suffered through the party. "Thank you."

"Make the tea and I'll fetch it," she offered, disappearing past the trunks of clothes in the hallway, towards her bedroom.

By the time the tea had brewed and I'd tracked down some plain chocolate digestives in the bread bin, Therese had returned, suit hanger in one hand, and a pair of bottle green stiletto-heeled sandals dangling from the fingers of the other. "You're going to sink into the grass," she said, depositing the clothes on the table and the shoes on the chair, "but it'll be worth it. Necklace and earrings are in the clutch bag in the holder."

"You're a marvel," I said, pouring her tea. "Thank you. Speaking of, can I hold on to the blue dress from last night a little longer? I thought I'd wear it again for dinner tonight." Dressing for dinner might have a range of meanings at Rosewood – as evidenced by Nathaniel's tendency to come down either in a dinner jacket or a bright orange jumper – but none of the officey clothes or jeans and tops I'd brought with me felt quite right.

"Absolutely not," Therese said, clanking her cup down on its saucer. "Wear the same dress twice in the same company? Not a chance. I'll go and find you something else." And, digestive biscuit clenched between her teeth, she bustled back off towards the bedroom again.

I felt a bit guilty, raiding Therese's vintage collection in this manner, but the truth was, I really didn't want to go to this dinner as myself. I wanted that feeling I'd had the night before, with my hair curled and my lips a bright red they'd never been before. The feeling that I was someone else, watching this family I had no ties to, no obligations. No guilt, I suppose, was the main thing. I just wanted to be someone else, until I was welcome back at Rosewood as myself again.

If I ever was.

Luckily, Therese wasn't inclined to ask questions about my motivation; she was much more interested in helping me dress the part.

My outfit for the evening was of a later vintage than the previous one – a white, 1950s print dress with big red roses across a wide skirt. Therese pulled my dark hair back into a high ponytail and slicked red lipstick across my mouth. The off-the-shoulder style of the dress meant that she also confiscated my bra, leaving me self-conscious, until I put on the high red sandals and looked in the mirror; I looked like an all-American cheerleader. I looked entirely unlike myself.

"Perfect."

Therese had chosen her outfit sympathetically, in a more sedate navy blue, but with her usual style of nipped-in waist and flared skirt. Together, we headed out to the terrace where the others were drinking gin and tonics in the early evening sunlight.

"You don't look old enough to drink in that," Nathaniel said, pouring me a gin and tonic anyway. He dropped a slice of lime into the glass with a flourish. He looked like he'd stepped out of a black-and-white movie, straight onto the Rosewood terrace. Tonight was a dinner jacket night, and I was glad I'd made the effort.

"I think she looks wonderful." Therese squeezed me around the waist.

Nathaniel snorted as he handed me my drink. "You would. You dressed her."

"She's my doll," Therese said airily.

Nathaniel turned to me. "You know, even when we were children, she loved dressing up her dolls. She once cut up my school tie to make a belt for one of them. Mother was not pleased."

"But the outfit was fabulous!" After giving her brother a kiss on the cheek, Therese breezed off to talk to Edward, who was leaning against the trelliswork at the terrace's edge, well out of the way. He caught my eye and raised an eyebrow, staring at my bare shoulders. I looked away, staring into my glass, as I remembered he'd seen much more than my shoulders when I lost my towel on the balcony the night before. Was he remembering the same thing? I glanced back up, but Edward had been swept up in conversation with Therese, and I no longer had his attention.

I contemplated going to try to make nice with Mum and Ellie, but then I spotted the corner of Caroline's bright yellow sundress disappearing into the Rose Garden, so I headed over for some less awkward conversation instead.

"What you doing?" I asked, plonking myself down on the bench beside her.

"Ghost-watching," Caroline said, in a surprisingly matter-of-fact voice. "I was thinking that, since it's summer, it doesn't get dark until much later. But she died in winter, so maybe she doesn't realise that. And in winter it gets dark by the time I'm finishing school, so maybe she'll turn up earlier."

I thought about it. There was a logic, of a sort, in there somewhere. "Could work."

"It was early morning when I saw her last time. If it was winter, it would have still been dark." Caro had obviously put a lot of thought into this. I blinked as her words registered fully.

"Caro, have you seen things here before?" I tried to picture the figure I thought I'd seen when I arrived. Had *I* seen her before? Somewhere in the back of my mind was a half-forgotten memory that I couldn't quite grasp. Was I remembering something I'd seen as a child, or just the storybook that Nathaniel gave me?

Caro shrugged. "Just the ghost, yesterday morning. I never thought to look here before, until Granddad told us that story."

"But other places?"

"Of course. There's the fairy ring in the woods, that you can only see when the dew's still wet, and the tree with the man's face – that's only there at dusk, I think, although I've never checked at dawn." She twisted on the bench to look at me. "Haven't you?"

And suddenly it occurred to me; I had. All through my childhood. I nodded. "There was a tree with golden acorns, somewhere west of the fairy ring. And the gravestone of a giant on the path towards the village." And a man who loved me, even though he was marrying my sister.

Caro wasn't crazy; she was a child. And in fact, she was just the same sort of child I was – over-imaginative and creative. We'd both inherited it from the same place: Nathaniel, who, for all that his books were full of human weakness, betrayals and lies – at least, according to the media – had also created wonderful tales of forest maidens and elf kings for me as a child.

Maybe Ellie had shown glimpses of it, too, when she was very young, playing with me in the woods. Maybe it was just one of those things you weren't allowed as an adult – like playing in ball pits, or choosing from the children's menu, or believing in Father Christmas.

Beside me, Caro sighed, as if hearing my thoughts. "It doesn't look like she's coming," she said, as Dad's voice called down to us, gathering us in for dinner.

"We'll try again tomorrow," I promised.

Chapter Four

*The trees shimmered with tiny lights, and
music floated up from the terrace on the
summer breeze. In the Walled Garden, the
flowers were in bloom – peaches and cream
to match her complexion. Just beyond the
walls, our friends and acquaintances chatted
of inconsequentialities, and drank themselves
stupid on the champagne I'd had delivered
from France.*

*But inside the walls of the garden, the world
was ours entirely. We were alone in Eden,
and the world was new.*

*"Bella." I felt in my pocket for the ring.
"Beloved. I have something I need to ask you."*

Biding Time, by Nathaniel Drury (1967)

"Have you seen your grandmother?" Mum asked me, sidling close as I reached the top of the terrace steps. Ellie, I noticed, was hovering in the doorway, dressed in the same cotton skirt she'd had on that morning, although she'd changed her T-shirt for a beige-coloured camisole that almost disappeared against her skin. She looked washed out and miserable, making me feel guilty for forcing our confrontation in the Orangery.

"I haven't seen her since this morning," I told Mum, and she sighed.

"Neither has anyone else." She leant in closer, the green glass beads around her neck clinking. "And I think your sister's about to lose it," she added in a whisper.

Since I thought pretty much the same thing, it appeared it was time to make myself useful. "I'll go and see if I can find her."

I didn't realise that Edward had followed me into the house until he spoke. "Is everything okay?"

"If you mean, is it my fault that Ellie looks like she's about to scream, I assure you that I have been on my best behaviour all afternoon," I told him, not turning round.

"I didn't, particularly." He drew level with me as I headed up the stairs. "I was just wondering what all the whispering was about."

"Curious fellow, aren't you." I turned left at the top of the stairs, rather than right towards my own room, and Edward said, "Are you looking for Isabelle?"

I stopped just short of knocking on my grandmother's door. "Do you know where she is?"

Edward shrugged. "I dropped her off at that swanky hotel down the road this afternoon. She had some treatments booked, apparently. Something about sea salt and scrubbing."

"Leaving Ellie to panic over all the last-minute details." I sighed. Looked like I wasn't the only one being selfish today. "Did she say when she was coming back?"

Edward looked awkward. "I take it she didn't tell Ellie she was going?"

"Apparently not. Come on, you'd better tell her."

Back downstairs, the evening's drinking was continuing apace at the dining table, as Dad dished up the food. I shook my head as Mum looked up questioningly at me, then I slipped into my seat beside Nathaniel. Edward, I saw, was already whispering to Ellie at the other end of the table, presumably explaining the situation.

He sat down opposite me, as Dad handed round plates of curry, which Isabelle would have hated anyway.

"Is there anything Ellie needs us to do?" I asked, reaching across for a naan bread.

Edward shook his head. "Not until tomorrow, anyway. She found a note from Isabelle in the kitchen, while we were upstairs, by the way. Apparently your grandmother felt it would be bad luck to see the groom before the wedding." He passed me a plate of vegetable pakora. "She does realise this isn't an *actual* wedding, doesn't she?"

"At this point, who knows?" I sighed. "Perhaps she just wanted to get out of here for a while. I suppose I can sympathise with that." Except I'd already been away too long. I didn't need to escape, any more. I needed to find a way home.

When we were down to just the poppadom crumbs, Nathaniel clanged his wine glass with his dessert spoon and we all duly stopped talking. "In the absence of my lovely wife, I would like to say a few words."

Almost instinctively, my shoulders tensed.

"Isabelle has apparently taken herself off to become even more beautiful, before we go through this rigmarole of a party tomorrow. I have no doubt that she will return, fresh and relaxed, just in time to meet her guests.

"The speeches, of course, are for tomorrow – and believe me, I have quite the announcement planned for you all." The smile on my grandfather's face was downright frightening and, across the table, Edward was looking very nervous. There was definitely something going on there, something I probably didn't want to know about until I had to, I reasoned. Plausible deniability, and all that.

"It occurs to me that, if we are to treat tomorrow as my second wedding day, then tonight, by all accounts, must surely be my stag night!"

Down the table, Ellie squeaked in alarm, doubtless seeing her plans for helping hands in the morning drowning in a pool of whisky. Nathaniel ignored her. "And as none of you were able to join me for the last one, by virtue of not having been born yet, I insist that you all celebrate with me this evening!"

Downing the rest of his red wine, Nathaniel led the charge to the drawing room and the drinks cabinet.

Things really only went downhill from there.

Three glasses of wine and a hefty dose of Nathaniel's best brandy later, I noticed that Ellie had disappeared. That wasn't fair, I thought. It wasn't fair that she should feel so uncomfortable in my presence that she miss her own grandfather's pseudo stag night. And, my fuzzy head insisted, it was time that I told her so, no matter what everyone else thought.

I drifted towards the doorway and slipped casually into the hallway, the others too busy watching Nathaniel juggle shot glasses to notice. Ellie wasn't in the kitchen, which had been my first guess – she had a tendency to seek out tea in times of stress. Neither was she getting fresh air on the terrace, or hiding out in the back drawing room watching telly.

She'd probably gone to bed, I realised, to get an early night before the party. I headed back into the hallway, only to be stopped at the bottom of the stairs.

"You're looking for Ellie," Edward said, a statement rather than a question. "Again."

I stared down at him, perched on the second step, his long legs folded up so that his knees almost reached his chest. "I just wanted to apologise for earlier. And, well, everything."

"Haven't we had this conversation before? Quite recently?" He sounded surprisingly sober for a stag night attendee. Much soberer than me, I realised. Soberer. Was that even a word?

"I just… I need to…" I scrubbed a hand across my forehead. "I need to tell her that I'm sorry. That she wins. She gets Greg and Rosewood and the family and you. I'll leave if she asks me to. She can have whatever she wants…"

"As long as she forgives you." Edward reached up and pulled me down to sit next to him.

I rested my head against his shoulder. "Don't you have your own family to drive you crazy?"

Edward huffed a laugh, and I felt it in his chest. "I think I'm the one who drives *them* crazy."

"I can't see how." Edward was, quite possibly, the steadiest, most sensible person I'd ever met.

"Right now, they think I'm having an early mid-life crisis," he said, with a small laugh. "Jacking in everything to come and live here at Rosewood, as an assistant to an ageing Great British Writer."

It hadn't really occurred to me that Edward must have had another life, before he came here. Rosewood was always in its own little reality bubble. The outside world ceased to exist once you were inside it.

"What did you do before?" I asked. "And what made you come here, anyway?" Had he left another job? Did he have a wife and kids secreted away somewhere else? He could be anybody, I realised. All I knew about him was that he could withstand Nathaniel's whims and tempers, and that he disapproved of me. Not a lot to go on.

"Nothing half as interesting." He shrugged. "As for why I came... maybe I'll tell you the whole long, boring story. Another day."

"Nowhere else is ever as interesting as Rosewood. It always was my favourite place in the world."

"I can see why," Edward said. "I mean, obviously. I haven't left yet, have I?"

"You're lucky that way." I sighed. "I just want things to go back to the way they were when we were little."

"We've already talked about that. You know it can't happen." Edward slung an arm around my shoulders, a show of camaraderie, which suggested he had at least sampled the brandy. Or maybe his disapproval really was starting to fade. It was probably the towel incident that did it. "Time only ever moves forward."

"I know." Sober, I suspected I'd be hideously embarrassed that it was Edward I was opening up to, the only person in the house not actually related to me. But even drunk I was a little grateful he had kept me from making things worse with Ellie. Again.

We sat in silence for a long moment, and I focused on the thrum of Edward's pulse where my cheek lay against his throat to keep the world from spinning.

"You know," Edward said, thoughtfully, "I think I saw some really excellent whisky in Nathaniel's drinks cabinet. Want to see if there's any left?"

I nodded, and he hauled me to my feet, tugging me back towards the drawing room. I'd just have to try to make it up to Ellie tomorrow.

Getting up the next morning was not easy.

Downstairs, there was coffee brewing in the kitchen, and a list laid out prominently on the table in Ellie's neat handwriting, detailing responsibilities and delegations.

Pouring myself a cup of strong, black Colombian, I sat down to read through the list.

Edward and Greg were charged with supervising the set-up of the tables and chairs, and the catering tents. Dad was looking after the caterers; Mum was making sure the cake was delivered and set up correctly, and looking after the musicians when they arrived.

"Are those our orders for the day?" Nathaniel asked, shuffling into the room and towards the coffee machine. "What am I down for?"

"Staying out of the way and making sure your bow tie is tied straight," I told him, reading from Ellie's list. "Possibly also greeting guests and stuff."

He groaned. "Well, I'm all right with the first part. Especially since it means I can go back to bed for a while." Taking his mug with him, he shuffled back out again.

I turned back to the list. In Isabelle's absence, Therese was in charge of all the last-minute straightening and tidying the house required, even though it had been cleaned from top to bottom by professionals the day before, and despite the fact it was a beautiful day and the entire party was planned to take place outside. Ellie was looking after the florist, and all the other decorative bits.

I wasn't on the list.

Putting the sheet of paper back for the next lazy slacker with a hangover to find, once they dragged themselves out of bed, I picked up my coffee and headed outside to see how I could make myself useful.

Greg and Edward obviously had stronger heads than I'd thought, or were even more afraid of upsetting Ellie than everyone else because, despite the considerable amount of Nathaniel's best whisky I'd watched them consume the night before, they were both up and lugging tables and chairs across the grass. Not actually feeling up to manual labour myself, I decided to seek out Ellie instead.

She wasn't hard to find. The florist's van was parked outside the side door, and Ellie was watching as obscenely large arrangements of yellow and white flowers were offloaded and dragged down to the party area.

She still didn't look happy.

"What's the matter?" I asked, sidling close before she could realise I was there and manufacture some excuse to disappear.

Ellie jumped at the sound of my voice, then sighed, the same tired, world-weary sigh she'd been using all week. "There was a mix-up with the order. They forgot the table decorations."

"Oh."

"Isabelle's going to be furious." Which was a bit of an understatement, I felt.

"Well, perhaps they can..." I tried, but Ellie cut me off, and I heard a hint of the temper she was back to keeping under wraps.

"They can't do anything," she snapped. "Apparently they've got an actual wedding this afternoon, and the bride and her mother are a lot scarier than me."

"Then we'll fix it ourselves," I said, wracking my brain to think of a way to do that.

"How?" Ellie asked, impatiently. "Do you happen to have a flair for flower arranging I don't know about? And some, oh, I don't know, flowers?"

I grinned. "No to the first, but absolutely to the second." And, grabbing her arm, I dragged her towards the Rose Garden.

"Isabelle was planning on only using the Rose Garden flowers in the house," Ellie said as together we surveyed the few remaining yellow roses.

"Isabelle's not here." I handed her one set of the gloves and secateurs I'd liberated from the gardener's shed, and pulled my own gloves on. "Besides, no one's going to be going inside. It's gorgeous out here."

Ellie kept staring at the flowers. To encourage her a little, I started snipping off flower heads.

"Wait!" she shrieked, grabbing my wrist as the first flower fell. "What are we going to put them in?"

"Water?" I said helpfully. Ellie raised an eyebrow at me and dropped my arm. "Okay, well, glasses then. Or bowls. You've hired in crockery and glassware for outside, after all. How many tables are there? Ten?" Ellie nodded. "Perfect, then. We use the glass dessert bowls we had the mango sorbet in last night, fill them with water and float rose heads in them. That way, we won't even need that many." Which was just as well, as Isabelle had decapitated most of them already, for the many vases that now littered the inside of Rosewood.

Ellie considered it for a moment, then smiled for the first time that week, that I'd seen. "Okay, then."

It was strange, cutting flowers with Ellie, for all the world as if it were ten years ago, and Isabelle had sent us out for roses for the dinner table before a party. In fact… "Do you remember how we used to do this as kids?" I asked, softly, hoping Ellie was in the same nostalgic place I was. Ever since we were tiny, I'd followed Ellie around those gardens, picking flowers and chasing butterflies. I'd have followed her anywhere, I knew. I'd thought she hung the moon and lit it.

Maybe I still did.

"We'd crush the petals with water to make perfume, and put it in Isabelle's tiny glass bottles," I went on, lost in the memories of happier times. A time when my sister was my whole world, and I was the person she loved most in it. "We thought it was the most beautiful fragrance ever. It probably smelled terrible! But Isabelle would wear it, whenever we gave her a bottle, do you remember?" Ellie smiled – just a small, half-smile, an absent gesture, but it warmed my heart to see it.

But then the smile faded. "I remember the last time we did this," she whispered back, her voice tight. "The day before my wedding. The day after you slept with my husband."

Ellie had woken me up really early, I remembered, far too excited to sleep. We'd picked the white roses for Isabelle to tie into a bouquet for Ellie, and a few golden yellow ones for me to hold. We'd talked about the future, about their plans, and mine. And I'd almost forgotten about Greg, until Ellie asked me what was wrong, why I was quiet. And I didn't tell her.

"I should have told you that day," I said, now, finally. "I should have told you the minute it happened."

"But Greg told me instead, later that morning. You just ran away the minute the confetti was thrown." She snipped another rose head free of its stem, and it felt like she was cutting my heartstrings. Apparently forgiveness was still firmly off the cards.

"And I think that's all the roses we need." Gathering up her flowers in her arms, Ellie headed away from me, towards the house.

I followed her, as always.

Once Ellie and I had distributed our makeshift centrepieces, I headed upstairs to get changed, luxuriating in the feel of the pale green silk of my dress against my skin, and hoping I could stay upright in the heels. With the matching headband and my slick bob, I felt just like a 1920s flapper girl.

As I teetered down the stairs, I spotted Greg standing in the hallway below, and my heart beat twice in one moment as I stopped, halfway down. I'd been home two days, and I still hadn't been alone with Greg yet. Part of me had been grateful not to have to go through that – trying to find the right words, if any, to say. And part of me had been desperate for it, just to know for sure that everything between us was in the past. Perhaps even to learn how he'd managed to be forgiven – why he deserved forgiveness and I didn't. So, did I stay or did I run?

Greg looked up and saw me, and the choice was out of my hands.

Swallowing, I resumed my descent. "Any sign of our missing matriarch?"

Greg shook his head, slowly, staring at me until I began to feel uncomfortable. "What?"

"Nothing." He caught my eye as I reached the bottom of the stairs. "You just look nice, is all."

God, what I'd have given to hear him say those words two years ago. I could picture it perfectly, if I tried. But I wouldn't. This wasn't two years ago. I wasn't going to blush prettily for him and try to deny it. I wasn't going to smile shyly at the compliment.

It wasn't even three, four or five years ago, when we were all friends, growing up with the world at our feet and sure that we would explore it, the three of us, together. I missed that feeling, but even I was realistic enough to know it wasn't coming back.

This was now, and Rosewood was a different world, these days.

"I'm looking for your wife," I said, pointedly. "Any ideas where she's got to?" If Isabelle still wasn't back, then Ellie was probably going frantic.

"Join the club," Greg said. "I'll help you look."
Which wasn't quite what I'd intended.

He followed me out into the bright sunshine; it was
half past ten, and the sun was creeping higher over the
house. Guests were due from midday. If Isabelle didn't
come home soon, she'd risk missing her own party.

It felt strange, being alone with Greg. Like we should
be sneaking about, watching out for anyone who might
see us. Except we'd never done that, even back then.
It wasn't how things were between us.

Over on the lawn, the tables and chairs had been
set out perfectly according to plan, and decorated
with white linens, chiffon sashes and our makeshift
centrepieces, a splash of yellow in amongst the white.
Places were laid with the hired white china and polished
silver cutlery that glinted and sparked in the bright sun.

Backing onto the woods, even the catering tents
looked starched and bleached. Outside each entrance
was a pedestal flower arrangement filled with white and
yellow flowers, and deep green leaves. From inside, some
very tempting aromas were already drifting out as the
food was assembled and reheated.

There was plenty of activity: I could see Mum settling
the musicians on one side of the dining area, and Dad's
voice was clearly audible from inside the tents, asking
questions about ingredients. But there was no sign
of Ellie.

Greg didn't seem bothered. "I'm glad I've got this
chance to talk to you, actually," he said, as I walked
purposefully towards the Orangery, Greg ambling along
behind. "There hasn't been an opportunity since you came
back. And I think there are some things we need to say."

I knew what he meant. Even if I'd wanted to talk to
him, with my family running interference, there wouldn't

have been the chance. Ellie wasn't the only one they were steering me away from. But I didn't want to talk to him. I didn't want the conversation. Didn't want to discuss our mistakes, or talk about how in another time or place things might have been different. How we just weren't meant to be, right here and now. I just wanted to pretend that two years ago never happened at all.

I'd thought that Greg would feel the same, but apparently not. And that made me very nervous indeed.

Suddenly, our meeting in the hallway seemed less serendipitous. "Greg, this really isn't the..."

"Actually," he interrupted, his voice sharper than I'd ever heard before, "I think it's the perfect time."

The Orangery was empty, and I was running out of places to look. "Maybe we should try the catering tents."

As I spun on my heel, sinking into the grass, Greg grabbed my arm and said, "Saskia," his voice firm.

I sighed. "Greg, we don't have to. Really." As I turned and looked up at him, I half expected all the old feelings to come flooding back. The obsessive need to watch him, to read his smiles, to catch his eye. The heat that touched my skin every time he looked at me. The connection we hadn't been able to deny. "Look, we made a mistake, we both know that. We... we fell in love, when we weren't free to do that. We shouldn't have acted on it, but... we couldn't help how we felt. But it's over now."

Greg let go of my arm with a laugh – a harsh, bitter laugh that grated against my ears. "Do you honestly still believe that?"

I blinked. "Believe... what? That's what happened."

"That's the story we told ourselves to try and make what we did less horrific," he said. "I guess you've been telling it to yourself so long you really believe it."

"I don't know what you're talking about." We'd fallen in love. We'd given in when we shouldn't. We'd made a mistake. What was I missing?

"That wasn't love, Saskia," Greg said, and my stomach dropped at his words. "And you know that, deep down. We were selfish, lonely people who thought that Ellie was ignoring us while she was so caught up in all the wedding stuff. I was scared about the future, about everything changing. And yes, I wanted you. And I knew you wanted me too – you weren't exactly subtle, you know. I was looking for some comfort, Ellie wasn't around and you were, and I was weak. I gave in. I risked everything that mattered to me in the world for a few minutes of feeling better, and it was the biggest mistake I ever made."

I stared at him, unable to speak, unable to process his words, unable to even *think* beyond the realisation that he was right.

Greg shook his head. "If you think *that* was love, Kia… then you haven't got a clue about what love really means. Love isn't roses – it isn't long glances across a room or secret rendezvous or any of the stuff we had. Love is owning up, saying sorry, and working like hell to make things right again. It's sticking around to fix things, even when it's the hardest thing in the world to do."

"Ellie said…" The words came out raspy, and I swallowed and started again. "Ellie said you tried to call off the wedding."

"I had to give her the option to walk away, with all the information. I'm just grateful as all hell that she gave me another chance."

And maybe, if I'd stayed, if I'd confessed that morning in the Rose Garden… maybe she'd have given me one, too. But it was too late now. I'd never know.

I turned, wrenching my heels from the grass, and walked away. I couldn't look at Greg another moment, not now I'd realised the truth. I didn't love him. I never had. And he'd never loved me. No wonder it hadn't hurt to come back and see him here, happy with Ellie.

It was all just a story, a way to make my peace with what I'd done. Only now, I knew there was no truth in that fiction.

The truth was I'd done the worst thing I could imagine to one of the people I loved most in the world. I'd betrayed her, and she was right not to forgive me.

With that one act, I'd torn myself away from Rosewood, away from my family. I'd run, and no one had followed. I'd slammed that door behind me, and I might never be able to go back through it. It wasn't just my relationship with Ellie I'd ruined – it was with everyone. Nathaniel, Isabelle, Therese, Mum and Dad, Caro… Things could never be the same between us, ever again. Hell, it had even coloured any friendship I might hope to have with Edward. The first and only thing he knew about me was that I betrayed my sister. Not a great start.

I heard Greg calling after me and picked up my pace, until I was running across the grass on my tiptoes, racing towards the edge of the garden.

I slowed as I reached the trees, slipping between them into the cool dark of the woods. Without needing to think about it, I ran my hands along the bark of the trunks, counting trees as I went. One, two, three… Six and seven. I stopped. Seven trees in and four across. Easy. I turned right after the seventh tree and counted along another four and I was there.

When I was small, I was desperate for a place that was mine, a secret, hidden place where no one could find me.

I wanted to be private and mysterious. And Nathaniel, my doting grandfather, indulged me.

One weekend, very early, we sneaked out into the woods and found the perfect tree, just the two of us. It was bigger around the trunk than even Nathaniel could reach, and its lowest branches were far above his head. It was summer, and the leaf canopy was impenetrable, shading the whole area in darkness and magic.

We had to enlist some help, because my grandfather has never been very good with his hands, except when there's a pen in them. Luckily, his assistant at the time was a young man called Graham, who couldn't have been more than twenty-one, fresh out of university, and whose father was a carpenter.

Since Nathaniel and I both knew that Graham probably wouldn't be around by the next month, we thought he was a safe bet. And so, in addition to Graham's other duties (dealing with letters from readers, looking up obscure books, making tea, being shouted at, that sort of thing) he was shanghaied into building an eight-year-old girl a tree house.

And, true to form, Graham quit two weeks after it was completed. As far as I know, he never told anyone else in the family about the tree house. Neither did I, and neither did Nathaniel.

Which meant, when I reached my tree and found the secret ladder already lowered and smoke blowing out of the window, there was really only one person who could be in residence.

I paused at the bottom of the tree, catching my breath after the rush through the woods, trying to stop my head spinning from my conversation with Greg. I'd wanted to be alone, to get away from Rosewood and all the horrible realisations it brought up. But now

I was there, I wanted my grandfather. I wanted the comfort of Nathaniel's presence, the warmth of his voice, the reassurance of his hugs… even the distraction of his stories.

I'd been alone for too long already. I wasn't going to miss this chance to be with my family, however hard it was.

"You know, this wasn't built as a smoking house for you," I called up, putting my foot on the first rung of the rope ladder. Now I thought about it, perhaps Therese's vintage silk dress and matching heels weren't the ideal costume for climbing trees.

Nathaniel stuck his head out of the doorway. "Who paid for the wood? And the labour? And where is the gratitude? I ask you." He took a good look at me. "Are you coming up in that?"

Grasping the rope, I swung my left foot up onto the next rung. "Apparently."

The tree house was fairly basic: a square base of tightly joined wooden planks, with just enough space for Nathaniel and I to squeeze in together, more plank-made walls, with gaps left for doors and windows, and a few more planks over the top at an angle as a roof. In essence, a wooden box.

When I was eight, I thought it was the most perfect place in the world.

I hoisted myself through the narrow doorway, ducking my head to avoid the ceiling, and slid onto the low stool Nathaniel held steady for me beside the sloping shelf beneath the window.

"We used to fit in here better," he observed, taking another puff on his pipe.

"I appear to have grown up." I smoothed out my skirt under me, and hoped I wasn't ruining the fabric.

"Indeed you have." Nathaniel caught my eye. "So why don't you tell me why a grown-up like you is hiding out in a child's tree house."

"I could ask the same of you," I pointed out.

Nathaniel spread his arms as wide as the walls of the tree house allowed. "Ah, but I have never really grown up. Proper writers never do."

"So, who are you hiding from?" I asked. "Isabelle isn't even back yet."

"I'm not hiding," Nathaniel said, sounding affronted. "I am rehearsing."

"Your speech?" Truth be told, I was starting to get a little nervous about Nathaniel's speech. My grandfather had a tendency towards long, obtuse but somehow insulting oratory. I was just hoping he'd wait until most of the guests were plastered before he started. At least some of the cleverer, crueller insults might pass over their heads that way. "Is it going well? Do you want to practise in front of a live audience?" If I knew who he was planning to offend, perhaps I could distract them.

"It will be the highlight of the year," Nathaniel announced, waving a few dog-eared notecards around. "And you're just going to have to wait and listen with the rest of them."

"You're all about the dramatic tension, aren't you?" I said, fondly.

"Of course!" He placed his notecards carefully on the floor beside him, out of my reach. "So, what can I do for you?"

I didn't want to admit that, actually, I hadn't been looking for him at all – I'd been running away from Greg. From my own mistakes. So instead, I leant back against the smooth wood of the wall and said, "Tell me a story."

He raised an eyebrow. "Aren't you a little old for story time?"

"Is that even possible?"

"I suppose not." He smiled around his pipe. "So, what sort of story are you after?"

"One about Rosewood," I decided. If I had to leave again, as it seemed I would, I wanted to take as much of this place with me as I could. "Not about the ghosts and the history. A story of you here at Rosewood."

"A story about me. My favourite subject." Another joke. For all that his books featured versions of himself and his life, I knew full well that none of those characters were the real Nathaniel. In fact, I suspected they were a screen for him to hide behind – more fiction than truth. A way to keep his true self private, even in the face of intense public scrutiny. My grandfather, I reflected, was a complicated man.

"Okay," he said, at last. "I have it."

He gave me a look I couldn't quite read, and I frowned for a moment. But then Nathaniel settled back on his stool, pipe clamped between his teeth, left a dramatic pause, removed the pipe and began his story.

"Once upon a time, there was an incredibly handsome and talented young man who had a very beautiful and intelligent wife. They lived in a tiny London flat in the most fashionable area, and she made it up to look twice the size it really was."

"I thought this was a story about Rosewood?"

"Patience," Nathaniel said. "Now, the lucky couple loved nothing more than throwing wild parties and showing each other off to all their friends. And their parties became renowned. Famous. Even notorious."

Would this party, this Golden Wedding, be one of those parties? I'd had an inkling it would, back in Perth, when he called and asked me to come. And, looking at his stack of notecards on the floor, I felt even more certain that it would. Nathaniel had never used notecards in his life; he just told a story, whenever he needed to speak in public. And his stories had never needed index cards.

What was he going to say in his speech? And what would it mean for all of us? I was almost too nervous – or excited – to ask.

"Are you still listening?"

"Of course!" I straightened up and started paying proper attention again.

"Tales of the parties they held filled the social pages, not to mention the conversations in all the most artistic haunts. People angled for an invite to the next one whenever they spoke to someone who'd been there. The themes became more outlandish, more spectacular. Until the day the couple announced that they were moving house."

"To Rosewood?"

Nathaniel silenced me with a look. "Moving to a charmed mansion in the English countryside, complete with a Rose Garden, a fountain, an orangery and a tiny, splintery tree house."

"Poetic licence already?" I asked. "The tree house didn't exist whenever you're setting this story."

"I'm just glad you didn't query the 'handsome and talented' part earlier. Now, shut up and let me tell the story." I obediently shut up.

"Their new house would allow them to throw even bigger and better parties, the woman declared. It was, she said, the 'absolute perfect house for parties.'" I could almost hear Isabelle saying the words as he spoke them. "They decided that they would hold the best ever party, to celebrate moving into their new home. They invited everyone who was everyone, and quite a few people who weren't anyone at all. It was *the* party of the season, and people fought tooth and nail for an invite.

"The day of the party arrived, and the woman spent all day – hell, all week, all month! – preparing for it, while her husband was writing. She dressed in her finest clothes, while he forgot until the last minute then couldn't find his cufflinks. The guests arrived and the champagne flowed. The band struck up a song, and people danced. And as the night went on the champagne flowed faster and the conversations got louder and the band grew tired and went home. But still the party went on, long after the moon had risen and fallen again. The sun came up and still the party continued. The champagne ran dry, but they just moved on to spirits. The house was filled to overflowing with people and fun and laughter…"

A pause, just a small one, and I realised Nathaniel was trying to decide the direction of the story. What would happen next? How much of this was real? I wondered. And how much part of his imagination?

And if it was real, what was he avoiding telling me?

"The party seemed like it might never end. People slept where they sat, and woke up and started all over again. The bedrooms were taken over by guests too, but very few people were sleeping in them. The sun set on the second day, and still the party went on. Until…"

"What?" I asked, as desperate as always for the next part of the story. "What happened?"

Nathaniel refocused his gaze on me. "Like I said, the house was overflowing. It spilled out onto the terrace, into the gardens, and even out the front door onto the steps. It felt like the party might just keep growing and take over the whole land… until suddenly a scream cut through the celebrations."

I flinched, and Nathaniel reached across to hold my hand. His fingers smelt like tobacco, and I knew mine would too, afterwards. I didn't mind.

"All the guests ran towards the sound, and the man wondered for a moment if the sudden shift would cause the house to tip. Silence fell – an eerie, painful silence that rang in the ears – as they all stared at the figure of a man lying at the bottom of the white marble steps, blood streaming from a gash on the back of his head."

Yeah, this one really wasn't suitable for Caro. But what I wanted to know most was, was it true?

"And in moments, the house was empty. The party was over, and only the man and woman were left. Well, just them and the body and the police.

"And that was the last party they ever threw."

His voice faded away, and all I could hear was the wind in the trees around us.

"Did that... Is it a true story?" I asked, half expecting him to laugh. Of course it couldn't be true. Apart from anything else, I knew for a fact that Nathaniel and Isabelle had held *plenty* of parties at Rosewood since they moved in.

"Aren't they all true, one way or another?" Nathaniel said, with a shrug. "It just depends on your interpretation."

"Yes, but—"

"And now, I believe I have another party to attend," Nathaniel interrupted. Bending over he collected his index cards, then stood up with a groan. "I'm too old for this, Saskia."

"You'll never be too old."

He smiled, then leant over and kissed the top of my head. "And you will always, always have a home at Rosewood," he said. "Whatever you do. Don't you forget that."

With a final puff on his pipe, he placed it on the rickety shelf and descended the ladder, cards flapping in his hands.

How did he do that? We'd talked about his speech, about some mythical party at Rosewood and a possible death, and his age. Not a word about me or Greg or being home. And still he'd known, without even having to ask, exactly why I was hiding out in the tree house.

I just hoped that what he said was true.

I blinked away my tears and, after a few moments alone with the quiet and the stale smell of smoke, I followed my grandfather back down the ladder and through the woods to the house.

It was nearly midday, after all. Time for the party to begin.

Chapter Five

*"A wedding day should be a magnificent
affair,"* Bella said, staring down at the small,
sad bunch of wildflowers in her hand.
"A celebration. A display of love."

"Our wedding day is all of those things,"
I assured her. The elopement was, of course,
my idea. *"And more. Because it's us,
for ever."* I kissed her forehead. *"And so
we don't need anyone else. Ever."*

Biding Time, by Nathaniel Drury (1967)

I caught up with Nathaniel on the front drive, just as
a large, black taxi cab pulled to a stop in front of the
house, and Isabelle stepped out. Caroline had beaten
us both, and was standing with her hands on her hips
watching the proceedings.

"Nathaniel, darling, have you got any cash on you?"
Isabelle asked, hooking her pale cream handbag over her
arm. "Kia, my bags are in the boot, if you wouldn't mind."

I stepped forward automatically and opened the
boot, as Nathaniel paid the driver. Isabelle, meanwhile,
sashayed her way towards the house, looking for all the
world like an ageing film star.

She'd obviously had peace and quiet and assistance
to prepare herself for the party: her silver-blonde hair

was perfectly waved and pinned at the back of her head, her make-up was flawless, and her cream shot-silk suit glittered in the sunlight. She looked every inch the bride she'd decided to be for the day.

The guests were starting to arrive, too, by the time I'd stashed away Isabelle's bags. In just moments, the chaos of tents and family members shouting instructions at each other had melted away, and a real wedding-y atmosphere had emerged.

Over by the trees, the string quartet were settling in for the long haul, starting off with the ever popular Pachelbel's Canon. Waiters in three-piece suits were circulating with trays of champagne, Kir Royale, and Pimm's, which were being grabbed up gratefully by guests as they stepped out of their cars. Ribbons tied to chairs and tables and tents and flower arrangements fluttered in the slight breeze, as puffy white clouds floated across overhead. Mum and Ellie were standing alongside Isabelle to shake hands and kiss cheeks, and the air was awash with the scent of roses and too much perfume. Greg hovered at Ellie's elbow, ready to cater to her every whim, I supposed. Every now and then she'd twist and smile at him, and the light that filled his face almost made me jealous. Not jealous that she made him that happy – I was past that. But just that I'd never had that effect on anyone.

Ellie and Greg were truly happy, and I was so glad that was the case. But it didn't stop me wanting some of that happiness for myself, with my own right person. If I ever found them.

"Saskia!" I turned at the sound of my name, only to find myself suddenly accosted by a gaggle of women – old friends of Isabelle's. I'd never been able to keep them all straight when I *lived* at Rosewood, so the chances of me remembering their names now was slim. Fortunately, they didn't seem to need me to talk at all.

"Well, darling, this *is* a nice surprise!" A woman in a green straw hat pressed a powdery kiss to my cheek. "We weren't at all sure that you'd be back for this little party you know."

"Isabelle did say that with your very important job she wasn't sure you'd be able to get away," another woman, this one dressed in flamingo pink, said. Of course Isabelle wouldn't have wanted to let on that she hadn't invited me. That there was a potential, scandalous reason why I might not be welcomed back at Rosewood.

Mrs Pink frowned. "What is it that you do again, dear?"

"I'm a reporter," I said, but no one was listening.

"Never mind her job," Mrs Green said. "What we all want to know is where your young man is!"

"I'll be honest," a third lady said. I dubbed her Mrs Poppy, as her dress was liberally covered in large poppy prints that did nothing to disguise her very ample curves. "I always thought that the next wedding we'd be attending at Rosewood would be yours, Saskia."

"Well, it's not really a wedding…" I started.

"So, where is he?" Mrs Pink asked, prodding me with a bony elbow. "Your young man, I mean."

How to answer that one? Did I say 'Perth' and continue the Duncan fiction? But that would only lead to more questions about why he hadn't come with me. Did I claim I didn't have one? Or would that just earn me pitying glances or – worse – attempts to set me up with their grandsons. I'd already been through that when Ellie and Greg got engaged, thank you very much.

Fortunately, I had an unlikely saviour.

"Saskia?" Edward appeared at my side, and put a hand at my waist. Isabelle's friends all awwed. In fact, I think Mrs Pink honestly swooned. I couldn't really blame her. Dressed in a charcoal grey suit, his hair neatly combed, Edward was the epitome of a classic English gentleman. "I think your dad is looking for you."

"Excuse me." I gave the gaggle a suitably polite smile, then walked quickly in the opposite direction, my hand tucked through Edward's arm. "Thank God for that," I said, the moment we were a respectable distance away. "Is Dad really looking for me?"

"No idea," Edward said cheerfully. "But you looked like you were about to rip that woman's hideous green hat off and stamp on it, so I thought I'd better get you out of there."

"Good call. Isn't green unlucky for weddings, though?"

"Why would I know?" Edward asked. "Besides, this isn't actually a wedding."

"Right." No service to attend, no Master of Ceremonies to boss us about. "So, where are we going then?" We were still striding across the gardens, after all.

"The bar. Where else?" Edward flashed me a grin, and I returned it.

Maybe the day wouldn't be entirely awful, after all.

In the end, it was everything a pseudo wedding should be, until the after-dinner speeches.

I'd been seated, with a slightly less professional name plate, exactly where Edward had written me onto the table plan – just apart from the rest of the family, on an extra chair shoved in between some second cousins, Edward and my godfather.

Pat Norris had been the family lawyer long before he took responsibility for my religious upbringing, and we were all very fond of him. The fact that he retained us as clients, despite having retired to the Welsh coast years ago, suggested that he felt the same about us.

"How are things in Perth?" Pat asked, pouring me a glass of white wine from the ice bucket in the centre of the table.

"Fine." I took a large gulp. "The usual. Busy."

"I keep asking your grandfather when I'm going to see your name on a hardback in the shops. You were always determined to be a writer like him when you were little."

Beside me, Edward had a curious eyebrow raised. Time to change the subject. "I don't suppose Nathaniel mentioned his speech for today in any of these little chats?"

Pat shook his head. "He's being most secretive. Not secretive enough that we don't all know he's planning *something*, of course..."

"Of course. What would be the point of that?" I turned to Edward. "Have *you* read the speech?"

Edward shook his head, but his eyes never left the top table, where Nathaniel was pulling out Isabelle's chair for her. "But I've got a suspicion about what he's going to say," he murmured.

He wouldn't say any more. And when, an hour or so later, Nathaniel clinked his fork against his glass and stood up to speak, I understood why.

"When I met Isabelle, over fifty years ago now, she was the most beautiful woman I'd ever seen. As you can see from looking at her today, that hasn't changed." Nathaniel reached down to touch Isabelle's hand, and my grandmother made an attempt at a modest look down at the table. At the family table, I saw Therese roll her eyes.

"Fifty years of marriage is a huge achievement for anyone," Nathaniel went on, pulling away from his wife and addressing his audience head on. "And I cannot claim that it has always been an easy journey." I winced, and Edward patted my hand where it rested on the table.

"It's not going to get any better," Edward murmured in what he may have misguidedly thought was a comforting tone. "You might want to pour yourself some more wine." I took his advice.

"But, as all writers know, that's where the best stories lie – in the trials and the tribulations, the scandal and the betrayals. And what is life, if not our greatest story?"

All of a sudden, I had a terrible premonition of where this was going. "He's not planning to…" I started to say, but Edward put one long finger to his lips and shushed me, a crooked smile on his face.

"Which is why it gives me great pleasure to announce, here, in front of all the friends and family who have gossiped about us over the years, that you will finally have the opportunity to find out the truth behind the legends – and all for the low price of eighteen ninety-nine, I expect."

Rustling and whispering ran around the tables, and Isabelle had a rictus grin fixed on her perfectly made-up face. Two tables over, Ellie was whispering urgently in Mum's ear.

"I can see most of you have caught on by now," Nathaniel boomed, amusement in his voice. "That's right – the next book I publish will be my own memoirs. An accurate, and hopefully entertaining, rendition of my life, my marriage, my family and my work – not that I think any of you will be reading it to find out about my writing habits!" There was a ripple of laughter among the outer lying tables – the ones occupied by people who knew they wouldn't appear between the pages of Nathaniel's memory.

"I have found, however, that writing an autobiography requires a different mindset to that of fiction. The research, surprisingly, is far more in depth, as I desperately try to remember the name of my first cousin – the one who got shot in Chicago – or who else attended the party we threw upon moving in to Rosewood." He didn't even glance down at Isabelle as he said that, but her face grew even tighter and more still. Was that the party he'd been talking about in the tree house? How much of what he'd told me had been story – and what on earth was the truth?

"It became quickly apparent to me that I needed a research assistant. But, as my family will testify, I haven't had the best of luck with assistants in the past." Another chuckle, from those who'd heard the stories of past assistants, but not from those of us who'd actually lived through it. Edward, I noticed, had refilled his own wine glass, and was drinking it steadily down.

"What I needed this time, I realised, was someone who understood what I was trying to do, someone with experience in this field. Someone who could turn my recollections into true biography." Nathaniel looked over in our direction. "Well, stand up, boy! Everyone, I'd like you to meet my collaborator in this project. The esteemed biographer and excellent writer in his own right, Edward Hollis."

As soon as I heard the name, I wondered why I'd not figured it out sooner. No author pictures on the covers of his books, I suppose. Edward staggered awkwardly to his feet, very briefly, before dropping back down in his chair. Esteemed biographer indeed, I thought. The name Edward Hollis was synonymous with unflinching accuracy and truth, even in his biographies of national heroes and historical giants. No one ever came out sparkling clean in a Hollis biography, but no subject could ever claim defamation or slander. He might ruin careers and reputations, but Edward Hollis was scrupulously truthful and fair.

And I was terrified what truths he would find to tell of us.

I turned to ask him what the hell was going on, but Edward was already halfway across the marquee, headed towards the bar.

"Did you know he was going to do this?" Therese asked, dropping into Edward's suddenly vacated seat. I peered around her and saw Nathaniel collaring his collaborator saying, "Edward! Come and meet Cecil." My grandfather, at least, was in his element.

"No idea," I said, topping up the wine glass she'd brought with her. "You don't seem too bothered by it."

Therese shrugged. "I know what he'll say about me, about my life. Nothing he hasn't said to my face over the years."

"I wish I felt as confident," I said. Therese chuckled. Over at the next table, the rest of the family was holding what looked like an emergency summit. "Should we be part of that?"

Therese glanced over. "I wouldn't. They're bound to repeat themselves endlessly over the next few days anyway. Isabelle especially. In fact, if you really wanted, I could probably recite every one of her arguments for you right now. They all add up to 'I don't want my husband telling the unvarnished truth about me'. You know your grandmother – hates to be seen without her stage make-up." She took a suspiciously large gulp of wine. I got the feeling she wasn't quite as unflustered by Nathaniel's announcement as she wanted me to believe.

"We're not missing anything. May as well enjoy what's left of the party."

But as the evening wore on, I realised that something *was* missing – Edward. I glanced around the marquee, checking on each family member. Dad stood at the edge of the tent, Caro at his side, pointing up at various constellations. Mum sat nearby watching them, a glass of wine in her hand. Therese was chatting to the barman as he topped up her glass, and Isabelle was at the heart of a gaggle of her friends. Ellie and Greg were the last couple on the dance floor, lost in each other's arms as they swayed to the music. I jerked my gaze away to find my grandfather in another corner, deep in conversation with Pat. Presumably, they were discussing the legal ramifications of his plans.

But Nathaniel's collaborator was nowhere to be seen.

Hardly surprising, I supposed, since the tent was full of people who either wanted to yell at him for his part in the plan, or find out what secrets he knew. He'd lied to my family, by omission if nothing else. Right then, Edward was even less popular at Rosewood than I was.

The realisation sparked a sense of solidarity in me. I snatched up an almost-full bottle of wine and set out to find Granddad's biographer.

He wasn't hard to find. On my way towards the terrace doors, I heard a large clunk from the Rose Garden and found Edward sitting on the bench, an empty wine bottle dropped on the shingle at his feet.

"Need some more?" I waved my bottle at him.

Edward looked cautious. "Have you come to yell at me too?"

"Family not happy with you?" I sat myself down beside him. "You do realise that I'm the only other person nearly as unwelcome here as you?"

Edward grabbed the bottle from me and took a gulp from the neck. "You're family. You're always welcome here. It's your home."

I shook my head and took the bottle back. "Even Greg practically told me to leave today."

"Ah, but he just married in. He doesn't count."

We sat together in silence, passing the bottle between us and listening to the noises of the party. It was getting late; the sky was growing dark. "Surely they've got to go home soon," Edward said, relaxing again after a couple of partygoers who'd strayed too close to our hiding place staggered back towards the drinks tent.

"My grandparents' parties have been known to go on all night." And into the following day, if the story Nathaniel had told me earlier had any truth in it. "Haven't you covered any of the parties in the book so far? Like… the one they threw when they moved into Rosewood?" If anyone knew the truth behind the story – apart from Nathaniel – it would be Edward, right?

But he just signalled for me to be quiet as we heard footsteps on the gravel again.

"We need a better hiding place," he said, once the crunching had faded away.

I thought for a moment, then said, "I know somewhere."

The attic was still stuffy, despite the hour, and I forced the window open as Edward worked the cork out of a bottle of brandy he'd liberated from Nathaniel's study on our way up. "He got me into this mess, after all," he'd justified.

"Who does all this stuff belong to?" Edward asked, kicking out at a box underneath the window from his cushion seat.

I peered at the box in question. "Well, that one's mine, anyway. Most of this stuff near the door is. Further back…" I shrugged "… anyone's guess."

For a moment, it looked like Edward was about to get up and investigate, but instead he slumped back against his cushion. I dropped down to sit beside him and grabbed the brandy from his hand. "Why's all your stuff up here?" he asked.

I shrugged again and as I raised my shoulders, I could feel the warmth of his arm against mine, the rub of his shirt against my bare skin. I hadn't realised we were so close. Was it his nearness or the wine making my blood buzz?

"You know why," I said, shifting a little to my left to try and maintain some distance, at least. "You already admitted that Ellie told you all the gory details."

Edward stretched out his left leg so it ran along my right and, suddenly, somehow, his shoulder was touching mine again too. "She told me about you and Greg – about what happened." He turned his head to look at me, and I could feel his breath against my neck. "Doesn't seem very like you."

"I like to think I was a different person then." I didn't say that the problem was knowing that it was still *me*. Or realising that everything I'd believed about what had happened had just been a story. Accepting the truth was even worse. "Younger, for a start. And particularly stupid."

"Or just in love?" Edward asked, passing me the bottle. I winced at his words. "How did it happen? Not the… I mean… I don't need the *actual* gory details, or anything…"

He trailed off, and I sighed. "We were always close, the three of us, from the first time she brought him home. I was worried that I'd, I don't know, lose her, now she had Greg. But he went out of his way to include me, too. We did everything together, and I adored them both. Then when they got engaged, Ellie was so busy with the wedding plans, Greg and I ended up spending a lot of time together, just talking. About the future, our hopes, dreams, that sort of thing. I always wanted to be more like Ellie – you know, petite and blonde and lovely, instead of tall, dark and difficult. Greg made me feel like it was okay to just be me."

But if anything, what happened next had only made it more obvious than ever that I would never be Ellie. Ellie would never have done what I did.

"That summer..." I paused, my conversation with Greg still echoing through my mind. I couldn't tell the story the way I always had before, in my head. I knew better, now. "Greg and I... I thought we were in love. Or I wanted to believe we were. And I imagined that Ellie knew, deep down. That she... I don't know. I guess I told myself enough stories until I convinced myself that it was okay, somehow. That it was still just the three of us." I shook my head. "Doesn't matter. She's my sister." I took a long slug of brandy, and absently wondered just how much I'd had to drink already. "I slept with her fiancé, two days before their wedding. I betrayed her, she's never going to forgive me, and I just have to accept that."

Edward was silent for a long moment, staring out towards the window and the ongoing party. Noises still floated up: music and voices and clanking crockery. They must be on to the sausage and bacon baps Ellie had ordered, in lieu of an evening buffet. "I think she'd like to," he said, eventually.

"Hmm?" I asked, drowsy from the brandy and the long day.

"Ellie. I think she'd like to forgive you. She'd like to move on. She just doesn't know how."

"Do you think she'll ever figure it out?" My voice came out smaller than I'd intended, and Edward snaked an arm around my shoulder, just like he had the night before.

"I hope so," he said. Then, "I think she will." He sounded more certain that time, and I allowed myself just a little bit of hope.

"It's nice that she has you here," I said, leaning into his embrace. "Rosewood's a long way away from pretty much everywhere else. It's hard to make friends."

"She has Greg. She doesn't need me," Edward said. "Is that why you left? To make new friends?"

"I left because I couldn't stay," I said simply. "After what I'd done... Ellie was so upset, and she wouldn't tell anyone why but they knew it was my fault. I knew it was my fault. And when she married Greg anyway... they had enough to sort out between the two of them. Me being there could only make things harder. So I left."

"To try and make her happy?" Edward shook his head a little. "Do you ever think that if you'd stayed you might have made up by now?"

"No." Because if leaving was the wrong thing, and staying would have been the wrong thing, what else could I have done? But I couldn't stop hearing her words, *You just ran away the minute the confetti was thrown*. Had she wanted me to stay?

I turned my body inwards, resting my head lower down on Edward's chest, listening to his heart beat through his thin dress shirt. "I thought you were going to hate me, when I first arrived. I thought that Ellie had told you everything, so you'd despise me."

"So did I." Edward sounded surprised, almost rueful. "In fact, you're pretty much the last person I ever thought I'd want to get to know better." That would have stung a hell of a lot worse if he hadn't tightened his arm around me and added, "I'm still not quite sure how you won me round."

"So you're not just gathering material for the memoirs, then?" I asked, wondering how I'd managed to forget about them, even for a short time.

Edward shook his head, and I felt the movement more than I saw it. "I think Nathaniel's got more than enough for that already."

"Why do your family think you're having a midlife crisis?" Time to shine the spotlight on his life, for a change. "I mean, aren't you just doing your job, same as always?"

"Not exactly. Usually, the subjects of my biographies are long dead, for a start. But this time… I guess I needed a new direction, for a while."

"You mean you're running away from something too." Except he got to run *to* Rosewood, instead of away. Lucky Edward.

"I suppose I am," Edward admitted. "Life out there in the real world got kind of screwed up for a while. And when Nathaniel asked me to come here… I jumped at it. Left everything else hanging and jumped on the next train."

"That doesn't sound like you either."

"It's not. Hence the midlife crisis accusations."

I tilted my head to look up at him, his arm sliding down to wrap around my waist until I was practically lying in his lap. "Are you glad you came?"

"Very," he said. "I just hope I'm allowed to stay, now it's all out in the open. That Isabelle won't talk him out of the memoirs project, I mean. I hadn't expected to find, well, a place here at Rosewood. But now I have…"

"You don't want it snatched away," I finished for him. "Trust me, I understand that." Except Rosewood hadn't been snatched from me, had it? I'd thrown it away.

"The memoirs… Is… What happened with me and Greg. Is it in there?" Because it was one thing for Edward and Ellie to know what I was, what I'd done, and quite another for my family and friends to find out, at the same time as the rest of the British reading public. God, my parents. Whatever they suspected, it would kill them to read it there in black-and-white. And Caro, when she was old enough. How could I bear that?

"I don't know," Edward said, slowly. "We haven't got that far yet. I don't know if he…"

"It doesn't matter. Well, it does, but we don't have to talk about it."

Edward twisted around on his cushion, and pulled me closer, up his body. "You said it yourself: you're a different person now."

"The people reading it won't know that, though, will they?" To my horror, I could feel tears burning behind my eyes. I blamed the brandy, and swore to myself that I absolutely was not going to cry in front of this man.

"They don't matter," Edward said and, ever so gently, kissed the top of my head. "They really don't."

"Easy for you to say." I gave a watery chuckle. "All anyone ever says about you is how truthful you are, how factual, how honest. It's the people you write about…"

"People like your family." He sighed. "I wouldn't be doing this if Nathaniel hadn't asked. I… Well, he helped me out, a long time ago, and I owe him, I guess. But it's up to him what he wants to include. I won't… I'm not trying to ruin your family, or anything."

"I know that." And strangely, I did. I barely knew this man – mostly because he'd been keeping his true identity a secret from me and almost everyone I cared about until today – but I knew that, lies aside, he didn't want to hurt us. Whatever his initial response to me returning to Rosewood, I got the feeling that Edward might even be on my side.

It was nice to think so, anyway.

"Good. I wouldn't want you to think…" He sighed. "God knows why, but I'd hate for you to think badly of me."

I looked up at him in surprise. "I don't."

Edward stared down into my eyes. "I'm glad to hear it," he said, his voice low and warm.

And then, out of nowhere, he kissed me.

"I'm sorry," he murmured, pulling away. "I shouldn't…"

But he should. He really, really should.

I slid a hand up his chest to the back of his neck and held his mouth against mine, just long enough to let him know that I really wasn't objecting to his kisses. His mouth felt cool in the sultry summer night air, and the sheer quantity of alcohol consumed certainly hadn't affected his kissing ability.

"You're sure?" he asked, and I just kissed him again. This was where I wanted to be – here in this moment, away from the rest of the family, from the party, from reality. With Edward.

Long, clever fingers methodically unfastened the row of tiny buttons at the back of my dress, running all the way up my spine. The fabric fell away, and I arched my back as his fingers ran across it, my nerve endings shivering.

God, I wanted this man. I wanted the oblivion of a night in his arms. I wanted the freedom, the closeness, the acceptance. And then, in the morning…

The thought was a bottle of cold champagne poured over my head.

In the morning, I'd be leaving Rosewood again. Going home to Perth. To Duncan.

I'd be running away from another ill-advised liaison, straight back to the man I'd spent days telling everyone was my boyfriend. And even if he wasn't, I couldn't deny that he was *something* to me. I owed him more than this.

If I wanted to start putting my life in order, become the Saskia who could come home to Rosewood with my head held high, it had to start here.

Not to mention the small fact that, very soon, this man would be writing my life story in my grandfather's memoirs.

Edward's fingers stopped stroking my skin, and he pulled back a little. This time, I let him go. "What changed?" he asked.

I swallowed, looking up into his eyes. "I'm sorry."

He gave a small nod, then got to his feet, moving around me and pulling me up too. "You're leaving tomorrow," he said, as he began to fasten up the dozens of ridiculously small buttons on my dress again. "This is bad timing."

"Yes," I said. I wanted to explain more, but the words were gone. All I knew was that, for all it felt incredibly right to be kissing him, this wasn't how I wanted it to be. Not secretly, hiding away in an attic from the rest of my family, cheating on my not-really-boyfriend. Edward deserved more than this.

Hell, I deserved more than this.

"I should go to bed." My voice was too loud, and I spun round to face him too fast, my head buzzing.

"Yeah." Edward's chin dropped to his chest. "I'll just… wait it out up here, I think."

I nodded mechanically. "I'll... see you tomorrow. Before I go."

I was out the door before he had a chance to respond.

I stumbled along the corridor, down the stairs to the first floor, then slammed to a halt when I heard the voices, almost too late to avoid being seen.

"You're selling our secrets!" Isabelle shrieked, and I pressed myself closer to the wall by the stairs. "Sharing our private moments with the world. And why? Because you can't come up with your own stories any longer?"

"This is an important project, Isabelle," Nathaniel replied, his voice a low growl. "It matters to me."

"And what about me? It's my history too, remember." They came into view as Nathaniel approached his study door, just a couple of metres away past my hiding place. Isabelle trailed behind him, still talking. "You promised me, Nathaniel. You swore you'd never—"

"It's a biography! Of course I need to tell our history, that's the whole point." He swung round to face her, his back to me. They were both still dressed in their Golden Wedding outfits, same as me – although I suspected my dress might be rather more rumpled after my moment in the attic with Edward. I tried to straighten it without drawing attention to myself. The last thing I needed was my grandparents catching me sneaking out after snogging Nathaniel's biographer in the attic. Everyone at Rosewood already thought badly enough of my romantic choices.

"You already made a fiction of our courtship," Isabelle said, desperation in her voice. "Why do this? Why turn our whole marriage, our lives together into nothing more than a story?"

Nathaniel shook his head. "I knew you wouldn't understand. But you'll see, when you read it."

Isabelle's face turned hard. "So, you're doing this. Even though your whole family thinks it's a bad idea."

"I'm doing this because it matters. I want our story told, the way it should be – not the way some stranger would write it once I'm dead." He turned away from her and I saw the determination in his eyes. He strode towards me, and I shrunk back further into the shadows – but he didn't even glance in my direction as he passed. Instead, he threw open his study door and walked through, ignoring Isabelle's wail behind him.

"I hate you, Nathaniel Drury!" she yelled, as he slammed the door behind him. Then she spun on her heel and stormed off back down the corridor to her rooms.

I stood, silent and still for a long moment, until I was sure the coast was clear. Breathing too fast, I picked up my shoes and ran barefoot towards the Yellow Room, very afraid that Nathaniel's memoirs might tear apart my family more irreparably than even I'd managed.

Chapter Six

The morning after a raid was always quiet –
a hush over the village as we all lay low,
waiting to be outed. Waiting to be caught.
Caught and taken away for ever.

Rebecca's Daughters, by Nathaniel Drury (1998)

My train left from Chester at four-thirty the following afternoon, and it was after eleven before I even woke up. Rather than go looking for any party survivors, I decided that a shower and packing were the order of the day.

I was still trying to figure out why I'd brought six pairs of shoes for the week, and only worn one, when Ellie appeared in the doorway. But instead of looking tired and pale as she had most of the time I'd been home, there was colour in her cheeks and fire in her eyes – just like the morning in the Orangery.

"When are you leaving?" she asked, her stare hard as she stood in the doorway. Was she just here to check that I really was going again? I wasn't sure.

"The taxi's coming at four o'clock," I answered, as mildly as I could. Whatever she thought or felt, I wasn't here for confrontation. I folded one of Therese's dresses neatly and put it to one side on the bed. I was going to miss the extended wardrobe, when I got back to Scotland.

Ellie nodded, but somehow gave me the impression that she wasn't taking anything in. She wasn't good at confrontation – never had been. She got too upset, usually. There was a reason I'd been able to just leave the minute the wedding was done and never have an actual argument with her in the two years since. I'd told Nathaniel I needed to go and, by the time Ellie came home from her honeymoon with Greg, I had a new job, a new flat, a new life up in Perth. My grandfather had friends everywhere and knew exactly which strings to pull.

Ellie fiddled with the empty glass perfume bottles on the dressing table, holding them up in the sunlight to watch them reflect. I carried on packing, and waited for her to speak again. One thing my many conversations with Edward had made clear to me – Ellie needed to figure things out in her own time. Hopefully, my visit had convinced her that I had no despicable designs on her husband, and that I was willing to make amends, whenever she was ready. Maybe now she could work towards forgiving me. Maybe.

"Are you going to speak to him before you go?" Ellie asked suddenly, and for a dreadful moment the anger in her voice convinced me that she meant Greg.

"I'm sorry?" I paused in packing a pink top that had gone from suitcase to wardrobe and back again, unworn, and looked up at my sister.

"Edward," she clarified, staring me down. "I saw you two disappear into the house together last night. And then you were both still missing when the party ended… I can put two and two together, Kia. Especially now I know what I'm looking for."

"We didn't… It's not what you think, El." I stumbled over the words, determined to get my truth out. Edward was Ellie's confidant, her friend. It was important she know what really happened.

"What? Did you just conveniently forget that boyfriend you're supposed to have in Perth? Or do partners not count when they're more than a mile or two away?"

My heart felt like stone, sinking through my body. Two years and we'd never had this argument. And when we did, it wasn't even about Greg. It wasn't even about something I'd actually done.

I made the right decision this time! I wanted to scream. *I did the right thing and walked away. I was a grown-up. A drunk, lust-driven and seriously annoyed grown-up, but still...*

But Ellie wasn't listening.

"I thought you'd grown up, Kia," she said, her voice dripping with disappointment, and also a hint of being proved totally right. I was used to disappointing people, but I'd only really let her down once. One colossal, awful time. Apparently she'd grown used to it fast. "I thought, when you came back, that maybe you'd spent your two years away thinking about what you'd done."

"I did! And I *have* grown up!"

"Really? Sneaking off to cheat with another man, acting on impulse, not thinking about the consequences, or other people... Sounds like the same old Kia to me." I'd never heard that cynicism in her voice before, and it broke my heart to know I put it there. "It doesn't matter to you that Edward's got his own problems. His own heartbreak. Does it? Not when you can just run away to Perth again, the minute it all gets too difficult."

"I left because I thought you wanted me to!"

"You ran away because that's what you do. You always have." Ellie slammed the empty bottle in her hand down on the dressing table, and I winced, hoping it wouldn't smash. "Even when we were little, if you were in trouble or something broke or went wrong, you'd run. Into the woods, or the attic – or to Nathaniel. Because you knew he'd protect you." She shook her head. "Perth is just the same thing, all over again. So run, Kia. Run and don't look back. Let those of us left behind pick up the pieces. We're used to it."

She swept out of the room, slamming the door behind her so hard that the perfume bottles rattled.

"I have grown up," I told the empty room. "And I'm not running away."

I'm not sure even I believed myself, though.

Maybe I'd made one right, grown-up choice – not sleeping with Edward. But look where it had got me. Right back where I started.

Eventually, all the things I'd brought with me, and a couple of precious things from the boxes in the attic, were all tucked away in my pull-along suitcase, sitting on the bed beside a pile of vintage clothing and accessories.

"It's not that I'm not going to see Edward," I told myself. "I'm just going to drop these back to Therese first."

Downstairs, the family had apparently taken some sort of hangover vow of silence. They were spread out across most of the rooms of the ground floor, all quietly reading, or just sitting, and staying out of each other's way. Which seemed like a fine idea to me.

"What time's your train?" Dad called quietly from the kitchen as I passed the doorway. "If it's later this evening, I might have got my blood alcohol level down far enough to take you."

"No chance," I said, smiling as much as my headache would allow. "Got to be at Chester by four-thirty. Don't worry; I've called a cab."

Dad nodded, and dropped his head back to the table. "Might be for the best," he mumbled into his arms.

Outside, it was another glorious sunny day, which seemed mean and unnecessary, really, given everyone's sensitivity to light and sound. Caro was enjoying it though; she was sitting out on the front steps, sorting through a small pile of books.

"What're you doing?" I asked, shielding my eyes from the sun as I looked at her.

"Research," Caro said, gathering up the collection. Looking closer, I realised they were all books on the paranormal.

"I'm going down to Therese's cottage," I said. "Want to come with?"

Caroline nodded, and ran to put her books inside on the telephone table before joining me on the path.

Therese seemed to be suffering less than the rest of the family; she was already out in the garden, pulling up weeds, when we arrived.

"Just returning your beautiful outfits," I explained, holding up the armful of slippery fabrics and sparkly jewels.

Therese held her head on one side as she looked at me, then nodded sharply. "I'll look after them until you come home next," she said. Which made no sense at all, since they were hers to begin with.

"Can I help you in your garden?" Caro asked, tugging on a honeysuckle stem. "Everyone up at the house is supremely boring today."

Therese smiled, and untwined Caro's thin fingers from the plant. "Of course you can. Let's start in this bed over here." She led her to a more sparsely populated bed, and began instructing Caro on how to tell the difference between plants and weeds.

"I'll just put these in the kitchen, then," I said, and Therese waved a hand at me.

"Thanks, Kia. What time's your train?"

"Four-thirty," I answered.

Therese twisted her head around to nod at me and said, "I'll come up to the house to wave you off."

Which left me all out of excuses. I deposited the clothes inside the cottage, and set off to find Edward. Not because of what Ellie had said, but because I wanted to see him, one last time, before I went.

In the end, finding him was much easier than it had any right to be.

I slid onto the shady bench Edward had chosen, and looked out across the Rose Garden at all the denuded branches and stems.

"Sorry I ran out last night," I said, quietly. "I was just… I suddenly realised some stuff, and it didn't seem like such a good idea."

Edward smiled softly at me. "Saskia, it's okay. You're right. It was a stupid idea. We were drunk and lonely, that's all." *We were selfish, lonely people…* Greg's words haunted me.

But this time it was different. That *wasn't* all, not to me. My heart ached at his words. I hadn't stopped because I didn't want him, I'd realised, tossing and turning in my bed alone that night. I'd stopped because I wanted him too much to have him that way – a drunken one-night stand before I went away again. If I were ever to have a chance with Edward, I wanted it to be real. Although, right then, I couldn't see any road that led to that happening at all.

But maybe he didn't mean it either. Ellie had said something about heartbreak, hadn't she? And he'd said, last night, that I was the last person he should want to get to know. Maybe he had his own grown-up reasons not to fall into bed with me.

"Ellie said…" I started, then stopped. After all, I didn't really want him to think I only came to find him because of my sister.

"I heard the yelling," he said, drily. "That's one of the reasons I headed out here. It's never good to hear oneself talked about in anger."

"I'm sorry." Colour flooded my cheeks. He'd heard all that? Not that I imagined it was anything Ellie hadn't said to him about me before. Still…

He waved a hand. "It's fine. And I can guess what happened after I stopped listening. Ellie told you that I'm damaged by previous relationships, and you have to be very careful," Edward surmised. "I'm not actually that delicate, you know."

"I know." Except I didn't, really. I hardly knew anything about him at all.

"Besides, you have a boyfriend." Edward raised his eyebrows at me and I shivered, even in the sunshine.

"Duncan," I said. "Yes." Edward was silent, perhaps waiting for me to go on. "I mean, yes, that's one of the reasons I stopped… everything, last night. But no, he's not my boyfriend. Not really. He's my boss, and sometimes we—" Oh God, I really didn't want to be having this conversation. "It's not a relationship, nothing like. And I think it's over now, anyway. Or it will be, when I get back."

"Oh?"

"Yeah. I… I realised last night that it's time for me to grow up. Move on."

"Not have sex in attics with strange men."

I laughed, amazed at his ability to break the tension, even now. "Something like that."

"And you don't see Duncan as part of your grown-up life?"

"Definitely not." I'd got a glimpse of what I did want in that life the night before, in the attic, but I wasn't telling Edward that. Not if he believed that last night was just two outsiders with too much alcohol.

For me, it had been more. Lots more.

It wasn't just his hands on my body, or the patient way he'd undressed me. It was the way he'd listened, the way he'd understood. Even just the way he'd kissed my hair and soothed me.

I wanted that. Even if I couldn't have it with Edward, I knew it had to be out there somewhere. And I intended to find it.

Maybe Ellie was right about one thing. It was time to stop running away – and start running towards something.

Edward got to his feet and held out a hand to pull me up. "Well, I hope you find what you're looking for, Saskia Ryan."

"So do I." I took his hand, letting the sensation of his skin against mine ripple over me, one last time. "And I hope everything goes well here. With the memoirs, I mean."

"Me too," Edward said. "Speaking of... have you talked to your grandfather at all this morning?"

I shook my head. "I don't think he's surfaced yet." The last time I'd seen him, he'd been slamming his way into his study. Given the row he'd had with Isabelle, I rather imagined he might have spent the night in there, and had no plans for coming out until tempers had cooled all round.

Edward glanced down at his watch, his palm sliding away from mine. I felt colder for the lack of contact. "What time's your taxi coming?"

"Four o'clock," I said, for the umpteenth time that morning.

"Then we'd better get you on your way. Let's go find your adoring family, so we can get on with the tearful farewells," he said, and I laughed out loud as I followed him up to the house.

It was almost a relief to settle into my seat on the nearly empty train – the first of three taking me home to Perth.

Home. Strange to think of someplace other than Rosewood as that.

I supposed I'd have to get used to it. If I'd learned nothing else that weekend, it had to be that – whatever Nathaniel thought – there wasn't a place for me at Rosewood right now. Maybe one day I'd be welcomed back there again, but it wasn't yet. Not with Ellie so angry, and everybody up in arms about the memoirs.

The memoirs, of course, made me think of Edward, which didn't help matters either. But I'd only known him four days, and Ellie my whole life, so as much as I might want to go back and see him again, maybe make a better go of things than the awkwardness in the attic, she had to come first.

But I still needed to talk to Duncan. Call things off once and for all. I hadn't been lying to Edward; I was ready for something more now. Something better.

I'd moved on from Greg, and Rosewood, and everything that had happened over the past two years. At twenty-six, I was finally ready to be a grown-up, and find my real life, at last.

The tears caught me by surprise, and I fumbled in my bag for a tissue – finding instead a book, shoved in the outside pocket of my handbag. A book I definitely hadn't put there. I tugged it out, sniffing, and stared at the cover while I continued to feel for a tissue.

Biding Time. By Nathaniel Drury.

Of course it was. Who had slipped it in there? My bag had been left in the hall while I said my goodbyes, so anyone could have. But I could only think of two who would – Nathaniel or Edward. And Nathaniel still hadn't surfaced to face his hangover like a man by the time I left.

I flipped through the pages, looking for a note, an explanation, anything. When nothing fell out from between the pages, I opened it at the first page and started to read.

It was then I noticed the pencil notes.

Every page was annotated in sharp, hard pencil lines. Even if I hadn't recognised the handwriting from the table plan, I'd have known the notes were Edward's in a heartbeat. Each questioned the reality or truth behind a fictional event in the book, and I could hear his wry humour in every one.

Biding Time was famously supposed to be the story of how Nathaniel met Isabelle, how they married, moved to Rosewood, and started their lives together. Nathaniel always claimed there was more fiction than truth in it, and Isabelle always declined to comment. Edward, however, had apparently tackled the text as the biographer that he was, looking for the real story behind the book.

Nathaniel would approve, I decided.

With the green and pleasant countryside whistling by outside the window, I turned my attention back to *Biding Time*, and tried to lose myself in the story. But Edward's notes kept jumping out, distracting me. I'd read the book often enough to be familiar with the text; Edward's notes, however, added a whole new dimension to the story.

Mostly they were factual, but every now and then one would offer more insight into Edward himself than the book. I found myself looking out for those nuggets, savouring them, considering them, and matching them up with what I already knew about him.

For instance, what did it mean when he wrote *Love at first sight?!* in the margin of the scene where Charles meets Bella for the first time? Was that incredulity, disbelief? Or amazement?

Did Edward believe in love at first sight? I might never get to ask him, now.

I could call him from Perth, I supposed, but what would be the point? I'd be hundreds of miles away, and he'd be tied to the one place I couldn't go – Rosewood.

Better to make a clean break, I decided, fumbling for another tissue. The second train had rattled over the border now, anyway. I was back in Scotland. A whole other country.

I'd run away again, just like Ellie told me to.

Instead of a tissue, my fingers hit my phone this time, and I pulled it out, half hoping there might be a message, an explanation from Edward for the book. Anything to give me a connection back to Rosewood.

I blinked at the screen. Twelve missed calls. Eight voicemails. Twenty-four text messages.

As I stared, it began to ring again. And with my heart in my mouth, I answered.

"Kia?" Edward's voice sounded too far away, the family nickname too familiar on his tongue. Just for a moment, I let myself believe that he was calling because he missed me, because he regretted how we left things, because he wanted to see me again… But only for a moment.

"Kia, I'm so sorry, sweetheart. You've got to come home. Now. It's Nathaniel."

Chapter Seven

*The day of my father's funeral was the day
I began writing my first book – a new story
for a changed world.*

From the notebooks of Nathaniel Drury

This time, when I arrived at the station, Edward was waiting for me, despite the ungodly hour, his arms folded tight across his chest as he leant against the window of WHSmith. The Caledonian Sleeper had whisked me back from Scotland without me ever reaching Perth, and deposited me back in Chester before seven a.m. But I couldn't shake the thought that, for all I'd rushed straight back, shivering the whole way on the sleeper train, it was still the next day. Nathaniel had been dead since *yesterday,* and I was only just getting there.

Nathaniel *had been* dead. *Was* dead. Wouldn't ever be alive again. How could that be a truth? How could I have not been there for his last moments?

And I'd spent my last minutes with him hiding in the shadows, watching him argue with Isabelle, because I'd been too ashamed of what I'd been doing in the attic with Edward. I'd missed my chance to have one last talk, one last hug, one last second with him.

Nothing about this day was right, least of all the empty feeling inside me that threatened to consume every part of me.

I lugged my case down the last few stairs before Edward spotted me and lurched forward to assist, in that way of his. Too long being Nathaniel's assistant, I supposed. Even if that was never all he was. Even if he'd never be that again.

It was crazy to think that less than a week ago he was taking this same suitcase up the stairs to the Yellow Room. That so much could change in so little time.

"Hi." He took the handle from me and set the suitcase straight on the concourse. He lifted one hand, as if he were about to touch me, brush my hair out of my eyes, something. Anything. I held my breath, but he stopped, busying himself with figuring out the pull-along handle on the case instead. "Was the journey okay?"

"Fine," I lied. Four hours up to Glasgow, two hours stuck in the station waiting for the train back home after his call, then eight hideous hours back again on the misleadingly named Caledonian Sleeper. "Thanks for coming to get me." My voice was dry and cracked after the long train ride, after crying all night, after not sleeping and not speaking to anyone. Edward didn't comment on it, although he must have noticed. Edward, I'd decided after reading his notes, noticed everything. Especially the things we wished he wouldn't.

Just ten hours since he called me. Less than a day since my grandfather died. Less than an hour before I had to face my entire family, again.

And only two days since I almost slept with the guy wheeling my suitcase out of the station. But if he wasn't going to mention it, neither was I.

I had heavier things on my mind.

Edward loaded my suitcase into the boot, then held the passenger door open for me when I just stood staring at it. "Are you sure you're okay?"

I nodded, finding it easier to lie without words. Of course I wasn't okay. Nathaniel was gone, and no amount of storytelling or rewriting or even wishing in a fairy ring could change that.

He shut the door behind me once I was seated, then moved around to his own side. As his door shut, the car seemed to close in on me, a metal box with no escape, and I opened the window for some much-needed air.

"What... what happened, exactly?" I asked, and Edward's hand fell away from the ignition without starting the engine. "I couldn't... The phone line wasn't very clear."

"I know," he said, "and I didn't want to tell you everything over the phone. It can wait, you know, until we get back to the house. You don't need to rush this."

"Nathaniel's not going anywhere." The joke came out cracked, just like my voice, and I choked back a sob.

"It was a heart attack," he said, quietly. "Quick and sudden. Nothing anybody could have done."

Even if I'd been there. Which I wasn't. Because I'd run away again, even after Nathaniel told me that Rosewood was my home. How could I have left? How could I have not been there when it happened?

I turned my face away from Edward and let the tears fall again.

"Let's get you home," he said, and turned the key. "I have to warn you, though... It's all... a bit tense back at the house."

"I assumed it would be." I stared out at the familiar sights of Chester running past the windows. It seemed like months I'd been away, not less than a day.

"Yes, of course." Edward ran a hand over his thigh before changing gear, and I wondered what had him so nervous – my arrival, my family, or his continued employment.

"It's just..." he went on, as we pulled out onto the roundabout. "It's not necessarily the usual kind of tense. People have been reacting... oddly."

I'd been awake for what was almost two days, at this point. I was grieving. I was worried about my family. It wasn't inexcusable for me to lose my temper, just a little. "A person's response to grief is an individual thing," I said. "I don't really think it's appropriate for you to be..."

Edward shook his head. "No. No. That's not... Look. Never mind. You'll see what I mean when we get there."

That sounded ominous. I bit my lip and tried not to imagine how much worse going home to Rosewood would be this time.

The marquees were still up.

The first thing I saw, as Edward pulled up outside Rosewood, was the looming shape of the marquee tents from the Golden Wedding, still occupying the south lawn. Flower displays still bloomed outside them, waiting for a celebration. There was probably still leftover food, maybe even champagne.

It felt like Rosewood didn't know that the celebrations, the parties, were all over, now. Like the house itself was waiting for Nathaniel to appear from his study, still in his white tie and tails, pipe in mouth, demanding more brandy. As if any moment someone would announce that it was all just a joke, a publicity stunt, a hoax, a story.

Except Nathaniel never did publicity stunts, and his stories always had more truth in them than lies.

This one more than most.

The front door to the house opened, and my Dad emerged, an apron wrapped around his waist even at seven-thirty in the morning. Comfort cooking, I knew.

Whenever he didn't know what to do, or say, Dad cooked. We ate extremely well during times of stress and turmoil, and everyone knew that a favourite dish was really Dad saying, 'I'm here, I love you, it'll be okay.'

I had no idea what he thought he could cook to fix this.

With a deep breath, I pulled the handle of the car door and stepped out. As I moved towards the house, I could hear Edward opening the boot, presumably retrieving my suitcase.

"Didn't expect to see you back so soon," Dad said, wrapping his arms around me. "I'm so sorry, Saskia."

I sniffed against his shoulder; he smelled like bacon. "How's everyone else?"

"Ah… a little crazy," Dad admitted.

Edward, passing us with my suitcase in tow, gave me a small, sad smile. "Told you so," he said.

Once Edward had disappeared into the house, I pulled away from Dad and looked him in the eye. Time to find out what was really going on. "Crazy, how?"

As it happened, I needn't have bothered. Dad was reluctant to go into detail and, in fact, the craziness was blatantly obvious from the moment I entered the house. I began to feel mildly guilty for yelling at Edward.

"Kia, thank God you're here," Isabelle said, as soon as I made it through the front door. For a brief moment, my heart filled with something other than grief, just to be wanted. To be welcomed home again. Then Isabelle went on, "You can help me," and the feeling dissipated.

"Help with what?" I shrugged off my light jacket and Dad took it from me, escaping back to the kitchen to hang it up by the back door and, coincidentally, avoid whatever it was Isabelle wanted.

"Your grandfather's study!" Isabelle grabbed hold of my arm and began dragging me towards the staircase.

She was, I noticed as I lurched across the hallway, not looking her usual immaculate self, which I suppose was understandable, given the circumstances. Still, it was strange, seeing my perfectly groomed grandmother with unstyled hair scraped back from her face, and a blouse that didn't quite match her shoes.

Grief takes us all in different ways, I reminded myself, and prepared to be calm and comforting in the face of craziness.

Luckily, Edward was waiting for us halfway up the stairs, and able to spare me from a morning of doing that. "Isabelle, you know you can't go in there," he said, and my grandmother gave out an actual, honest-to-God wail. The sound caught in my chest, proof positive that nothing was the same. Nathaniel wasn't about to appear from his study, demanding to know what the commotion was about. If the inhuman noise that came from Isabelle hadn't called him back, nothing could.

"It's my house!" she yelled. "Who are you to tell me where I can and cannot go? What are you still doing here, anyway? In case you hadn't noticed, your employment has been terminated. So why don't you just *get out of my house*!" The last part of this was screamed at the top of her voice, and accompanied by the throwing of the papers in her hand against the wall.

Edward stood silently still on his stair, and looked at me. Time to do something, apparently.

"Okay, then, I think we could all do with some coffee." Possibly an Irish one, if I thought it would settle her nerves, even if it was not quite eight a.m. With one arm around her shoulder, I managed to steer Isabelle back down the few stairs we'd climbed and towards the drawing room. It was only then that I discovered we'd drawn a crowd; Greg and Ellie were standing behind us, and Dad was back in the kitchen doorway, spatula in hand. Ellie was pale, but Greg's arms were around her waist, holding her close. I looked away. Ellie deserved that comfort, that love, and I was glad she had it. Glad, too, that Greg had found that absolution, and his place here.

I just wished it wasn't at the expense of my own.

As I turned, Ellie stepped forward, away from Greg and towards me. Her hand came up, as if to reach for me, and for that brief second my heart stopped. Was this it? Was this the moment she let me back into her life? I started to move towards her – until her hand dropped and she shifted back into Greg's arms again.

I looked away. Apparently even our grief wasn't enough to bring us back together. Ellie must be every bit as heartbroken as I was – but she had Greg to help her through it. She didn't need me.

Even if I still needed her.

It took a little time to get Isabelle settled in the drawing room, but things moved quicker once Ellie and Greg came to help. Eventually, I was able to slip out without being noticed, two coffees in my hand, letting the door click shut behind me.

Edward was sitting on the stairs, where we'd left him, hands clasped across his knees, staring at the closed front door. He didn't even look up until I waved the coffee under his nose.

"All sorted?" he asked, taking the cup from my hand.

I settled myself onto a step a few below him and blew across the surface of my coffee to cool it. "For now. You really meant it when you said things were crazy, didn't you?"

"I did." He sighed, his head hanging low and his shoulders hunched. "You see what I mean, now."

"Yeah. I'm sorry." I loved my family dearly, but they weren't always the easiest people to live with.

Edward gave a small shrug. "All part of the job, I suppose."

It wasn't, though. Whatever the terms of his employment, I was pretty sure Edward could walk out whenever he wanted. He'd *chosen* to stay, to help my family when they needed him. Even if Isabelle didn't appreciate that, I did.

"Where's everyone else?" I asked, looking to distract him from Isabelle's awfulness. How Edward would know, having only just arrived back with me, I'd no idea. But he did.

"I think your mum is down at the cottage with Therese. She stayed there last night. Therese was... hysterical."

I tried to picture it, but couldn't. Therese was poised, funny, had a great line in biting commentary, tea and biscuits and perfect clothing. But in the twenty-six years I'd known her, I'd never seen her hysterical. But then, I'd never seen my grandmother in a mismatched outfit before, either. "Worse than Isabelle?"

"Different. More distraught than angry." I could understand that; her brother had just died, after all. Except, surely Isabelle should be the same. Her husband was dead. And, if I was right, her last moments with him were spent in anger. Her last words were that she hated him.

Maybe that was why she was losing it, why she was focusing on getting into the study. Denial. Or delusion; a desperate wish to rewrite the ending, before it was too late.

I could understand that, too. I wanted the same.

Edward was still talking, and I made an effort to tune back in. "And Caro's probably hiding out in the attic; she says it's quieter up there."

The mention of the attic should have been awkward. On any other day I'd have been thrown back into memories of our evening together, of his hands on my skin, of kissing him. But there were bigger things to think about today.

"How are Mum and Caro taking it?" It seemed absurd that it was only a day since Nathaniel died, that people were still only just reacting, that no one had thought anything through yet. Perhaps it was the distance I'd travelled that made it seem like so much longer.

"Badly," Edward said. "Just like everyone else. Your mum... I think she'd love to just fall apart, but with everyone else acting so crazy, she's having to hold things together. Her and Ellie, who looks absolutely drained."

Poor Mum. Normally she got to be the flighty, dramatic, emotional one. But not today. And Ellie... she'd looked so pale, so exhausted. Like she always did after a long journey, as a child, when she suffered from travel sickness. All she probably wanted to do was lie down in a dark room and wait for everything to pass. But that wasn't an option for either of us. Not when everything at Rosewood felt so *wrong*.

We sat in silence for a while, sipping our coffee, and instinctively, I rested my head against his knee. After a few moments he reached up a hand to stroke my hair.

Something inside me that had been curled tight since he called finally started to relax, just a touch. I wanted to stay there in the quiet with Edward for the rest of the day. Maybe longer. As long as it took to stop feeling so broken without Nathaniel there to mend me.

But eventually, I needed to start figuring things out. "Why is she so furious with you? Isabelle, I mean. Is it the memoirs?"

I could almost feel him sigh behind me, as if all the air had been flung out of his body. "Amongst other things. But yes, mostly that."

"What happened?" Edward pulled his hand away from my head and, twisting on my step, I watched him put his elbows on the step behind him and lean back. His empty coffee cup was safely stored two steps further up.

"It only started this morning," he said, staring straight ahead again. "Yesterday... When I..." He stopped, and took a breath. "I was the one who found him, you see, in his study. Which was... Well, I wouldn't have wanted any of your family to have to do that, so I suppose it was for the best. Somehow."

"I'm sorry," I said, reaching up to touch his knee. It hadn't occurred to me to ask how Edward was in all this. After all, he'd probably spent more time with Nathaniel than the rest of us combined over the last year.

"He hadn't come down, you see. To say goodbye to you, I mean. I checked his room and he wasn't there, so I figured he was working. I left him to it until dinner time, but when I let myself in..."

"He hadn't been down at all?" Edward shook his head, and my head buzzed with the confirmation of what I'd already suspected. I'd been the last person to see him, even if he hadn't seen me. And I was probably the only person who knew about the row between him and Isabelle, that last night.

God, if I felt this dreadful from having hidden from him, wasted my last chance to spend time with him, how bad must Isabelle feel? No wonder she was losing it.

"He was lying there, collapsed over his desk. He still... he was still wearing his white jacket from the party." Edward swallowed so hard I could see his Adam's apple bob. "Anyway, what with the doctor coming and having to tell everybody... Isabelle was just very quiet, even when they took him... when they took the body away. We fed her some brandy and put her to bed, then I called you..."

"Why did *you* call?" I asked, thinking aloud. "I mean, why not my parents, or something?"

"Therese asked me to," Edward said with a shrug. "Before she suddenly lost it and insisted on leaving Rosewood. Your mum went to look after her."

"And everyone else had somebody else to look after too," I finished. Of course they did. Greg would have been taking care of Ellie, just the way he was supposed to. Mum and Dad had each other, and Caro. Even Isabelle had Therese... except, Therese hadn't been here, had she? She'd gone back to the cottage, taking Mum with her, leaving Ellie and Greg to deal with Isabelle and Dad to look after Caro. Why would Therese insist on leaving when things were so crazy? Surely she'd want to be with the family?

I'd only been back at Rosewood an hour, and already everything felt wrong. And it wasn't just the lack of Nathaniel's booming voice in the hallways.

"Anyway, so I called you, and then we all sat up drinking whisky until far too late, and I slept very badly and when I woke up this morning and it still didn't seem real, Isabelle was clawing at the locked study door and demanding I give her the key."

"Which you didn't," I guessed, and Edward nodded. "Why not?" Surely it wasn't too much for her to ask – to see where her husband had spent his last moments. The room where he spent most of his time, in fact. The study, more than anywhere else at Rosewood, simply *was* Nathaniel. Of course Isabelle would want to go there.

Edward sighed heavily, something I suspected might become a bit of a theme. "Because he made me promise I wouldn't."

Under the circumstances, 'he' could only mean Nathaniel. And unless Nathaniel was issuing orders from beyond the grave... "He knew he was going to die?" My voice came out shaky and small, and Edward reached out again to touch my hair.

"He suspected, I think. It wasn't... there wasn't any diagnosis, no warnings from doctors, as far as I'm aware. I think he just knew he might not make it to the end of this project. So, one night, a few months before the Golden Wedding, he got me buzzed on his best Scotch and made me promise that, if he died before the memoirs were published, I'd lock his study door and keep it that way until his lawyer told us to open it." He pulled a face. "His lawyer, apparently, has more specific instructions and, more importantly, doesn't have to deal with your grandmother right now."

"What did he think she was going to do? And why?" Because, while Isabelle wasn't always the sanest of people, I hadn't really pegged her as the "burn down my dead husband's office" type or anything. But then I remembered her screaming at him in the hallway the night he died, howling about him telling secrets he'd promised to keep... Maybe she would. Maybe she'd destroy everything to stop the memoirs being published. Nathaniel obviously thought it was a possibility.

"Who knows? Nathaniel certainly wouldn't say." Edward looked down at the rapidly cooling coffee in my cup. "Are you going to drink that?" I handed it up to him and he swallowed it down, before putting my cup to join his on the higher step. "I imagine that there's something in there – no idea what, mind – that Isabelle wouldn't want included in the memoirs, and he didn't want her finding and destroying it." I didn't have to imagine. I knew it, deep in my bones. Somewhere in Nathaniel's study was a secret that Isabelle didn't want getting out.

"But what does it matter now? He's dead, after all." I swallowed the sudden lump in my throat. I hadn't said it out loud before, I realised. "There won't be any memoirs."

"No," Edward said, too slowly. "Perhaps not."

With a sudden movement, he was on his feet, empty coffee cups in hand. "Come on," he said, pulling me up. "It must be nearly time for breakfast. Let's go and find your mum and Therese."

The path down to Therese's cottage was littered with reminders of the party that had just been. While the obvious detritus – bottles, plates and so on – had been cleared away by the team Isabelle hired, there were still plenty of things that the family obviously hadn't got around to before... just, before. Looking at the flowers, tables, and chairs, it felt like time had stopped. That the timeless bubble of Rosewood had frozen, even in the early morning sun, pausing everything around us while we caught up with the idea that Nathaniel was gone. That the heart of the house had stopped beating.

Would we ever come to terms with that? I wasn't sure.

We crossed from the main path to the gravel entrance to Therese's front garden, roses around the cottage door blooming pink and warm and welcoming.

"She'll be glad to see you," Edward murmured as I knocked on the wooden front door, and I assumed he meant Therese. Until my mother answered the door.

"Oh, thank God you're here," she said, ushering us both into the cottage. Another welcome home I'd missed the first time, but I knew better this time. Mum, like everyone else, wanted me here to do a job. A job I wasn't sure I'd ever signed up for. "I'll leave you to it, and go make sure everything's ready for breakfast."

"I definitely smelled bacon," Edward said helpfully. "Which I took as a good sign."

"Great." Mum yanked her cardigan from the rack and shoved her arms into it. "You can come and help me set the table."

Edward winced. "I'm not sure Isabelle…"

"Ignore my mother," Mum said, waving a hand. "The rest of us do. Come on." She looked over at me. "Kia, Therese is in the sitting room. Do try and get her to come up for breakfast, won't you?" She paused and then, unexpectedly, she folded me into her arms. "Oh, Kia. He loved you so much, you know." She sniffed, and I realised my cheek was damp with her tears.

She pulled back, and wiped her eyes. Then, with a kiss on the cheek for me, she dragged Edward back into the cold morning air and left me alone with my great-aunt.

"Therese?" I let myself into the sitting room, and found her sitting in a hard-backed armchair beside the window, looking out at the flowers. Even though it was August she was wrapped up in a thick, woolly cardigan and had her slippers on. For the first time ever that I'd seen, she had no make-up on, and her clothes looked shapeless and thoughtless under her cardigan – no sign of her usual nipped-in waist and fifties style.

She looked old, I realised. Or at least, older than she had when I'd left, the previous day.

Therese looked up as I came in, and gave me a watery smile. "Kia, darling. So lovely to see you again, even under such tragic circumstances."

She didn't seem hysterical, or losing it like Isabelle had. Therese just seemed incredibly sad. Like all the life and spirit had flown out of her with her brother's death.

I slid into the chair opposite her, displacing a number of tiny throw cushions. "Mum wanted me to bring you up to the house for breakfast." *Like you do every time Dad's making a fry-up*, I thought but didn't add. Clearly there was something going on here, too – and I wasn't sure it was just grief. Not after everything I'd seen up at the house.

Therese shook her head slowly from side to side. "I'm not sure that's such a good idea, dear," she said, her voice wobbling. "After all… better to wait until my position here is clear, I think."

"Your position?" I asked, because I'd had a very long couple of days and really didn't have the energy to try to riddle it out for myself.

"Of course." Therese turned her attention to the landscape outside the window again. "I came here as my brother's guest, after all. And with Nathaniel gone…"

Which was all a little too much "destitute Victorian widow" for me. "Oh, for heaven's sake, Isabelle's not going to throw you out! You're part of the family."

"Your family, certainly." Therese sighed again. "But Isabelle never really wanted me here, you know."

"I'm sure that's not true," I said, despite having a suspicion it probably was. Still, Isabelle might roll her eyes when Nathaniel and Therese were sharing some sort of secret joke or memory, and the two women did have a tendency to snipe at each other, or make comments behind the other's backs. But that wasn't the same as throwing someone out of their home. "Has she said something? Did something happen?"

"Not yet. But she will," Therese said, ominously. "I've known her for more than fifty years, remember. I know that woman. I know what she'll do."

How had Rosewood changed so dramatically in just a day? Nathaniel had been gone for twenty-four hours, and already we were falling apart. And somehow, it seemed to be my job to pull us back together again.

"Well, she hasn't done any of it yet," I said, leaning over to help her up from her chair. "And besides, she's far more likely to toss Edward out on his ear than you, particularly today."

Therese brightened a little. "That's true."

Time to push my advantage. "Dad's making full English for everyone. There's probably black pudding."

"It is a time to be with family," Therese conceded.

"Excellent! Then let's go."

Breakfast was a stilted affair, during which we all took the time to savour the sausages, rather than actually talking about anything. It wasn't until we were clearing up that Mum leant over to me and said, "Pat's coming this afternoon, to read the will. Wants to get things sorted as soon as possible, he said." I wondered if Edward had helped speed things along with a begging phone call, or if Nathaniel had primed his lawyer to get in as soon as possible to try to forestall a nervous breakdown by Isabelle. He seemed to have predicted the chaos that had descended after his death better than anyone else.

No one lingered over coffee after breakfast. Instead, with a mug in hand, I made my way up the stairs and along to the Yellow Room, to unpack the clothes I'd so recently put back in my case.

It wasn't much of a surprise to find Edward loitering on the landing. "Did you hear?" I asked, as I drew close. "Pat Norris will be here later today."

Edward nodded. "One good thing, at least; that part will be over soon." He leant against the railing that surrounded the stairs, and I rested myself against my bedroom door. Somehow it was safer talking to Edward in the communal spaces, rather than in private, I realised. "Then, if your grandmother still wants me to leave, I can do so with a clear conscience." I frowned at the idea. Rosewood was coming apart at the seams. I couldn't help but feel that the moment the first person left, it would start an exodus. Mum and Dad would go home to Manchester – they'd only come to stay for a couple of weeks to help with the Golden Wedding, after all. They'd take Caro with them. And Therese... would Isabelle really kick her out? Could she, even? Maybe we'd find out in the will. Ellie and Greg... they lived here now, but would they always? Surely they'd want their own place eventually. And I had to go back to Perth, to my job, my real life, sooner or later.

What if Isabelle was left alone here, rattling around an empty house, looking for echoes of her dead husband? I shuddered, just thinking about it.

And it would all start with Edward's departure. Suddenly, it seemed vitally important to keep everyone there, at Rosewood, until things were mended.

Except, how could they be? Nathaniel was dead.

Maybe it would be best for Isabelle to simply sell the house and never look back.

"I suppose there's not much reason for you to stay," I said, thinking about all the real-world things like friends and work and family that he must have put on hold in order to set up camp at Rosewood for eighteen months. He'd told me he'd run out on everything. Maybe he was thinking it was time for him to be going back. And who could blame him?

But Edward gave me a strange, assessing look in return and said, "Well, maybe there might be some."

And I, because I'm a fool, flattered myself into thinking he might mean me.

I wanted to say something, make some reference to how we'd left things between us. We'd said goodbye – quite firmly and finally. I'd hardly expected to see him again ever – let alone the next day. And yet, here we were, the awkwardness of our abortive night in the attic lying between us, and the only thing holding us together the death of my favourite person in the world.

I should say something, I knew. But instead, when I opened my mouth, I just yawned.

Edward gave me a small, half-smile as I covered my mouth. "The sleeper train wasn't so good for sleeping, then?"

I shook my head. "It was freezing. And uncomfortable. Besides… I don't think I could have slept, wherever I was." I'd been lucky; my seats had been at least a little way apart from the other, sleeping passengers. I hoped that no one had been kept awake by my sobbing, at least. I wrapped my arms around my middle. "I still can't get warm."

"You're exhausted," Edward said, as I yawned again. "And reality is setting in now you're here. You need to rest."

"I can't. I just need another cup of coffee, and to unpack, and I'll get back down there and deal with Isabelle, and everything."

But Edward was already steering me through the doorway of the Yellow Room, his hand warm on my elbow. "You need to sleep. Don't worry about the rest of them. I'll deal with them."

You shouldn't have to, I wanted to say, *they're my family.* But all that came out was another yawn. With gentle fingers, Edward stripped my cardigan from my shoulders, and slipped my feet from my shoes. Then he pulled back the bedcovers.

"I'll wake you up when the lawyer arrives," he promised, pushing down on my shoulders until I sat on the bed, and tucking my feet up under me. It was easier to go with him than to fight him, and before I could even object, I was curled up in bed with Edward tucking me in.

Not exactly how I'd imagined any potential next meeting between us where there was a bed involved.

Bending down, he kissed my forehead, staying there just a moment too long. Long enough for me to breathe in the scent of him, soak in the warmth of his lips.

Then he pulled away, and I realised my eyes were closing.

"I'll be back before lunch," he said, and my eyes flickered open long enough to see his long, lean form moving away from the bed, towards the door.

I was asleep before I heard it close.

Chapter Eight

Item 7: Ghosts

*There are lots of different sorts of ghosts –
poltergeists, crisis apparitions, vengeful
ghosts – even ghosts who don't know they're
dead yet.*

*I think the Rose Garden ghost must be a
ghost with unfinished business.*

I wonder if Granddad will be one too.

Excerpt from "Caroline Ryan's List of the Unexplained
(with notes)"

I woke to Edward's hand on my shoulder, and a fresh glass of water on the bedside table.

"Pat Norris just pulled up," he murmured, his voice bedroom soft. It made me want to reach my arms around his neck and kiss him again, but I managed to restrain myself. "I'm just going to round up the others."

I nodded, and struggled to sit up as he left again, as quietly as he'd come.

I washed and changed clothes quickly, pulling on jeans and a T-shirt from my case. My make-up had worn away hours before, and my eyes were too sore from all the crying to think about redoing it. I ran a brush through my hair and called it job done.

Downstairs, I found the family all nervously perched around the drawing room, sipping tea and not eating biscuits.

"How about some anniversary cake, Pat," Dad tried, but Nathaniel's lawyer shook his head. He was, very clearly, here for one purpose only, and keen to get it over and done with as quickly as possible. I didn't blame him. I wasn't sure I wanted to spend the day with my family in their current temper, either.

"Shall we begin?" he asked, and we all nervously nodded, except for Isabelle, who continued to stare out of the window as if none of it mattered at all, really. I knew my grandmother, though. She was listening most carefully.

Mr Norris started with the usual explanations and disclaimers – when Nathaniel had last updated his will (more recently than I'd have expected – just two weeks ago) and what instructions he had left, which at least vindicated Edward's insistence that the study door remain locked until Mr Norris's arrival. Isabelle scowled briefly, before regaining her expression of bereaved indifference.

"Now, the actual bequests." This part, at least, seemed straightforward – almost everything went to Isabelle, including the rights to all his books. There was also a generous allowance made to Therese, until her death, along with the deeds to her cottage. Isabelle scowled at this too, but Therese's face and shoulders relaxed for the first time that day. I let out a small sigh of relief. One less thing to worry about.

There were bequests to Mum and Dad, and smaller ones to us grandchildren. Caro's would be held in trust until her eighteenth birthday. As a favoured granddaughter, Caro was also left Nathaniel's collection of his own first editions, all signed. But there was nothing in there to really upset Isabelle.

Until we reached the section about the memoirs.

"To Saskia Ryan and Edward Hollis, I leave the notes, files and existing work achieved on my planned memoirs, on the understanding that they complete and publish the work according to the plans I leave. Should they not be willing to undertake this task, the files will be boxed, sealed and delivered to my lawyers, to be auctioned off in twenty years' time, with the money going to my nominated charity. If they do complete the work, they are to share equally any profits made."

Absolute silence.

Shortly followed by absolute chaos.

"That impossible man!" Isabelle shrieked, slamming her teacup down so hard a crack spread out from the base. "He cannot *possibly* have done this!"

"Saskia, you're not really thinking of taking over writing the memoirs, are you?" Therese asked, calmer, but with a similar edge of panic in her voice. I started with surprise. I'd thought that Therese, at least, didn't care about the memoirs – but it seemed she was as apprehensive as everyone else. Why?

"I... I didn't know he'd done this," I said, staring at Edward, but no one was listening to me.

What had Nathaniel been thinking? He must have known how this decision would go down with the family. Why would he put this on me? And why on earth hadn't he *told* me?

Edward's gaze darted away from mine and I wondered, had he known? Had Nathaniel warned him?

"But, how can *you* write them, Kia?" Mum asked, frowning. "I mean, not that you can't write, sweetheart.

But you weren't there, were you? You don't know. It would be irresponsible to try and tell a true story you don't really know."

Irresponsible. The word leapt out at me. Didn't they all already believe that was what I was? And weren't they right?

Whatever Nathaniel had intended by naming me in his will this way, he certainly hadn't made my coming home any easier.

"Nathaniel has left very comprehensive notes," Edward said, his voice calm. Unlike the rest of the room. "Along with his diaries and journals, which chronicle his life from an early age. With Saskia's family and personal knowledge, and my experience in writing biographies... it shouldn't be too hard to put together an accurate picture of his life."

He might have been talking to the room at large, but he was watching me as he spoke. Edward wanted me to do this, I realised. He wanted me to risk alienating my surviving family, to honour the last wishes of my grandfather. And, of course, make Edward's career. I couldn't ignore the fact that he had a professional reason to want me on board with this.

While my family, apparently, had myriad personal reasons for wanting me to refuse. I just wished I knew what they were.

But Edward's words were too much for Isabelle.

"*You!* You really think you can write my husband's life story after knowing him for, what, eighteen months? Fifty years of marriage, not to mention the twenty-six before that, and you think *you* can condense everything important into a couple of hundred pages? A few pithy anecdotes and some heart-wrenching sob stories? You're a hack, Edward, and you're crazy if you think we're going to let you tarnish Nathaniel's memory with your words."

Edward's face turned ghost-white, the same colour as his knuckles as he grasped the back of the chair in front of him. The rest of the family fell silent – whether in shock or agreement, I couldn't be certain.

But I sure as hell wasn't letting Isabelle get away with that, grief or not. Just because she was beating herself up about her last moments with Nathaniel, that didn't give her permission to treat Edward that way.

"Stop!" The word came out louder than I'd intended, and suddenly all eyes were on me. I swallowed, and tried to sound like I wasn't making it all up as I went along. "Nathaniel left this project to *both* of us. He obviously believed that we could produce the book he wanted. There's no need to attack Edward just because Nathaniel trusted him with this. It's his decision whether *he* thinks he can do it. Not ours."

"Well, actually, it is a bit *yours, Saskia.*" Pat Norris lifted the paper in his hand with a small smile. "The terms of the will are very clear. You and Edward *both* have to agree to proceed."

"Well, it's decided then," Isabelle said, crossing her arms firmly over her chest. "They won't be doing it. Saskia would never betray her family like that. Would you, Kia?"

The pointed look she gave me, followed by the glance at Ellie, stabbed straight to my heart. I knew what she was saying, even if the words she used were different. *You've already betrayed your sister. Surely you wouldn't hurt the rest of us this way, too. You wouldn't let us down again. Imagine how your parents would feel. Imagine telling the world what you did, in print. Imagine your friends and family finding out what you are in the pages of a book. You'd never be welcome at Rosewood again.*

I stared at Edward, willing him to find the right answer for me. Nathaniel had wanted me to do this. But it could cost me everything.

"Saskia, we just don't want you to jump into something and make a mistake," Mum said. "You have to think of the family, darling."

"Isabelle does have a point," Therese added. "I know you loved Nathaniel very much, but you *weren't* there for most of his life. And you've never written anything like this before. You said yourself that you mostly just type up press releases." I winced at her description of my job, accurate as it was.

"And really, Kia, do you honestly think it's a good idea to air *all* our dirty laundry to the public?" Ellie's voice was sharp, and filled with as much hidden meaning as Isabelle's had been.

Reality sank in. Not only did no one *want* me to take on the project of Nathaniel's memoirs, no one even believed I *could* do it.

Nobody except Nathaniel, and maybe Edward.

And, as it turned out, my dad.

"Stop it. All of you." Dad came up and put an arm around my shoulders. I stared up at him in surprise. I don't think I'd ever heard him sound so stern, so commanding, in my whole life. My dad wasn't the one who argued, who shouted, who got involved. He was the one who brought biscuits.

Apparently there was a side to my dad I'd never expected.

"Nathaniel left this choice to Saskia and Edward, correct?" Dad looked over at Pat Norris, who nodded. "So it's up to them to make it. Not you, not me. Them."

"Tony, really. You don't understand," Mum started, impatiently, but Dad stopped her.

"I understand perfectly, Sally. You're all angry with the wrong person. You're all furious with Nathaniel for deciding to write his memoirs, and for leaving the job to Saskia and Edward – not to mention dying in the first place. But shouting at them isn't going to change anything. Nathaniel wanted his memoirs published. He wanted those stories out there. And however scared you all are about facing the consequences of your history, of seeing your secrets down in black and white, it's out of your hands now. *It's not up to us.* It's up to them. They're adults, capable of reason and sensibility. So I suggest we sit back, let them talk about it, and wait for them to tell us their decision. Okay?" There was no room for argument in Dad's tone, and when no one spoke, he nodded, and placed a kiss on the top of my head before letting me go. "Good. Now, who wants a biscuit?"

"I suppose any decisions should wait until after the funeral, anyway," Mum said, and the others nodded their agreement.

"Great," I said, my palms still sweating, despite my father's faith in my adulting abilities. "Then we can just... wait. That sounds good."

I might not be able to put the decision off for ever but, right now, I'd take what I could get.

"Then, if we've finished discussing this point, there are a few more bequests to discuss," Pat said, as calmly as if it had been a small debate about a porcelain figurine, or something. "Mostly smaller items, left to family and friends who particularly admired them. Plus, a few charitable bequests."

While the rest of the room settled down to eat biscuits and listen, I caught Edward's eye and tipped my head towards the door. He gave a small nod, and followed as I slipped out into the hallway. As the door shut behind us, I heard Isabelle exclaim, "Why would he leave anything to *her*?"

"How long do you think this will go on?" Edward asked, as we took up familiar positions on the staircase and listened to the noise through the closed door. As much as I didn't want to be in the room, I also didn't want to be so far away I couldn't step in and separate people if it started to sound like Mr Norris's life was in danger.

"No real way of telling," I said, looping my arms over my knees. "We've never actually been through something like this before."

We listened in silence for a few more moments to the muffled discussion beyond the door. I doubted Isabelle really objected to anything else in the will. Any anger from her now was just misplaced from the memoirs. I wasn't fool enough to believe that Dad had defused that bomb for good. Still, out here, with Edward, everything felt calmer, as if the pressure weighing down on me from my family had been lifted, just for a time. Just while Edward was there to carry some of it.

"You knew, didn't you? Nathaniel told you what he'd done?" I tilted my head to look up at him as I waited for a response.

Edward sighed. "Not exactly. I knew he wanted you to work on the project with us. I thought he was planning to ask you while you were home."

"He didn't." At least, not in so many words. But when I looked back at our conversations… I could see every one of them leading to this moment.

"He should have done."

"Yeah."

More silence, punctuated by the odd exclamation through the door.

Then, "What are you thinking?" Edward asked, leaning forward with his elbows on his knees, his breath tickling my ear.

"We should have brought the brandy with us."

He laughed almost silently, a huff of warm air against my throat. "I meant about the will. About the memoirs."

Ah. A slightly trickier proposition than whether or not to just get drunk and ignore everything else.

"I'm not sure," I answered, which was at least honest. "On the one hand, it was practically his dying wish. But on the other…"

"Everyone will hate you?" Edward guessed.

Not just hate me. I'd be an outcast again, even more than I already was. Deciding to take on the memoirs with Edward might mean giving up any hope of ever being welcome at Rosewood again.

"That's definitely part of it. Plus the fact that I still can't be sure if Nathaniel didn't only want to have his memoirs published to piss everyone else off."

Edward laughed again, louder this time, a short, sharp bark of a laugh that felt like he cut it off just in time to make sure that none of the family heard and came out to physically attack him. "Yeah, I could see that," he said, quieter. "But I don't think that's why. I worked with him for over a year on this. He wanted this story to be told for it's own sake, I think. Like all the stories he told before. He wanted other people to be able to know it."

I twisted around to face him, leaning my back against the hard wood rails of the banister, feeling them press against my spine. "You say he told you he wanted me to work on the memoirs with you. What about the will? Had he told you he was going to do this?" My voice was still calm and quiet, I realised, despite the bubbles of confusion and frustration and anger that were bouncing around inside of me.

"No." I must have looked disbelieving, despite the strength in his voice, because Edward went on. "Honestly, Saskia, I didn't know he'd done this. I thought... I thought that maybe he'd have made some arrangement with his publisher, that maybe they'd want to hire me on to finish the job, but I really didn't expect..."

"Okay. I believe you." I sat straight again, fixing my eyes on the drawing room door.

"Is it... Are you worried that it will be awkward, working with me?" Since it appeared from his voice that it was awkward for him to even ask the question, I wondered how much of his concern also applied to him. "I mean, after... Well, you know. The other night."

"Edward," I said, stopping him before it got more excruciating for either one of us. "I assure you that I am much more concerned about my family's collective mental health than I am about working with a man I almost slept with."

"Oh," he said. "Good."

"That said," I carried on, turning back to face him again, "I am glad you're still here. I wouldn't want to have to do this without you." For some reason, my voice came out a lot softer than I'd intended, and my hand found its way to Edward's knee, ostensibly just for a quick, reassuring pat. But somehow his hand was covering mine, and the warmth and reassurance seemed to be flowing the other way.

What would I have done if Edward *hadn't* been here? If Nathaniel had left this responsibility only to me, and I'd had to make these decisions in the face of family uproar? If they'd all had one more reason to hate me?

As he held on to my hand, I let myself accept for the first time how really very glad I was that Edward was there to share the misery with me.

I looked up as the drawing-room door opened, but Edward didn't let go of my hand until Ellie was already out of the room in the hallway, staring at us.

"Right," she said, sounding pretty much done in. "Sorry." And with that, she turned and walked out of the front door into the summer afternoon.

"Damn it," Edward said, mostly under his breath, and got to his feet. "I'd better go and see if she's... See where she's gone, anyway."

My jaw felt suddenly tight, and I realised I was gritting my teeth at the reminder that Edward was Ellie's friend, first. He wasn't here for me – he was here for Nathaniel, for Ellie, for the family, for the work. I was just incidental.

In a few long strides he was down the stairs and on his way out the door. I stayed where I was, arms wrapped around my knees again, listening to my family tearing itself apart in the other room.

"Are they nearly finished in there?" Caro appeared in the doorway from the kitchen dressed in a pair of yellow shorts with flamingos on, pink glittery shoes, and a T-shirt that announced to the world that, tomorrow, she planned to be a mermaid. In her hand was a bare cupcake. "Only, Dad said he'd help me decorate these later."

I looked at the plain cupcake, then at my little sister. Maybe I couldn't fix my relationship with Ellie, and maybe I was about to destroy my relationships with the rest of my family too, if I chose to take on the memoirs.

But I was still Caro's big sister. And that was a relationship I could strengthen, right now.

"I've got a better idea," I said, getting to my feet. "Come on. I want to show you something."

"Wow!" Caro's eyes widened as we reached the ladder at the bottom of the tree house. "How did I not know this was here?"

I grinned. "It's a secret. Nobody knew about it except me and Nathaniel. And now you."

"Can we go up?" Caro asked, turning to me with a bright, excited grin.

"Of course! That's why we came here. Go on. You first." I watched her disappear up the ladder, her glittery shoes gripping tight to the wood, before I followed.

It felt strange, watching Caro flit around the inside of the tree house, discovering all the treasures I'd left there over the years – and one of Nathaniel's old pipes, too. She handed that to me, and I held it in both hands, as if it might carry answers from my grandfather from beyond the grave.

It didn't.

"Who made the house?" Caro perched on a small stool, pulling her feet up onto it and hugging her knees. "Was it the fairies?"

I tried to imagine Graham the Assistant as a fairy, and failed. "Probably," I said. "I used to play here when I was younger. I thought that you might like to, now."

Caro frowned. "Don't you still want it?"

"I'll be going back to Perth soon." Although, honestly, camping out in the tree house seemed like a viable alternative at the moment.

"I wish you didn't have to," Caro said.

"So do I." If I said no to the memoirs, would I be able to stay at Rosewood? Maybe. But then, maybe not. Making the decision my family wanted this time didn't undo the harm I'd done before. And could I really stay, knowing I'd let my grandfather down at the last? I wasn't sure.

I had a life in Perth. It might not be the one Nathaniel had planned for me, but it was mine. And I couldn't just give that up. Could I?

"So, what do you want to play?" Caro asked. "Elves and fairies? Ghost hunters?"

I smiled across the small wooden room at her. Whatever happened next, right now I had Caro beside me, and games to play. "Why don't you tell me about how your paranormal research is going."

Caro's face lit up again, as she jumped up and pulled a pink notebook from her pocket. "Do you want to go alphabetically or in the order I discovered them?"

"Whichever you like," I told her, and settled back against the wooden wall to listen.

By the time Caro and I made it back up to the house, Dad was waiting with a bowl of buttercream icing, and the news that Mr Norris had declared he had a long drive back to the coast, and sitting there listening to everyone arguing wasn't getting him there any sooner. Therese, meanwhile, was waiting for me. It was around this time that Isabelle realised that Edward still had the key to the study, and I could hear her demanding to know where he was from behind me as Therese dragged me out of the front door and down the path that led to her cottage. As Ellie and Edward still hadn't returned, there wasn't much I could say to help, anyway.

My great-aunt clearly wasn't in the mood for conversation, so I allowed myself to be taken down to the cottage, where Therese set about making tea with the maximum possible amount of clashing of crockery and clanging silverware.

"Can I help with anything?" I asked, finally, as Therese spilt milk all over the tea tray.

"No," she bit out, mopping it up with a tea towel. "Go have a seat in the sitting room. We're going to have tea."

It seemed safest to do as I was told.

"Did you all get anything sorted out?" I asked, when we were finally seated and Therese had slopped tea into both my cup and saucer.

"Yes," Therese said, snatching up a chocolate biscuit. "I decided that your entire family are self-absorbed fools, who are interested in nothing beyond their own petty secrets."

Which seemed a little harsh, but not entirely untrue.

"And they are most certainly not interested in mourning my brother or making his dying wish a reality," she went on, spraying biscuit crumbs. I'd never seen Therese talk with her mouth full before. It was certainly an experience.

"I thought you didn't want the memoirs to be published, either?" It was dodgy territory, I know, but I reckoned that if I were going to make a decision about what to do next, I would need all the information I could get. Once that information could be conveyed at a reasonable decibel, and one piece at a time.

"I want the story it tells to be true and accurate," Therese clarified. "And it's not that I don't trust you, dear, but you weren't there. I'm not sure how you can recreate the childhood Nathaniel and I shared."

"Edward says the early years are pretty much finished, actually," I reassured her. "If we decide to go ahead, perhaps you'd like to read them through, see what you think."

Even that was dangerous ground, I realised. After all, what two siblings have exactly the same memories of how they grew up? Everyone remembers things differently. On the other hand, if Therese was upset by what Nathaniel had written, would I want it published anyway?

Therese paused in her destruction of the chocolate biscuits. "Maybe I would like that," she said, and returned her half-eaten biscuit to the plate. "We shouldn't be eating these, you know. Your father will be cooking a three-course dinner. Stress cooking, as usual."

I didn't point out that none of us had eaten any lunch, given the lawyer baiting that had been going on at the time. I wished Therese had waited long enough for us to snag a couple of Caro's cupcakes to go with the tea.

"Anyway," Therese went on, pushing herself to her feet. "I have clothes for you." Dad stressed-cooked, Therese stress-dressed, it seemed. Not that I was complaining, as the beneficiary of both.

I traipsed after her into her bedroom and discovered, inevitably, that these were no ordinary hand-me-down clothes.

"This outfit is for tonight," she said, handing me a hanger weighed down with a grey and duck-egg-blue tea dress with vines and tiny cream flowers climbing up it. It was cut in a forties style, and Therese had hung a duck-egg cardigan over it on the hanger. The matching cream handbag and string of pearls were wrapped around the hanger. "The earrings are in the bag," she added, passing over the cream heels that went with it.

"Do you really think we'll be dressing for dinner tonight?" I took the dress and considered it. It was sober enough to fit the mood at the house, but still far nicer than anything I'd brought with me.

"Why wouldn't we? Nathaniel would expect nothing less."

"Nathaniel would have shown up in his old orange jumper with the oil stains on and you know it." I still couldn't quite imagine that he wouldn't. That he'd never wear that jumper again. Isabelle would probably dress him in some awful suit he'd have hated for the funeral.

Maybe she'd be distracted enough to let Therese choose his clothes for that. I could just see him dressed as a thirties film star for the occasion.

"Nathaniel was a law unto himself," Therese said. "No reason to let our standards slip." She paused, her fingers brushing against a closed garment bag. "I'll have an outfit for you for the funeral, too," she said slowly. "But not just yet. I'll bring it up to the house when it's ready. I just want to make sure that it's right."

I hadn't even thought about the funeral. I certainly hadn't packed anything mourning appropriate when I came home for the Golden Wedding.

"You're coming up for dinner?" I folded the evening's outfit over my arm carefully.

"Of course," Therese said, closing her wardrobe door. "Especially now we've established that Isabelle is definitely too angry with you and Edward to notice that I'm there at all."

"Excellent," I said, trying to imagine just how horrible dinner was going to be.

"Now go and get changed. I'll see you up there."

And with that, I was hustled back out onto the sunny path, clutching my new outfit close to my body, like some sort of shield. At least Therese's outfits gave me an armour of sorts. Some protection against the fraught dinner ahead. As long as no one resorted to throwing food… Well, it should be fine.

Dad, obviously anticipating the general chaos that Mr Norris's visit would bring to the day, had started preparing dinner much earlier that morning, and chosen something that was easy, liked by everyone, yet could sit in the oven for hours while the family bickered over inheritance matters.

By the time I made it down to dinner, dressed in Therese's chosen outfit, the rest of my family were already sitting down at the dining table. Whether they'd skipped the pre-dinner drinks altogether, or if they'd all been steadily drinking since Mr Norris left, I had no way of knowing.

Regardless, it made it slightly easier to slip into the room unnoticed. Dad, out of loving kindness for his middle daughter, had kept the seat beside him, the one closest to the door, free for me, for which I gave a quiet vote of thanks.

From the other side of the table, Edward gave me a small, tight smile. I wondered how long he'd already been there.

"Right then," Dad said, bearing in a huge pot. "Pasta bolognese. With about a bottle and a half of red wine in it. Just the thing for tonight, don't you think?"

We all made the appropriate appreciative noises, and avoided looking at each other as we tucked in.

Dinner was, perhaps not surprisingly, a fairly silent meal. Isabelle, I noticed, ate as little as possible, pushing her pasta around her bowl and looking faintly sulky. Her loss, I thought, as I tucked into the bolognese with gusto. Dad might not have been able to heal all family rifts, but he certainly knew how to cook dinner.

The seat at the head of the table was, of course, empty, and as much as I avoided looking at it, I still felt the lack of Nathaniel keenly. It wasn't as though he'd have been able to make everything all better. On the contrary, he'd probably have gone out of his way to make things worse, purely for entertainment value, and at some later date snippets of the ensuing fight would have shown up, entirely out of context, in one of his books.

Something Nathaniel did fairly regularly, but never admitted to critics, was put his family into the background of his novels. We never appeared as main characters, or even any incidental character anyone would remember. But when the hero was sitting in a cafe, listening to a couple arguing, or the heroine was walking in the park and saw a small girl fall in the lake shallows as she tried to feed the ducks, her grandfather standing there laughing while her grandmother yelled – that was us. Every time.

As Greg swiped the last piece of garlic bread, Mum pushed her empty plate aside and put on her serious-teacher face. It never looked right on her. Mum was the opposite of serious and focused, but sometimes she liked to pretend, just for our benefit.

"We should talk about the funeral," she said. "Shouldn't we?" she added, belying the decisiveness of her words.

"We should," Ellie confirmed. "Apparently Nathaniel didn't leave much in the way of instructions. Isabelle, did he ever say anything to you about what he wanted?"

"Why would he?" Isabelle sounded astonished, and I exchanged a frustrated glance with Edward.

Because you're both in your seventies. Because you were his whole world, once. Because that's the sort of thing people do. Normal people.

People who believed they were going to die, anyway. I suspected that Isabelle just intended to go on for ever, and Nathaniel wouldn't ever have wanted to consider the possibility. Except that he had, with Edward. He'd made provisions to ensure that his memoirs were taken care of, and his legacy. Just not his body.

Typical.

"Did he have any favourite hymns?" Dad asked. "That's always a good place to start."

Isabelle perked up. "I always liked 'For the Beauty of the Earth'."

I glanced up at Edward again. Nathaniel had hated going to church, and everyone knew it. And yet, because her social circle would expect it, Isabelle would plan a traditional church funeral.

"*He* liked 'For Those in Peril on the Sea'." Therese added, which earned her a glare from Isabelle.

"I'll contact the vicar tomorrow," Ellie said, and Isabelle shook her head.

"No. He was my husband. Leave it to me." She pushed her chair away from the table and stood. "Now, if you'll excuse me, I have a headache. I think I'll go to bed."

"I think it's your bedtime too, young lady," Dad said to Caro, scooping her up from her chair. "Come on. I'll read you a story. I don't care if you're nearly ten, you're never too old for a bedtime story." Caro protested, but only for a moment. She looked as exhausted as the rest of us.

The door clicked shut behind the three of them, and I looked from face to face around the table. What happened now? I had no idea. I didn't know where to start. How did this work? How did we function without Nathaniel?

I worried for a moment that they'd want to talk about the memoirs again, but it quickly became clear that they all had bigger concerns.

"Are we really going to leave the funeral up to Isabelle?" Ellie asked.

Therese shook her head. "I wouldn't recommend it. She'll probably insist on funeral favours."

"She wouldn't," Mum said, sounding tired. "But if you could help her out, Ellie... She works so much better with you."

"Of course." Ellie didn't point out that Isabelle only liked working with her because she could boss her around, which I would have. "But what are we going to do after the funeral? Greg and I..." She trailed off, but I thought I caught her meaning. Living at Rosewood with Nathaniel and Isabelle and Therese had been one thing. Taking sole responsibility for Isabelle was another entirely.

"Let me talk to your father," Mum said. "We don't need to be back in Manchester, for the start of term, for another week or so. Maybe I can look at taking a leave of absence."

Ellie shook her head. "We can stay."

I should offer to move back. To take care of things. To be useful, for once. But I wasn't at all sure that they wanted me to.

Especially since, if I stayed, I'd be working on the memoirs. With Edward.

I glanced up at him again and found that, somehow, he'd disappeared from the room without any of us noticing. When? Had he followed Dad and Caro out? And where had he gone?

The answer to the last came to me easily. Nathaniel's study. Where else?

While Mum, Ellie, Greg and Therese talked about the future, I slipped out of my chair, opening and closing the dining-room door as silently as possible, and headed for the stairs – and the past.

Chapter Nine

An author writes to leave a legacy, a mark on the world. The stories we leave behind are our way of showing the insides of our heads – our thoughts, our beliefs, our loves. Never mind what truth there is in our words, what we send out into the world is greater than truth, and longer lasting. Stories, after all, survive far longer than facts.

From the notebooks of Nathaniel Drury

The door to Nathaniel's study had been locked since I came home again, but now, as I crept down the long hallway towards it, I could see the door was ajar. I stared straight ahead as I passed the place where I'd hidden, the night of the Golden Wedding, and pretended I couldn't still hear my grandparents arguing in my head. What was the point? Nothing I – or Isabelle – did could change those last moments now.

It occurred to me that Edward had probably commandeered one of the bedrooms at this end of the building – he seemed like the sort to want to be near his work. And that meant he had easy access to the study at all times. I wondered how much time he'd spent there over the last couple of days, without Isabelle noticing.

The study door opened in one smooth sweep. As I'd predicted, Edward was already there. Not in the seat behind the desk – Nathaniel's chair – but in a hard wooden seat to the side of the desk, one I imagined he must have used throughout the long months of working with my grandfather.

I bit the inside of my cheek as I looked around. Somehow, the whole room felt different from how I remembered. Emptier, despite the floor being covered in boxes and journals. Paler, somehow, like the lights had faded when Nathaniel did.

I stared at the chair behind the desk, empty except for an orange fisherman's jumper draped over the back. That was where Edward had found him. Where he'd died.

Knowing Nathaniel, I supposed he'd probably say it was the second best place to go. The best, I imagined, was next to the drinks cabinet.

I took a deep breath. I had to keep moving. Keep living. The moment I got lost in my memories, I worried I'd never find my way back to the surface again.

"We should probably lock this door," I said, shutting it softly behind me. "Someone's bound to notice we're missing eventually."

Edward looked up from the papers he was reading with a start, but relaxed quickly once he realised it was only me. I liked that he could feel relaxed around me. "Maybe they'll think I'm seducing you in an attic, or something."

"Unlikely." I grabbed a chair from the corner of the room, one covered in shabby red velvet that I remembered curling up on as a child as I watched Nathaniel work, and pulled it closer to the desk. "They'll all immediately jump to the conclusion that we're up here working on the memoirs." I took a deep breath. "Which it looks like we might be so, seriously, lock the damn door."

The look he gave me was long and assessing, but he did at least get to his feet and move towards the door.

As the key turned in the lock, I heard the tumblers fall into place and wondered just what the hell I was doing.

"Are you sure about this?" Edward leant against the closed door and kept on giving me his 'concerned and caring look.' It left me with the impression that he was slightly afraid that I might lose it at any second.

Which wasn't entirely unreasonable.

"Not even a little bit," I said with a sigh. "But I know that I can't make a decision on whether to publish or not until I know what we're talking about. There's obviously something Isabelle doesn't want included, and I don't know whether that's the same thing everyone else doesn't want written about or something else, and until I do... I just don't know. So I need to look at what Nathaniel left behind."

Edward nodded. "Makes sense." He crossed the room and settled back into his chair, shuffling the papers that were piled on the desk in front of him, before selecting a clip-bound-paper stack and passing it over to me. "This is what we'd got agreed so far."

What they had so far, from my brief look through, was Nathaniel's childhood and existence up until the point where he met Isabelle.

"'I saw her, and my world changed,'" I read. "That was the last thing he wrote?" It was almost a direct quote from *Biding Time*.

"Yep. Think it will make Isabelle feel any better disposed towards the project?" Edward tipped his chair back a little, his face lit by the faint remaining evening light forcing its way in through the window.

"Probably not." I clipped the pages back together. "I'll read through this properly tonight, but then I promised Therese she could take a look at it too."

Edward's face was unreadable. "What if she remembers their childhood differently?" he asked, making me wonder exactly what Nathaniel had said about growing up poor in North Wales.

"Then I'll take that into account when I make my decision."

"Okay, then." Edward let the front two chair legs crash to the ground. "So the question then is, what happened next?"

"Yep." I put the partial manuscript to one side, and gave Edward my full attention. "So, what do we have?"

"Mostly?" Edward stood up and crossed the study, pausing by a pile of file boxes, stacked haphazardly upon each other and looking frighteningly precarious. "What we have is this," he said, gesturing at the boxes.

"Fantastic." I sighed. "We'd better get started, then."

We made it through the first two boxes that night, sorting through Nathaniel's notes, journals, photos, clippings and miscellany. I wasn't sure I'd figured out the logic to the storage of the notes yet, but I hoped that Edward, who'd been working with them longer, would have a far better idea than I did.

Eventually, after I yawned for the eighteenth time in half an hour, Edward closed the lid of the box I was looking through and took the journal I was reading from my hands.

"We should get to bed," he said, placing the journal on top of the box.

At his words, a strange warmth flowed through me. "You seem to be saying that to me a lot lately." I meant when he put me for a nap, like a small child, that morning. But as soon as the words were out I was transported back to that night in the attic in my mind.

From the heat in Edward's eyes, he was thinking the same, forbidden, thoughts.

His Adam's apple bobbed as he swallowed, his gaze sliding away from mine. "You're tired."

Was that an excuse? A reason not to address whatever the hell this was between us? Or an easy let-down. A way to let me know that the spark didn't matter, not any more.

That seemed more likely.

I pulled back, hurrying to my feet, wanting to get out of there, fast. "You're right. And I need to call Duncan, before I go to bed."

Edward stilled at the name. "You haven't spoken to him yet?"

"I left a voicemail, explaining what had happened. About Nathaniel, I mean. I needed to let him know I wouldn't be at work for a few days."

"A few days," he echoed. "So you're still planning on going back?"

Was I? I wasn't sure. "I'll have to, at some point. I have a job. A flat. All my stuff is there." And besides, was there really a place for me at Rosewood? Especially without Nathaniel there to stand in my corner.

Edward's head bobbed in a jerky nod. "Of course. We'll carry on here tomorrow though?"

I gazed around the room at the endless unopened boxes. "I think we have to." What other way was there for me to figure out what happened next?

Duncan didn't take the news of my impending absence particularly well.

"So when will you be back?" he asked, impatiently. I wondered if I'd interrupted some sports event or another, or if he'd always been this grumpy outside of a bed and I just hadn't noticed.

"I don't know," I admitted. "We don't have a date for the funeral yet, and even then, there's a project he's left to me to finish…"

"A project more important than your job here?"

Wasn't that the million-dollar question? I thought of Edward, head bent over a fifty-year-old journal, soaking in every moment of my family's history. "I think it might be."

"I see." He sighed. "Well, take all the time you need. You can't rush grief. But, Sas… I can't hold your job indefinitely. Not even for you."

Not even for me. Speaking of which, there was something else I needed to talk to Duncan about. And if not now when?

"Actually…" I started, then trailed off.

Duncan laughed. "Don't tell me. Your grandmother has set you up with a date for the funeral, you've fallen madly in love and it's all over between us."

"No. Not exactly."

"But close? Sas, who has a date for a funeral?"

I sighed. "It's not a date. Just like whatever was between us wasn't, I don't know, a relationship."

"It was the closest thing either of us had had in a while," Duncan pointed out, which was truer than I'd like. "And it's over now, right?"

"Yeah," I admitted. "It is. I just… I think I'm looking for something more than that."

"You think a relationship will make you happy?" He made the idea sound ludicrous.

"Maybe. Maybe not. But I've never really had one, not as an adult. I think it might be time to give it a try."

It didn't change anything, not really. But somehow I felt lighter after I hung up the phone.

*

The next day dawned bright and warm even from the early hours.

The house seemed empty when I made it downstairs, so I assumed everyone else was having a lie-in. Deciding to enjoy the peace, I picked up the paper from the doormat and took it into the kitchen to read with my coffee. But as I flicked open the pages, I forgot all about my caffeine fix.

LITERARY COMMUNITY IN MOURNING.

I skipped the headline, my gaze locking directly onto the photo of Nathaniel next to it. He looked just as he had the last day I'd seen him, dressed in his white dinner jacket. It must have been taken at the Golden Wedding, I realised, running a finger across his face as my eyes filled. I blinked the tears away.

I needed to know what they were saying – about the family, about the memoirs. About everything.

For all that he was almost seventy-six, there was no warning of his demise. There was no long struggle with illness, no public decline, no reports of ill-health even. Quite the contrary, in fact – just the day before his death Drury had announced, at his own Golden Wedding Anniversary party at his home in Rosewood, his intention to write his memoirs – something the gossips and scandal-mongers of the aforementioned literary world have been waiting for impatiently for many years.

Whether the work will now be completed remains to be seen, but if they are published, we can all be assured of one hell of a story.

Well that, I supposed, was a given. I read on, through a brief recap of Nathaniel's early life and rise to fame – with the obligatory reference to *Biding Time* being a love story to Isabelle. She'd like that bit, anyway.

I met Drury only once, in London in 2013, at the Blackfriars pub – a personal favourite of his. I was supposed to be interviewing him about his latest book, The Tithing. *Instead, I found myself drawn into a conversation about one of his granddaughters, and her burgeoning career as a journalist.*

I sucked in a breath, then let it out fast. If I couldn't handle a passing reference to myself in the paper, how would I cope with my story being told in the memoirs?

"Do you think she will follow in your footsteps?" I asked, over a mouthful of game pie.
  "I think she will do anything she sets her mind to," he said. "Just as I did."

I didn't bother trying to stop the tears, this time. I couldn't ignore all the ways I'd let Nathaniel down, not lived up to what he wanted for me. Greg was only the start of it.
  It had to be different from now on. *I* had to be different. That much, I was sure of.
  The obituary finished with another line about the memoirs.

If Nathaniel Drury really wanted to publish his memoirs, perhaps it is presumptive to assume that he would allow even his death to stop him. Perhaps, somewhere in Rosewood, there is a manuscript box, all ready to be delivered to his publishers…

I smiled. If only that were the case. It would be a lot easier… but it would rob me of the chance to work with Edward on them. To make the project my own.
  And I had to admit, the idea of that had started to appeal to me.

"What are they saying?" Isabelle's voice came sharp from the doorway. "I bet it's all gossip."

"It's a nice piece, actually," I said, holding the paper out to her. She ignored it. "You should read it."

Isabelle's lips were pursed tight, the lines around them suddenly obvious in a way I'd never noticed before. She looked *old* all of a sudden.

"I don't want to read what *they* have to say about me. About my husband," she corrected herself, and I frowned. What was it Isabelle thought *they* were going to say? "He's barely cold and they're already digging. Already looking for scandal and lies. It'll only get worse, you mark my words."

With that, she wandered back out again, towards the Orangery. I stared after her in confusion.

There was *definitely* something weird going on with Isabelle.

Eventually, everyone else made it down to the kitchen, hunting for breakfast.

"I think we all need to get out of here for a few hours," Dad said, as he warmed croissants in the oven. "Especially Caro. The atmosphere around here is no good for a young girl."

He was right, I knew. So even though all I really wanted to do was curl up in Nathaniel's study with Edward and keep going through all the documents and photos he'd left behind, I said, "That sounds lovely. Who else fancies it? Edward?"

Edward raised his eyebrows at me across the kitchen counter, but I ignored him. He'd been stuck up in that study for too long already. Some fresh air would probably do him good, too.

And actually, it was lovely. Isabelle, when I took her coffee in the Orangery and explained the plan, insisted on staying at home in case of condolence callers, of which she expected there to be many, and to call the funeral directors. Mum and Ellie decided they'd best stay with her so, in the end, it was only Caro, Dad, Edward and I who ventured out, Dad with the picnic rucksack on his back.

Edward and Caro set off at a faster pace than the rest of us, and I could hear Caroline explaining about all the different creatures that lived in the woods – mice and owls and squirrels and fairies and even the occasional unicorn, apparently. Edward, to his credit, was not only listening attentively, but also asking insightful questions into the housing issues faced by fairies in today's disappearing woodlands.

"Well, we certainly know where that one got her imagination from," Dad said, stooping to pick up a long and sturdy stick, as if it would make him any more of a natural walker.

"Nathaniel," I said, fondly.

"He used to love her stories." Dad gazed ahead at where Caroline had dived into a pile of cut grass, and Edward was trying to pull her out. "She'd sit up in his study with him and Edward, pretending to help them work." He linked his arm through mine and tugged me close. "He used to say she reminded him of you."

I always knew that my grandfather loved me. I had some inkling, even as a child, that I might be something of a favourite. But I'm not sure I realised exactly how much he trusted and respected me until he died.

On the one hand, leaving me his notes and plans for his memoirs, and entrusting me to get them published, was always guaranteed to get me into hot water with the rest of the family. But what I hadn't really stopped to consider, until I got out of the house and away from the others, was that I was the only family member he chose to give this responsibility to. There was no one else, except his assistant, an outsider, and even then, I had the final decision on what happened.

We'd barely even started going through the boxes the night before, but I already knew it was going to be a hard slog. Nathaniel had, at least, managed to package things vaguely into decade-orientated boxes, but within those boxes nothing was really in order, and there was certainly no handy index to the life and times of Nathaniel Drury. Just figuring out what was in there, and what events each document corresponded to, was going to be a challenge. I hoped that the majority of the older documents were dated accurately, or we didn't stand a chance.

"Couldn't you have persuaded him to be a little more thorough in his archiving?" I'd asked Edward, as I pawed through what appeared to be a recent box. It included, amongst other things, my very first byline – something not even I had kept a copy of.

For the first time, I wondered how much of *my* past was in these boxes, beyond what I'd done to Ellie. And would I like it when I found it?

We returned to Rosewood in the early afternoon, stuffed full of Coronation-chicken sandwiches and feeling virtuous anyway for walking at least a few miles. In our absence, it appeared that most of Cheshire had stopped by with flowers and, while I was subjected to a detailed tour of our new floral arrangements, along with pointed comments from Isabelle about who was simply being ostentatious and who would probably sob all through the funeral, even though they'd only met Nathaniel twice, Edward escaped upstairs without even taking off his boots, leaving grass-stained footprints all the way to Nathaniel's study.

The funeral, Isabelle announced, was to be held in five days' time. Apparently she'd had a secret meeting with the funeral director, Mrs Dawkins, yet another old friend of the family, while we were out, and Mrs Dawkins had agreed to hurry things along. We'd established that Nathaniel definitely hadn't left any firm instructions for how his funeral should be handled in his will which, given Isabelle's tendency towards extremes, seemed a bit of an oversight to me.

I followed Edward up to the study once I'd fully admired all the flowers, and found him already elbow deep in paperwork. I shut the door behind me, then snapped my fingers at Edward. It took him a moment, but he eventually figured out what I wanted and tossed me the key.

Safely locked in, I felt comfortable enough to get stuck into my family history once again.

I wasn't sure if the family were just ignoring our absence, or honestly hadn't realised what we were up to. Given their ongoing complaints about the memoirs, I suspected they were just hoping we'd come to our senses and drop the whole thing.

As I took my seat, ready to pick up where I'd left off the night before, Edward spoke.

"I saw Ellie on my way up here. She's asked me to speak at the funeral."

I froze, halfway through reaching for Nathaniel's journal. Somehow, just picturing Edward standing up there, talking about my grandfather, made the whole thing seem real all over again. Like, while we were in his study, reading his words, Nathaniel wasn't really gone.

But soon, I'd be sitting in that church, mourning him, and I wouldn't be able to pretend any more.

I looked up at Edward, and took in the grey tinge to his skin, and the ways his hands shook, just a little, as he reached for the next box.

"Are you going to do it?" I asked.

"I guess." He shook his head, like he wasn't sure. "I just don't get why they want me to. Ellie said that Isabelle told her to ask me. Why would she do that? She hates me right now."

"No, she doesn't." He gave me a look. "Well, maybe a bit. But it's not you. It's what you represent. And that's exactly why she wants you to speak."

The majority of the congregation would probably be readers, rather than close friends – Nathaniel always had more of the former than the latter – and Edward was the only one of us who could talk with any confidence about his writing, or his professional life.

The more I thought about it, the more sense it made.

"What do you mean?"

"To most people, Nathaniel was his books. That's what she wants you to talk about. His legacy."

"As long as I don't mention the memoirs, you mean," Edward said.

"Pretty much. Think you can manage it?"

He sighed. "I can try."

We worked in silence for a long while, enjoying the warm summer sun lighting the room, and the rustle of papers. Occasionally Edward would pass a tattered old photo, usually with black-and-white figures staring at the camera, and I'd try and decipher Isabelle's scrawl on the back to puzzle out who they were. It was becoming more and more obvious to me that without the cooperation and assistance of my family, we'd never be able to uncover all the information we needed to write these memoirs.

Deciding to go ahead with the project wouldn't be enough. I'd need to convince my relatives that it was a good idea, too. And that sounded even more impossible than making sense of Nathaniel's boxes and boxes of notes.

"I'm learning a lot about you in these boxes." Edward handed over another, more recent, photo: me, aged around ten, wearing a glorious black-and-fluorescent-pink combination, with my hair cut much the same as it was currently – bobbed just above shoulder level.

"Maybe we should swap boxes," I suggested. Mostly, I'd been wading through book reviews and communications with publishers – interesting, sure, but not really very enlightening. More than anything, I was just amazed that Nathaniel had kept so much stuff, all these years.

In the back of my mind, I knew exactly what I was looking for – whatever it was that Isabelle was so afraid of. And my thoughts kept circling round to the story Nathaniel had told me in the tree house, the day of the Golden Wedding – the story of that first, possibly fatal party there at Rosewood. Was that it? Was that the secret? I still wasn't sure how much of Nathaniel's story was just that – a story. But I wanted to find out – and I was in the best possible place to do just that.

Edward pulled out my school report, circa 2004. "Absolutely no way I'm swapping." Flipping through the pages, he began to pick out some choice phrases. When he reached my PE teacher's comments, I shoved the box I was reading through off my lap and onto the floor, and launched myself at the report and, by default, Edward, landing half across the desk, and half across him, hanging on to the report for dear life.

Laughing, Edward relinquished his hold on the report, mostly so he could put his hands on my waist to stop me careening onto the floor. "I guess your old school reports don't have all that much relevance to your grandfather's memoirs."

"Exactly my point." I struggled into an upright position, failing to notice until I'd achieved it that it just left me sitting in Edward's lap, his arms around my waist and my heart pounding. I could feel the blood flooding to warm my cheeks.

"Good job that door's locked," he murmured, but other than that there was no sign, no move, no signal that he wanted to kiss me as much as I wanted him to.

But maybe he was just good at hiding his feelings. I mean, he'd wanted to sleep with me, hadn't he? Not even a week ago, so he must have found me vaguely attractive, right? And yes, okay, so we'd both been drunk and I'd run out on him, but still, it meant something. So maybe I should just kiss him, and forget all the waiting around to be kissed. Maybe this was what was meant to happen. Maybe I should just…

"What's that?" Edward leant forward, tipping me from his lap as he reached for a yellowing newspaper clipping that had become dislodged from a pile in our tussle. He held it up to me, and I shivered as I took it, despite the sun.

"It looks like it's a clipping from the society pages." I stared at the image of a twenty-something Isabelle, and an even younger Therese, both in evening dress, smiling out for the camera. Between them stood a man I didn't recognise, his grin bigger than either of theirs. And behind them all loomed Rosewood, unchanging and unchangeable.

Heart in my throat, I checked the caption. *Pictured: Isabelle Drury, Matthew Robertson, Therese Drury.* So, before Therese was married. My gaze flicked further down to the text underneath:

All eyes are on Rosewood House this weekend, home of literary darling Nathaniel Drury and his wife, as they prepare for their first party in their new home.

No explanation of who Matthew Robertson was. Could he have been Therese's beau? I smiled at the idea. He certainly looked nothing like Uncle George, from what I'd seen in photos. This Matthew was far more handsome. He looked the suave, charming sort. Had he romanced Therese? Maybe I'd ask her. I frowned at the photo again. Where was Nathaniel, though? Matthew had his arms around both my great-aunt and my grandmother, but my grandfather was nowhere to be seen.

"Did he ever talk about a housewarming party here at Rosewood?" I asked Edward.

"Not as far as I remember," he said, with a shrug. "But there's got to be something about it somewhere in these boxes."

I surveyed the mass of documentation and memorabilia. He was right, I realised. It had to be in here somewhere. All the secrets my family were keeping were. And, one by one, it was my job to find them.

"Everything okay?" Edward asked, and I snapped out of my trance to look at him again. Moments ago, I'd thought he was about to kiss me. Now all I could think about was what potential scandals my family were hiding, and Edward's reputation for uncovering the truth, every time.

I gave a sharp nod. "Everything's fine," I said, and got stuck back into my box of papers.

Whatever the truth was, I wanted to find it first.

The next few days passed in a haze of funeral preparations and research. I still hadn't turned up anything else on that fateful party but, on the plus side, neither had Edward.

He hadn't come close to kissing me again, either. I couldn't quite decide if this was a good thing or not.

The night before the funeral, we all endured yet another awkward family meal, during which nobody asked Edward or me where we'd been all afternoon, and Ellie gave me funny looks and Edward sat at the opposite end of the table to me, seemingly on purpose. By the time I was able to escape to my room I was tired, cross and tense. But then, I opened my bedroom door and found the dress.

It was obviously another Therese special, heralded by the tiny cream envelope tucked into the matching handbag which, when opened, yielded up a thick, cream card with the words 'For tomorrow, Tx' flowing across it in neat, black ink.

I sat back on the bed and looked at it. It was nothing elaborate, utterly unlike most of the other dresses she'd picked for me. It was, at heart, a simple, black Hepburnesque shift dress, eminently suitable for funerals, and much nicer than anything I had in Perth, even if I'd had the chance to go back and pack them. But there was something about it – maybe in the cut, or the trim, or the discreet diamond jewellery she'd included. Something that gave it a hint of something more, even if I couldn't put my finger on exactly what.

I just hoped it could give me the calm, grace-under-fire countenance that I'd need to get through the day.

The funeral was being held in the tiny local church, even though it was clear from the moment we arrived that there was no way everyone was going to fit inside. I'd walked down early with the rest of the family – except for Isabelle, Therese and Mum, who were following in the hired black car that travelled in convoy with the hearse.

"That's… a lot of people," Edward said, pausing at the church gates. I looked up. Apparently Edward was developing a fine line in understatement.

"Mrs Dawkins was reserving the front two pews for family," Dad said, gazing across the crowd.

"Reverend Tucker is looking a little shell-shocked," Greg commented, and Ellie gave out a small, inappropriate laugh, before she smacked a hand across her mouth.

"Well," she said, once she'd got herself back under control, "he's probably never seen so many people in a church before."

I squared my shoulders. "I suppose we'd better get in there."

It took a while to even reach the doors of the church. Everyone, even people I'd never seen before, wanted to offer their condolences, which was overwhelming at the same time as it was kind. I kept shying away, every time I caught a glimpse of someone I'd seen or spoken to at the Golden Wedding. It seemed wrong to be seeing them all again so soon.

Isabelle had requested donations to charity rather than flowers, but there were still countless more floral arrangements already making their way into the church. We pushed our way through the crowd and the flowers and into the church, and found our allocated pews. I kept Caroline close to me, and found Edward on my right, next to Dad. Ellie and Greg sat in the row behind. The rest of the family would fill up the empty pew on the other side of the chapel.

I fiddled with the service sheet I'd been handed at the door, and tried to figure out how Therese had convinced everyone that "For Those in Peril on the Sea" was an appropriate funeral hymn. The sheet slipped from my hand and floated to the floor, where Edward reached down and collected it.

"You holding up okay?" he murmured, handing it back.

I nodded. I was absolutely fine, of course. How could I possibly be anything else?

And I was. I was fine all through the service, even when Edward stood up and talked about the honour – and difficulties – of working with such a celebrated writer, and the pleasure of becoming part of his family. I was fine as we stood at the graveside, shivering in the sudden summer wind as we watched the coffin being lowered into the verdant ground. I was fine as we held court at the nearby hotel – because Isabelle couldn't bear the idea of having a rerun of her Golden Wedding celebration at Rosewood, but without her husband. I was polite and charming to the guests, sipping slowly on one glass of white wine when all I really wanted to do was swallow down the bottle and forget about it all until tomorrow.

I was even fine when we returned to Rosewood, sombre and subdued, and all gravitated towards the drawing room for whisky nightcaps.

In fact, I was still telling myself I was fine when Edward crouched down in front of my chair and took my empty glass from my hand. "Come on," he said, and I blinked at him. "Seriously." He stood up and took my hand. "Come with me."

No one else was paying us much attention: Therese and Isabelle had got the old photo albums out and were explaining to Nathaniel's agent, who'd joined us at the house, exactly who everyone was. Dad had taken Caroline up to bed, and Mum was sitting with Greg and Ellie, telling them stories about growing up at Rosewood. I realised, suddenly, that I had no idea how long I'd been sitting there.

Edward tugged me to my feet, and I followed him out into the hallway, through to the kitchen and into the small utility room where we kept all the coats and boots. Numbly, I let him shove my arms into the sleeves of somebody or other's jacket, and my feet into a handy pair of trainers that even I was aware didn't really go with Therese's carefully chosen dress. Fastening my laces, Edward nodded. "You'll do," he said, reaching for his jacket.

Outside was pitch-black and utterly quiet, but these things didn't really register with me. I was aware of them, but I didn't care or feel about them either way.

Edward kept a tight hold of my hand, and I focused on that instead – his skin against mine. Human contact.

"Where are we going?" I asked, finally, but Edward didn't reply; instead, he led me across the path towards the Rose Garden.

The Rose Garden didn't have a lot to recommend it, stripped of most of its flowers after the Golden Wedding, and especially since it was too dark to see anything anyway. Still, Edward led me inside, and sat us down on the bench just inside the walls.

"It's private here," he said. "No one's going to hear you or see you. I even brought the whisky, if you really want to keep drinking yourself into oblivion."

"I had one glass of wine at the hotel," I objected.

"And considerably more than one whisky back at the house." Edward shook the quarter-full bottle. "Don't forget, I was doing the pouring."

"I think I'm entitled to a drink, today of all days."

"Absolutely." He unscrewed the bottle top and handed the whisky to me. "And you'll notice I'm doing nothing at all to stop you."

I held on to the bottle but did not drink. "But...?"

"But I noticed that everyone else in the room was reminiscing – they were sad, but they were thinking about the good times. And you looked like you were thinking about Armageddon." Which wasn't strictly true. I hadn't actually been doing any thinking at all, that I could remember. "And I thought that maybe you needed to get outside, or at least out of that room, somewhere where people weren't watching you or worrying about you. I thought that maybe you were obsessing about keeping things together, and it might be good for you to fall apart for a little while."

"So you brought me to sit in the dark on my own, so that I don't bother anyone else if I decide to have a nervous breakdown?"

Edward took my hand. "Not on your own." His voice was warm and comforting, and I could feel the tears already building behind my eyes.

I looked down at our joined hands. "Yeah. Okay."

Tucking my head onto his shoulder, I let the tears come – quietly at first, as I remembered all the things that I'd never experience again, then louder as I thought about the next few days, weeks, months, years without Nathaniel. Edward simply wrapped his arms around me and let me sob – after moving the whisky bottle out of its precarious position between my knees.

It was some time before I felt calm enough to talk again. "How did you know?" I asked, wiping my eyes then nose with a handkerchief Edward had produced from one of his pockets.

We were still sitting so close that I could feel him shrug. "I was watching you. And I remembered what I needed when my dad died."

"I'm sorry." I contemplated the soggy handkerchief in my hands. I was really going to have to wash it before I gave it back. "I didn't know."

He shrugged again. "No reason you should. It was a few years ago now."

"Thank you," I said, after a while of sitting in silence. "This was what I needed, and I had no idea."

"Ready to go back in?" Edward asked, shifting his arm from around my shoulders.

I glanced down at my watch – it was almost midnight. "Yeah. I should get to bed. Lots of work to do tomorrow after all."

Edward creaked to his feet, rubbing some of the chill out of his knees and legs before turning to me and offering me his hand. "Oh I don't know, there's only another twenty or so boxes to go through." And one of them had to contain the information I was looking for. "Come on."

He was facing the wrong way, so he couldn't have seen it. But as I took Edward's hand and stood up, my own bones aching suddenly in the night air, I saw a figure just beyond him, on the other side of the Rose Garden. A woman in white, indistinct and ethereal. Caroline's ghost, again. Would Nathaniel return to haunt us here at Rosewood, I wondered hazily, through the whisky fog. I wasn't sure if I wanted him to or not.

"Come on," Edward said again. "Let's go in."

I nodded and smiled at him, and when I looked back, the figure was gone.

Chapter Ten

Sally came home last night. She brought with her a man I don't imagine I'd have spent more than a moment considering under normal circumstances. He shouldn't fit in here; he's not loud enough, or brash enough, or full of stories. You couldn't write a book about him. But to my daughter, he is everything. And to me... he is more than another character in our story. He's the hero.

From the journal of Nathaniel Drury, 1987

It should have been awkward the next morning. It should have been difficult to sit down at breakfast with Edward and everyone else and know that he'd seen me break down more completely than even my family ever had. But somehow it wasn't.

"I suppose you'll be starting work on the memoirs today, then," Isabelle said, glaring at us over her cup of coffee. "After all, he's dead and buried now. No point in waiting."

Edward gave me the "This one's yours" look. I gave him the 'Thank you very much' sarcasm glance in return.

"I'm not making any firm decisions yet, Isabelle," I said, calmly pouring myself another cup of tea. As strange as it seemed, I did feel much better after my crying jag in the Rose Garden the night before.

Even dressed in my own jeans and top and not a film star's outfit, I at least felt I could cope with the world. "In fact, I can't make any decisions without reading all the materials Nathaniel left behind. And we're still only about halfway through. So, yes, Edward and I will be working in the study today."

The rest of the family remained sensibly silent at that.

"Did you really mean that?" Edward asked, as we escaped up the stairs towards the study.

"Mean what?"

"That you still haven't made your mind up about the memoirs?"

Ah. That. I'd thought I was doing quite a good job of keeping everybody happy by hedging my bets every which way, but eventually I really was going to have to make a decision.

"Yes, I did."

"I see."

I waited. I was pretty sure that wasn't everything he had to say on the matter.

To his credit, Edward managed to keep quiet until we were in the study. Whether out of habit, or to stop me escaping without answering his questions, he locked the door behind us again. I settled into my usual chair and tried to look engrossed in the next box in the pile, but Edward was having none of it.

Perching on the edge of the desk closest to me, he said, "What's holding up your decision?"

I sighed, and put aside the box for the time being. "A number of things. First of all, I still don't know what it is everyone doesn't want broadcast to the public at large, so how can I say it's the right thing to publish them? I need to know exactly what we're talking about if I say yes to this." Most especially, I needed to know what secrets Isabelle had been talking about, the night of the Golden Wedding. Did it really all tie into the story Nathaniel had told me that morning? Did someone really die at a Rosewood party – and if so, how? I thought about the clipping again, and the way the guy in the middle had been looking at Therese. Who was he to her? And what did Nathaniel think about that? I couldn't help but think that if whatever happened was as innocent as I hoped, I'd have heard about it before now.

"Not to mention your own secrets." Edward gave me an assessing look. "Are you sure you're not holding back because you don't want to expose those to the whole world? I mean, that's understandable, I guess."

But I could tell from his expression that understandable wasn't the same as acceptable to him. Edward Hollis was all about the unvarnished truth. He'd never accept me keeping something back just because it made me uncomfortable. Even if it turned out that my family had something to do with a man's death.

"This isn't about me and Greg." Because that was what *he* was talking about, I knew. And it was almost the whole truth, too. "Not everything is, you know."

"Fine." He didn't believe me, I could tell, but he moved on anyway. "So what are your other reasons?"

I considered. What else was holding me back from committing to the job? Other than a possible investigation into a long-ago death, my own despicable behaviour, and the possibility of being banished from Rosewood for good? Wasn't that enough? "Well, there's the logistics of it all, I suppose."

"Logistics?" Edward hitched a leg up to rest on the pile of boxes and looked at me with interest.

"I do have a job, you know. And a life. Hundreds of miles away." Whether I liked it or not. "Either you and all this material would need to move to Perth, which doesn't seem very practical considering the input we need from the rest of the family, or I'd need to move down here permanently."

"That's what Nathaniel was going to ask you to do," Edward said. "At least, he planned to. I don't know what changed."

"Maybe he saw just how unwelcome I was here." Or maybe he changed his mind. Or perhaps… perhaps he had been asking me, in his way, that whole last weekend – and I just didn't notice until it was too late. "I'm not sure I *could* stay, without him here."

Edward gave me a sympathetic look. "Maybe we could come to some sort of arrangement, if you did decide to do it. Work by email in the week, when you had time around the paper, and try and get together every other weekend, or something. It would take longer…"

"But it would be better than nothing," I agreed. "Maybe. We'll see." For some reason the idea of only being a part of this on a part-time basis didn't appeal. If I took this on, it would have to be the whole thing.

I didn't let myself acknowledge that the idea of only seeing Edward every other weekend wasn't very appealing, either.

"What else?" Edward asked. When I hesitated, he went on, "Come on, Saskia. There's another reason, I can tell. So spit it out."

I looked away, taking in the mountain of information still left to wade through. "When I left, to go back to Perth… I had a plan. Ellie told me to stop running, remember? So I was going to try. I was going to find something new to work towards. A new life to live, for me. And instead…"

"You ended up back at Rosewood again," Edward finished. "And you don't think the memoirs could be part of that new life?"

I shook my head. "You wouldn't understand."

"Try me."

And the thing was, I wanted to. I wanted to explain it to him; I just wasn't sure I had the right words.

"Nathaniel said to me – before the Golden Wedding – he said he always hoped that I'd be a writer. Create my own stories. I never knew he wanted that for me. And I never told him how badly I wanted it for myself. We hadn't talked about it since I was a child."

"And the memoirs are his story, not yours."

I nodded. "I'll always be in his shadow, whatever I do as a writer. It's okay for you – you had your own career, your own name before you ever came here. But I'll always be Nathaniel Drury's granddaughter first."

"It's not a bad shadow to be in," Edward pointed out.

"I know." I looked down at my hands. "And I do want to do it. I just don't want it to be the only thing I ever do."

"It won't be." Edward sounded so certain, I looked up to seek the reason for his surety in his face. "I know you, Saskia. I know you're going to get there. Wherever you want to be."

The last person to tell me that was Nathaniel.

I hoped to God that they were both right. Because I knew for sure I couldn't stay where I was – outcast from my family, my home, working at a job that only filled my days, not my need for creativity, sleeping with a man I didn't love, didn't see a future with. I couldn't be this person any more.

Could working on the memoirs help me become the person I wanted to be? Maybe.

I had to admit, it was worth a try.

"We should get back to work," I said, and Edward smiled.

We'd fallen into a familiar rhythm with the job of sorting through the information for the memoirs; we'd each take a box, and try and assign each of the contents to a date, an event, at the very least a year. Documents relating to the same period of time were clipped together and annotated, as far as possible, to remind us later what we thought they were. Then we'd put the pile with the journal corresponding to the same period of time. My grandfather had been a sporadic journal-keeper. For some years we had detailed entries full of description and information. For others we had nothing but a few scrawled notes, or lists.

I was still searching for the journal that covered the year they moved to Rosewood. I wasn't entirely sure which sort I wanted it to be.

We were helped, to some degree, by the notes Nathaniel had left – pages of lined A4 paper covered in his sprawling script, detailing vague timelines that started abruptly and finished without warning and never linked to the next one. Each date or event had some scribbled notes beside them – words and sentences that would obviously have jogged Nathaniel's memory enough for him to be able to write it up fully, but all too often meant nothing at all to us.

"Well, I think I've reached 1987," Edward said, tossing a file onto the desk. "Although since I arrived here by way of 1954 and 2003, I have no idea which direction I'm going in."

I heaved the box in my lap onto the floor, and went to perch myself on the edge of the desk. "Ellie was born in 1988," I said. "So I'm pretty sure my parents were married in '86 or '87."

"Might make it easier to figure out the year," Edward agreed. "What date's their anniversary?"

I was already flipping through the file before I realised that I had no idea. "They never really celebrate it," I explained, pulling out a carefully clipped newspaper cutting. "But this should tell us."

Even thirty or so years later, the woman in the black-and-white photo was very clearly my mother. Same wide eyes, same pale blonde hair swept up on top of her head under a lacy veil, same broad smile as she clutched her bouquet of flowers to her flouncy white wedding dress. What was confusing, though, was that the man standing next to her was equally obviously not my father.

My heart started to beat faster. I'd been so busy concentrating on Isabelle's long-ago secrets, that I'd forgotten she wasn't the only one who'd objected to the memoirs.

"Hang on," Edward said, peering over my shoulder. "That's not…"

"'Miss Sally Drury, daughter of Nathaniel and Isabelle Drury, was married to Mr Robert Marks, son of Harold and Sheila Marks, at St Michael's Church, on Saturday, 26 April 1986.'" I read slowly, not really believing the words even as I said them. "That's… Ellie was born in January 1988."

"There's more here," Edward said, pulling a pile of envelopes from the file. "Letters from your mother, by the look of things." He handed them to me, and I took them with shaking hands.

How had I not considered that Mum had her own secrets, too? I'd assumed she was protecting Ellie, or even herself – not wanting her daughter's shortcomings out there in the world, in print. Not wanting to read the truth and have to believe in it. Not wanting that shame for Ellie, or her, or even me.

But how did a secret marriage, and lying to your children their whole lives, stack up against sleeping with your sister's fiancé? Was there even a scale for secrets like ours?

The letters had all been opened, read, put back in their envelopes then taken back out to read again many times, judging by the soft feel of the envelopes and the well-worn folds of the writing paper. The stamps on the envelopes were unfamiliar, from countries I'd never even heard of in some cases. How many times had my grandfather pulled these out and read them, missing his only daughter on the other side of the world? And what was in them to explain my mother's marriage to a man I'd never heard of? Perhaps, a small corner of my mind added, perhaps he'd read them so much because he wasn't sure if he wanted to include this story in the memoirs.

One thing was clear: I would have to talk to my mother about this. But first, I wanted all the information I could get.

I pulled my chair closer to the desk, still reluctant to sit in what would always be Nathaniel's chair, positioned in the bay window behind the leather-topped desk. In date order, I read my way through the letters, passing each page to Edward as I finished with it. After all, there was no way to keep the story from him, even if we did decide to keep it from the rest of the world.

They started off so happy. *Having a wonderful time in America! Robert has an interview for a lecturer's position here. We're still in New York – I've been exploring the city!* And then, a new name. *Robert's friend, Tony, has been such a great guide. He's British too, but studying here.*

"That has to be Dad, right?" I said, passing the letter to Edward.

He scanned the page. "Looks like. What happened next?"

"They had an affair?" I guessed. Maybe that was why Mum had never wanted to know what really happened between me and Greg. Too much of a reminder of her own past.

I miss you. Robert says that maybe we can come back next year. Or the year after.

And then, the last letter.

By the time you read this, I might already be home. I can't risk staying.

Risk. The word jumped off the page at me and I knew instantly that this was *nothing* like what happened between me and Greg. Whatever story I told myself about my own actions, I couldn't hold it up against my mother's.

By the end of the stack of letters, I was cold and my eyes were damp. There was just so much she didn't say, even right at the end when she wrote that she was pregnant and coming home with this man who wasn't her husband, this Tony Ryan. What had my grandparents thought then? Only a year or so after the wedding. But in everything she didn't say, I thought I could read a glimmer of the truth. She had married the wrong man – a destructive, terrible man – and she had got out.

But was that after Robert Marks got her pregnant? Was Ellie actually my sister, or only a half-sister? And did that make anything I had done to her any more excusable? The last, at least, I felt I could answer – no, not at all.

The lies, though. My whole life, my parents had lied to me – by omission if not in fact. My mother had a whole history I never even suspected. My father might not even be her husband at all. I felt like my whole foundation had shifted, and I wasn't quite sure how things would resettle. Or what my family would look like once they had.

"What do you want to do?" Edward's voice was quiet as he put down the last letter.

"I need to talk to Ellie, and then we need to talk to Mum." That much I knew, even if what would happen next was a mystery.

"Why Ellie first?" Edward asked, curiously, as I opened the file to return the letters. I frowned; there was something else in there. Another clipping. I pulled it out, my body shielding it from Edward's view. Was this another wedding photo? Or something else?

"Because she's my big sister. That's who you go to when family stuff turns crazy." I turned the clipping over and took in the headline. There was no photo this time, only the stark black text on yellowing paper: MURDER INVESTIGATION AT ROSEWOOD. Then, underneath, in smaller text: *Matthew Robertson, 25, was found dead after a party at the home of author Nathaniel Drury and his wife Isabelle.*

This was it. This was exactly what I'd wanted – and been afraid – to find. Suddenly, Nathaniel's last story – about the death at the first party at Rosewood – came flooding back. Was this what he'd been talking about? A *murder* investigation? And if so, who was the murderer?

Perhaps Mum's secrets were only the beginning, the prologue in a long list of truths I needed to uncover. And now I knew I absolutely had to find out what happened – before I told Edward. *If* I told Edward.

Edward moved closer, and I slipped the newspaper clipping into my pocket.

"Even now?" he asked, and I struggled for a moment to remember what I'd been saying. Ellie. Mum. The man who might be Ellie's father. That was what I needed to deal with first.

"Especially now. Give me the key?"

He reached into his pocket and handed me the heavy brass key. "Let me know how it goes?"

"Of course," I replied. "Wish me luck."

With a half-smile, he reached out and brushed the hair away from my face. "Good luck."

Of course, it wasn't as simple as just presenting the evidence to Ellie and asking her advice. I mean, it should have been. But the last proper conversation we had involved her telling me to run away to Perth – and me following her instructions. Could we just put that aside and deal with the crisis at hand? I wasn't sure.

"El?" I found her in the kitchen, chopping nuts. "Stress-baking?" Ellie might be most like my mother in many ways, but in others she definitely takes after Dad. Baking was one of those. Was cooking ability genetic or learned? Maybe, if we found out who Ellie's father really was, we'd have a better idea.

She didn't look at me as she replied. "Isabelle threw out what was left of the Golden Wedding cake. So I'm making coffee-and-walnut cake to keep us going." Which, I had to admit, did sound delicious.

I waited until Ellie had put the knife down and had turned her attention to blunter instruments – in this case a wooden spoon and a mixing bowl full of butter and sugar – before I spoke again.

"Look, I know we probably need to talk about a lot of stuff," I began.

Ellie sighed into her cake mix. "Saskia, really, do we have to? The funeral's over; you'll be heading back to Perth soon. Can't we just leave it?"

Always Ellie's preferred plan of action – ignore a problem until it went away. I might run, but she hid – and I wasn't sure that was any better.

Besides, this problem really wasn't going away.

"What if I decided to stay?" I asked. "At Rosewood, I mean. To finish the memoirs with Edward."

The wooden spoon stopped moving, but still Ellie didn't turn. "Are you going to?"

"It depends."

"On what?"

How to start… The best plan, I'd decided, was to start small. Build up to the shock and the horror. "Ellie, did Mum ever talk to you about anyone she dated before she met Dad?"

"Not that I can remember." Ellie turned at last and looked up at me. "Is this about Duncan? Or about…?"

"Neither," I said, hurriedly, before she could say the name that would take this from a conversation between sisters to a conversation between bitter enemies. "It's about Mum."

Ellie tipped the walnuts into the bowl and mixed them in. "Mum's fine." The tone under the words suggested, 'and I should know, because I've been here while you've been off gallivanting in Scotland.' Which wasn't really very fair, since I'd only left to save Ellie's sanity. And everyone else's.

"I know she is. It's not that. It's just…" I took a deep breath. "Edward and I have been going through Nathaniel's files, to help decide whether or not to go ahead with the memoirs." Ellie muttered something into her mixing bowl that sounded suspiciously like "bet that's not all you've been doing" but I charitably ignored it. "We found something this morning, about Mum. And I wanted to talk to you about it before

I spoke to her. Or, preferably, we both spoke to her. Together."

I had all her attention now, I could tell. Perfectly calm, Ellie tipped the cake mixture into the pre-lined tin and pushed it into the oven, before setting the timer. Then, she washed her hands, dried them on her apron, and took a seat beside me at the table. "Show me."

I waited silently as she read through the letters, watching as every emotion I'd felt passed over her face. In this, at least, we were still sisters, still as one.

"How could we not know this?" Ellie placed the last letter on the pile and looked up at me, her eyes wide with confusion. "I mean... this man could be my real father. I could be..."

"You're my sister," I said, fast, before she finished the thought. "That's all that matters. And this man, Mum's husband – God, that sounds strange – he's out of our lives. Hell, he was never even in them. He shouldn't matter any more. Not after what he did."

"No," Ellie said firmly. "He shouldn't."

Then she met my gaze, and I knew exactly what she was thinking. *Not all sins deserve forgiveness.*

I looked away.

"We need to talk to her," Ellie said, after a moment.

I nodded. "I know. That's why I brought these to you first. I think we need to, I don't know, present a united front? Show her that we just want to know the truth; we're not judging."

"I agree." She paused, then went on, "But, Saskia, you have to realise... she might not want this in the memoirs. She might not want to talk to *you* about it."

Not to me. Because I was something less than family now, wasn't I? I was the enemy – and for once, not because of my own actions, but because of Nathaniel's.

The idea cut through me, but I knew she was right. This had to be what Mum was afraid of, about the memoirs. I needed to show her she didn't need to worry.

"I'll explain. They're *Nathaniel's* memoirs, not hers. We can leave this out."

"How will Edward feel about that?" Ellie asked, in the sort of voice that told me she already knew the answer.

"It doesn't matter. They can't go ahead without my say-so." And given everything else I'd found out about the history of my family at Rosewood, I wasn't completely sure I'd be willing to give my approval anyway.

"Okay." Ellie gazed steadily at me, so long I started to feel awkward.

"What?"

"This… Mum, the memoirs, Nathaniel's death, all of it… It's bigger than what's between you and me," she said, eventually, and I couldn't help it. I started to hope.

"It is."

"I'm not saying I can forget what you did," she cautioned.

"Or forgive," I guessed. "I get that. But perhaps… perhaps we could come to an agreement?" It would be a start. And a million times better than the nothing I'd had so far.

Ellie gave a sharp nod. "An agreement. We avoid the subject of the past, and everything that happened. At least until everything else is decided."

"So we just… pretend it didn't happen?"

"No. I can't do that…" Ellie said. "But I can just about handle you being here, I think, as long as we don't talk about it. And I mean it, Kia. Not a mention, not a reminder, not a throwaway comment, nothing. We live as if it never happened. And only until we get things here sorted out."

It wasn't much – wasn't even a friendship. More like a shaky alliance. But I'd take it, because it was all I had of my sister.

"Fine by me," I said, and held out a hand to shake on it.

Ellie ignored the gesture, gathering up the letters instead. "Then we'd better talk to Mum."

I let my hand fall. "After dinner. When Dad's putting Caro to bed."

"Fine. I'll see you then."

And just like that, I was dismissed. I sighed, and left the room. Apparently things weren't all that different after all.

After dinner, once Dad had disappeared up to the attic with Caro and her stack of books on the paranormal, once Therese had gone back to the cottage, and once Isabelle had retired to her room again while Greg cleared up, I caught Ellie's eye and, together, we went to hunt down Mum.

We found her in the drawing room, collecting glasses for the dishwasher, and through some misdirection and hinting managed to get her upstairs to Ellie and Greg's room. Neutral ground, or the best we could do in a house crowded to the gills with family. Mum seemed so pleased to see Ellie and me in the same room being civil to each other, that she didn't really question our motives.

When Ellie and Greg moved in to Rosewood after their marriage, ostensibly because it was close to Greg's work and property prices were phenomenal in the area, and so that Ellie could help Isabelle and Nathaniel around the house in between supply teaching stints,

Isabelle insisted that they take on the front bedroom, the one with the huge bay window and at the opposite end of the house from the master suite, where our grandparents slept. As a result, their room had not only an en-suite bathroom, but also a sitting area in the bay window. Ellie had decorated it in creams and golds that gave an effect utterly unlike my own Yellow Room of Hell.

But it really wasn't the time for being jealous.

"So, girls, what's on your minds?" Mum asked, settling into one of the stiff-backed armchairs around the low, circular table. With a glance at Ellie, I took the seat on Mum's left, Ellie the one on her right.

"It's about Nathaniel's memoirs, Mum," I said, fingering the file of papers I'd carried up the stairs behind my back, hoping Mum wouldn't see them and ask what they were until it was time.

"You've decided what to do with them?" Now I was looking for it, I could hear the reluctance and concern in my mother's voice. She was just as worried as Isabelle; she was merely better at hiding it. How scared had she been, the last few days, waiting for me to find something that led me to this truth?

"Not yet." I put the file on the table. "I wanted to talk to you about some things I found when going through the files." No point mentioning to Mum that Edward knew too. This was bad enough as it was.

Mum opened the file, saw the wedding announcement, and slammed it shut again. "I see."

"We just want to understand what happened," Ellie said, sounding much calmer than I felt.

"You want to know if Tony is your father." Mum's voice was hard and blunt as she spoke to Ellie.

"That too," Ellie whispered, looking close to tears.

Some of the fight went out of Mum then. "He is. Both of you. Tony's your father, and Caroline's, just like we've always told you."

"Are you actually married?" I asked.

"No. We never... When I left Robert, I left him completely. Never spoke to him again, and he never tried to find me. So we never did get a divorce. So I couldn't marry Tony, even though I took his name." Which made sense. From what I'd read between the lines in Mum's letters, I wouldn't have ever wanted to see the man again, either.

"Did he...? I mean, Robert. He hit you, didn't he," Ellie said, reaching out to hold Mum's hand.

Mum tried to sound prosaic about it, but we could hear the tears in her voice. "Broke my arm, twice. And I don't want you to even have to imagine the rest. Tony was... He was Robert's best friend, but he couldn't bear what he did to me. So he became my friend instead, my confidant. And we fell in love." She shook her head, trying to brush away the tears. "When we found out I was pregnant... Robert would have known it wasn't his, couldn't be his. And we couldn't risk what he might do to me, to you." She clutched at Ellie's hand. "So we escaped. Came home."

"I can't imagine what you must have been through," I whispered. How had I thought for a moment that my own misdeeds could be measured against other people's? That a stupid, selfish, childish act could be anything like what my mother had lived?

"Your dad... he gave up everything, you know." Mum looked up, between the two of us. "You might not think it to look at him now, but... he was my hero. Robert... he came home, just as I was packing. Tony was there, standing guard for me, and when Robert tried to stop me... Tony knocked out his best friend with one punch, and then he took me away from everything. He left his job, his career prospects, his own dreams... He gave up everything to move back to Rosewood to be with me. With us." She took Ellie's hand. "Tony got a job at the university – a step away from the research he'd been doing in the States, but he made the most of it. And Mum and Dad looked after you, and later you, Saskia, while I went back to university. And eventually, we were able to pretend that none of it ever happened."

Except it had, and Nathaniel had planned to tell the world all about it.

"So you can see why I'm not very keen on Dad's memoirs being published," Mum went on. "It's a part of my life I just want to forget about. And..."

"And you're afraid that it would prompt Robert to come and find you," Ellie said. "Even though he never has before?"

Mum nodded. "It's ridiculous, I know. I'm exactly where I should be – he could have tracked me down at any time over the last thirty years. But if you write the truth... even though I swear it is the truth, he could sue for defamation. That's the sort of thing he would do. And the publicity... I'd just be so ashamed, to have my word questioned. To have people think that I lied, just to make my own adultery more palatable."

"It wasn't your fault," Ellie said, fiercely. "He didn't deserve your love, or your loyalty. He gave up any right to that the moment he hit you."

"I know, I know," Mum said. "At least, intellectually, I know that. But inside... I'm still a scared twenty-year-old, terrified my husband will find me out."

"We won't let that happen," I promised her, and even Ellie looked approving at the certainty in my voice.

"You're not alone, or far from home any more. We're all here. There is *nothing* he can do to you. Not with us protecting you."

Mum reached out to hold my hand as well as Ellie's, and gave us both a brave, but wobbly, smile. "I'm actually glad you know." She sounded surprised, and gave a little laugh. "I didn't think I would be, but I am. We'll have to tell Caroline, I suppose…"

"We've got time to work that out," I said, rubbing my fingers across the back of her hand. "Even if we go ahead with the memoirs, we don't need to include this. Not if there's a risk of Robert coming after you. I promise."

Mum hugged me, and then Ellie. "Thank you, girls."

I hugged her back, trying not to dwell on my promise. Edward wouldn't like it, I knew, but this was my family. This wasn't Nathaniel's life, it was Mum's, and she deserved some privacy if she wanted it.

And there wasn't a chance of me doing *anything* to bring Robert back into Mum's life again.

Chapter Eleven

*The cottage lay at the top of the cliff path,
looking out over the waves and the sand, and
the tiny village below. On a wild night, the
wind swept up from the sea, over the cliff, and
rattled the tiles of the cottage roof. But the
night that Rachel and Ursula met Sebastian
wasn't wild. It was warm, and clear: a classic
British summer's evening, with Pimm's in the
garden, the buzz of the insects in the long
grass, and the fading sting of too much sun on
one's skin. The night they met was perfect.*

*It was only after that everything started
to go wrong.*

On A Summer's Night, by Nathaniel Drury (2015)

It was late by the time we finished talking, but I had one more, urgent thing I needed to take care of.

Checking the hallway to make sure no one else was near, I let myself into Nathaniel's study. Placing the file with Mum's letters on the desk, I pulled the newspaper clipping about Matthew Robertson's death from my pocket. I needed to make sure Edward wouldn't find this until I was ready. Until I knew what had really happened.

I grabbed the photo of Isabelle, Matthew and Therese from the journal I'd hidden it in, and stuffed both clippings into an empty envelope. Then, with one last check over my shoulder at the locked door, I crawled under Nathaniel's desk and pulled up the loose floorboard I was pretty sure no one else knew about.

Nathaniel had used the hiding space for his secrets: for keepsakes he wanted to hide from the world, for notes on books so top secret he hadn't even mentioned them to his agent yet, for chocolates he wasn't supposed to eat, and an emergency bottle of whisky for when the writing got hard. He'd shown me the space under the floorboards when I was sixteen, swearing me to strictest secrecy.

If he'd had any other information about Matthew's death, information he'd wanted to keep from Edward, this was where he'd have put it. And it was where I planned to hide the little information I *had* found.

But when I looked, the hiding space was empty, except for a half-full bottle of whisky and an envelope with my name on it.

For a moment, I hoped it might be some final instructions from Nathaniel, sent from beyond the grave. But then I realised – the handwriting on the front wasn't his.

It was Ellie's.

I took the envelope and replaced it with my hurriedly sealed one. Then I stared at my name, written in Ellie's neat, precise hand. Whatever it said… I wasn't sure I was ready to read it. Not when we'd just managed to find our way to a sort of truce. I couldn't do anything that might unsettle that, not now.

I pushed it back into the hidey-hole and replaced the floorboard. Straightening up, I put my hands on my hips and stared around the study. If the information I needed wasn't there, then where was it? There was a journal or at least a diary with extensive notes for every single year since Nathaniel turned eighteen – except for 1968, the year he and Isabelle moved to Rosewood. It couldn't be a coincidence. Had he destroyed it? Or had Isabelle found it?

And, most importantly, what did it say?

I crossed the room to the large, heavy oak bookcase, situated between the door and the comfy chair where Nathaniel liked to do his reading. Running my fingers across the spines of his novels, I stopped at *Going Home,* and pulled it out. It was the book I'd been reading, the day Nathaniel called and invited me home for the Golden Wedding. I flicked through the pages, soaking in my grandfather's words once more, searching for... something.

Glancing at the clock, I knew it was past time for me to go to bed. But somehow, it seemed easier to curl up in Nathaniel's comfy chair and lose myself in Agnes and Grace's story again. If he hadn't left the answers I needed in his journals, I couldn't help but think Nathaniel might have left them in his fiction. He always claimed not to write about his life, but anyone who'd met him knew it wasn't true. Every single word he wrote said something about him, his life, his beliefs and thoughts. And even if they didn't solve the mystery of Matthew's death, perhaps they could tell me something else – what he believed about *me*. What I needed to do next, what he wanted for me in this world, what *my* truths were, from the man who knew me best.

At that realisation, I paused, my finger on the page. I was reading the wrong book. *Going Home* had been published in 1980, ten years before I was even born. If I wanted the truth, I needed to read his last book. Nathaniel once told me that the completion of one book was what led him to start the next – that as soon as the last words were down, he realised what he *should* have been writing about all along, and that was what spurred him to begin a new book, to try and say all the things he'd failed to in the last one.

I needed the book he'd written just before he decided to write his memoirs. Somewhere in those pages there had to be an explanation, a reason for his decision to publish the family secrets now. Something that would help me decide whether to go ahead with the project.

Rushing back to the bookcase, I replaced *Going Home* and pulled out the newest, shiniest hardback on the shelf: *On A Summer's Night*. The story of two sisters, stuck together in some crumbling seaside cottage, both in love with the same – married – man. The book had received middling reviews, I remembered vaguely. I'd only read it once, the day it came out, but it was too soon after leaving Rosewood, and too close to the bone, for me to take it in properly.

Now, I raced through the pages searching for something else – yet all I found was more of myself. The sisters weren't me and Ellie, not really. But there were flickers of familiarity spread through the book, enough to prick my conscience and distract me from my search.

"What are you reading?" Edward's voice from the door made me jump.

I held up the book. "Searching for the truth in fiction, for a change."

Edward perched on the arm of my chair. "You think the family secrets are in there?"

"Probably not," I admitted. "But I think I've had enough secrets for one day, anyway."

"How did it go with your mum?"

"Better than I'd expected." I leant my head against his side, and felt the warmth of him through his shirt. In moments like this, the quiet, private ones, I knew exactly what I wanted for my future. The rest of the time… I couldn't even admit that to myself. "She told us everything."

"And?"

"Ellie is Dad's daughter too," I said. Then I remembered my promise. "But… we can't include this story in the memoirs if we go ahead with them."

He froze beside me. "Why? Because she's ashamed? She shouldn't be."

I shook my head. "It's not that. I think she's honestly glad to have the truth out in the open." Would it be that easy with Isabelle? Whatever her secret was, once it was out, would it all be over? "But she's scared that her husband might come after her. Might sue, or try to discredit her – and the memoirs by association, I suppose."

"He clearly wasn't the most stable of men. I can understand why she'd be afraid. But Saskia… the truth is the truth. The past is a series of facts. We can't pick and choose which ones we include."

"I'm not going to do anything to put my mum at risk," I said firmly, and he sighed.

"No, of course not. And I'd never want you to."

"So we're at an impasse?" Would all my relationships be like this from now on? A series of negotiations, truces and deals, that never let me truly relax?

"So we'll wait and see what happens. Let me do some digging, before we make a final decision." I didn't know quite what that meant, but I was too tired to argue with him. Edward's fingers stroked through my hair, soothing and making me sleepy. I yawned, and he plucked the book from my fingers. "Save the rest of this for tomorrow. Come on."

Standing, he held out a hand to pull me to my feet. I took it, stumbling forward as I got up. Edward caught me, his arms around my waist in a moment, and suddenly I was pressed against him, so close I could feel his breath on my cheek.

"Kia…" he whispered, and I shook my head. I was done with words for today.

Stretching up on tiptoes, I pressed a kiss to his lips, long and soft. A promise, more than anything. And then I stepped back.

"Goodnight, Edward," I said. Then, taking the book from his hand once more, I walked out and down the corridor to the Yellow Room, my heart singing the whole way.

I didn't read any more that night, but I still managed to oversleep. In the end, I was woken up by my dad knocking on the door with a cup of tea for me.

"Your mum filled me in on last night," he said, putting the mug on my bedside table, and perching on the edge of my bed. "I'm not surprised you're all so tired."

I gave a small smile. "It wasn't quite how I was expecting my day to go when I woke up yesterday."

"Well then," Dad said, "who knows what might happen today." He paused. "Are we okay? You have to know… we never wanted to lie to you. It just never seemed like quite the right time to tell."

"I can understand that." So many secrets, so many lies, at Rosewood. Would there ever be a good time to spill them all?

I placed my hand over Dad's and squeezed. "We're fine," I assured him.

"I'm glad. Now, come down to breakfast when you're ready. I've made chocolate croissants." Then, with a kiss on the top of my head and a pat of my hand, he stood, and headed for the door.

"Dad?" I called after him, and he paused in the doorway. "Thank you. For everything. I hate to think... I'm just so glad Mum had you."

"So am I," he said, with a warm smile. "Besides, you'd all have starved if you'd been left to survive on your mother's cooking."

And then he was gone, before I could point out that without him, none of us would even exist. And Mum might have been trapped in a violent marriage for good.

I shuddered, and threw off the thought. I'd far rather think about last night's kiss, or even the memoirs. But actually, I lay back against the pillow and contemplated what I wanted to do with my day. After chocolate croissants, obviously.

Firstly, I decided I wanted a day off. A week of wading through Nathaniel's handwriting and inefficient filing was enough to make anyone need a break.

Secondly, I had something I wanted Edward to see. I'd shared it with Caro already, after all.

"Where are we going?" Edward asked after breakfast, as I strode ahead of him down the path. We'd left the others to their own occupations back at the main house, and ignored any suspicious glances from Isabelle as we left.

"If you want to understand my grandfather, and his writing, then you have to understand this place." I threw my arms out wide to encompass the house and the gardens and the woods.

"I have been living here for more than a year," he pointed out, catching up to me with long strides.

"Ah, but how far into the woods have you been?" He didn't answer that, so I carried on down the path, the morning air fresh and sweet as it filled my lungs.

"So what's so important about these trees?" Edward pushed a low-hanging branch out of my way, and I ducked into the real heart of the woods, where it got darker and damper and scarier, counting tree trunks as I went.

"How many of my grandfather's books have you read?" I asked, answering a question with a question.

"All of them," Edward responded promptly, as if insulted that there could be any doubt. "Repeatedly."

"Then you should already know." My hand brushed against the seventh tree, and I swung myself round to the right. Edward scrambled to follow my abrupt change of direction. "*This Day or the Next,* set mostly in…" One tree, two trees…

"A house in the woods," Edward answered, catching on finally.

"And best scene in *Underworld Dreams*?" Three trees…

"The night in the woods. Okay, I get it. They were all this wood." Give the man a medal.

Four trees. "Correct. And now we're here."

He looked around, confused, even as I reached behind the tree for the hidden ladder. "Where?"

"The place I wanted to show you." The ladder swung down, and I tugged to make sure it was still secure, before putting my foot on the first rung. "Nobody else knows this is here. Well, except for Caro. Not now Nathaniel's gone."

Edward followed me up the ladder into the cramped wooden box of a tree house, looking too tall and out of place as he stretched his legs out more than halfway across the floor and propped himself up against the wall.

I sat across from him, my arm resting across his ankles, and tried to remember why I'd asked him up there in the first place.

"You brought me to see your secret tree house," Edward said, folding his arms behind his head.

"Sort of." I tried to gather my thoughts, but it was hard when he was looking at me that way, with warm amusement and affection in his eyes and the lines of his body. "This tree house... Nathaniel built it for me, when I was small. Well, actually he conned his assistant at the time into building it for him."

"And I thought that shopping for an anniversary present for Isabelle was bad," Edward murmured.

I ignored him. "He wanted me to have a place that was my own, you know? Because we were down here for whole summers and the house was always full of people, and I wanted to have adventures and secrets because I was that sort of child..."

"Like Caro."

"Like Caro," I agreed. "And nobody knew about it except for me and Nathaniel, once the assistant left."

"And now me." Edward lowered his arms and wrapped one hand around my ankle. "And you brought me here because you wanted me to know more about Nathaniel?" Even as he said it, I could tell he didn't believe that was all there was to it.

"And me, I suppose. A bit."

He nodded. "I seem to be learning more and more about you."

"And I seem to know less and less about you." I shifted closer. "I don't suppose you want to redress the balance?" And that, I realised, was the real reason I'd brought him out here. Because he was uncovering my secrets and my family's secrets one by one, and I needed to have something in return. And the tree house was the best place I knew for secrets.

Edward smiled, a slow, lazy smile. "What do you want to know?"

My answer wasn't quite what I'd have expected it to be, if I'd spent any time at all thinking about it before my mouth blurted it out. "What's the deal with you and Ellie?"

From the look on Edward's face, it wasn't the question he'd expected either.

He sighed, and for a moment I thought he wasn't going to answer, or was going to fob me off with some half-truth, but instead, he started to talk. "When I first arrived here, I was... Well, to be honest, I was running away from my real life. Things had got away from me, fallen apart, and I just wanted to be as far away from it all as possible."

I suspected that this tied in to Ellie's comments about being careful with him. I also suspected that if I interrupted to ask, I'd never get the full answer to my question, so I let him carry on.

"Ellie... When I arrived, Ellie was still very angry. It had been hard for her, I think, not just dealing with what happened between you and Greg..." I winced. Nice to see he wasn't going to soften any of this for me. "But also because she's really very isolated out here. She wasn't working much at the time, and the only people she really saw were her grandparents, who she couldn't tell what was the matter, and her husband, who had cheated on her before they were even legally married."

The hand around my ankle tightened, just briefly, as though to reassure me that he was merely stating facts, not judgements. I wasn't really all that reassured, although it wasn't as if anything he was saying wasn't true.

"So, I think it was nice for her to have me around," Edward went on, loosening his grip on my leg. "Someone vaguely her own age who she could talk to. And with me having my own relationship issues... we bonded. Became friends."

I couldn't really bring myself to ask, "Just friends?"

Luckily for me, Edward answered it anyway, eventually. "It took a while for me to realise that our situations were actually very different. I'd been betrayed and humiliated by a woman I thought I loved. My ex... We were supposed to get married. Until I found out that I wasn't the only person she'd promised that to. She and my best friend were making plans to elope, before our booked wedding day. I guess she thought that once the deed was done, I couldn't try and talk her out of it. I don't know."

"That's awful." I knew I wasn't really the right person to censure another for their actions in relationships, but still. That was pretty cold, and my heart ached for Edward.

He just shrugged. "It was. And that's why I had to get away. When Nathaniel called and invited me here, it was a lifeline. A chance to live a new life, to step outside my reality for a while. And once I got here I realised pretty quickly that, while it still hurt, and it stung and I woke up thinking about it every morning, I was more angry with myself for being a fool than I was with her. And I didn't really have any interest in seeing her again or making things better; I just wanted to forget and move on." He shifted, pulling one long leg up against his chest. "Ellie, on the other hand, just wanted to be able to forgive and forget, and couldn't figure out why she wasn't able to yet."

"She still loved Greg," I said, with a certain amount of relief.

"And she still loved you," Edward said, his voice quiet and soft.

That, inevitably, was when the sob that had been fighting its way up my throat found its way out. Suddenly I was aware of the tears on my cheeks, and the fact that my nose was starting to run – not least because it was cool and damp in that tree house.

Edward shuffled himself round to sit beside me, and I found myself pulled into his arms, my face against his warm, broad chest. I have to admit, it did make everything seem just a little bit better.

"She doesn't want to be angry with you any more, Saskia. She's just not sure how to stop."

I sniffled, probably very unattractively. "She and Greg seem happier, at least."

Edward nodded; I could feel his head bob above mine. "I think it has helped, seeing you this summer. Seeing how little interest you have in him. Telling everyone that you have a new boyfriend – even if that wasn't exactly accurate."

"I tried to make it obvious," I admitted. "I wanted her to know that it was all over long ago. I hadn't even spoken to Greg since I left."

"So," Edward said, with the tone of someone changing the subject. His mouth was very close to my ear, and his breath was warm against my hair. "Do you feel you know something more about me, now? Like why you are the last person in the world I should be falling for, and why kissing you that night in the attic was the biggest risk I've taken in years?"

"I think so." I straightened up as much as I could, without dislodging his arms from around me, letting his words sink in. To his mind, I was exactly like his ex – worse, I'd already committed a terrible betrayal, so he already knew I was capable of it. No wonder he'd been keeping his distance. Until now...

"Good. Then I'd like to ask you one more question." I nodded to give him permission and, looking straight into my eyes, he asked, "What is the situation with you and Duncan right now?"

"Why do you want to know?"

Edward gave me his lopsided smile, one that warmed my middle even in the shady cool of the tree house. "I want to know if you're officially single yet before I kiss you again."

Well, in that case. "It's over. I ended it when I called the other night."

Every complaint my body had about the chill or the uncomfortableness in the tree house disappeared when Edward's lips met mine.

Eventually, however, even I had to admit that an outdoor structure with gaps for doors and windows and a large potential for splinters wasn't the best place for a romantic interlude. I'd stopped things in the attic because the time and place were wrong. The timing might have improved, but the tree house wasn't much better as a location.

"We should go back to the house," I murmured against Edward's neck, as his fingers trailed up my spine then snaked their way underneath my bra and moved around to my front.

"Absolutely," Edward said, making no effort at all to pull away.

"Really," I said, after another long kiss. Pulling back I bashed into a wooden box, which must have been tucked away behind one of the stools that we'd displaced with our antics. I frowned as the lid fell open to reveal a small black notebook, some polished gemstones, a few pens, flower petals and another of Nathaniel's old pipes.

"What's that?" Edward asked, his lips already at my neck.

"Caro's treasures, I guess." I turned back into his arms and kissed him again. "Inside. Really. We are not doing this in a tree house – especially not when Caro could arrive at any moment to retrieve her stuff."

"Good point."

We made it to the bottom of the ladder, eventually. Not a lot further, since Edward instantly spun me round to pin me against the tree trunk and kiss me again but really, as long as he kept kissing me, it could take us until January to reach the house for all I cared.

"We need to…" Edward pulled back and took a breath. "Unless you want your family following us up to your bedroom, we need to… pause."

With some considerable effort, I took a step backwards. "Your bedroom. Mine's too yellow."

"I really don't care."

We were lucky, in the end – everyone had made themselves conspicuously absent, although I suspected it wasn't actually for our benefit. Still, we sneaked up the stairs, trying not to giggle in my case, and dashed down the landing, avoiding the squeaky floorboards, and into Edward's room, letting the door crash behind us.

"Thank God for that," Edward murmured against my mouth, as he reinstated his campaign to remove as much of my clothing as possible in the minimum possible time.

And this time, I had no intention of stopping him.

It was strange, that night, sitting across the table from Edward, too far away to touch, too self-conscious about what the family would say to even make eye contact with him. Edward, at least, seemed to understand this. He rolled his eyes at me over the starters, then spent the rest of the meal entertaining Caroline with tales from his own childhood, growing up in some tiny seaside town that I began to suspect he might actually have invented.

"Then there was the year that the jellyfish invaded..." I turned my attention aside and tried to make pleasant conversation with Isabelle, instead.

Even that was hard.

"I suppose you've found all manner of fascinating things in my husband's study," Isabelle said, tapping her perfectly polished nails against her wine glass. "I appreciate, of course, that these items are in your power now. But, nonetheless, I'm sure many of them are my memories too. Perhaps, when you've finished pulling them apart..." She trailed off, looking wistful.

"Isabelle, of course you can look through them," I said, tiredly. "We're just putting them into order, at the moment, trying to make some sense of what happened when. As soon as we've got them sorted."

Isabelle leant forward across the table. "Are you working forwards or backwards?" she asked, her voice suddenly forceful. "I mean, chronologically. Are you starting from now and working back, or from the beginning?"

"Uh, a bit of both," I said, wondering why it mattered, "Nathaniel's files weren't really all that well organised."

"Perhaps I can help," Isabelle offered, brightly. Too brightly. Once again, I found myself wondering what it was Isabelle thought was in those files, and when we were going to find it. Was it Matthew Robertson's death? Did she already know the truth I was seeking? It would explain a lot. Or worse, was there another, bigger secret that I hadn't even sensed yet?

"I'm not sure… I mean, eventually we'll definitely need your help, identifying people in photos, things like that." I was waffling, and Isabelle was starting to turn pink around the cheeks. "The ones that aren't newspaper clippings, anyway."

"Newspapers?" Isabelle's nervous tone kicked it up a gear. Suddenly, I was certain that this had to do with the death at the party. What else would be newspaper worthy? "Did he keep many clippings?"

"Some," I said, carefully. "Isabelle, if there's something specific you want me to look out for… something that happened here at Rosewood, for instance…"

He gaze snapped to connect with mine. "What have you found?" she asked, her words a whisper.

"Nothing, yet." Not really, anyway. Nothing I could prove. But if the police had been investigating, there must have been something suspicious about the death. Something Nathaniel had known. And the only way he could have known for sure was if he'd been involved in it.

That was the part I was desperately hoping I could disprove, before Edward found out about it.

Isabelle gave a small, sharp nod. "Because there's nothing to be found. You just let me know when you're done rifling through my past." She pushed her plate away and turned to talk to Ellie, on her other side, but I caught her wrist with my fingers and stopped her.

"Isabelle… the night of the Golden Wedding. I was there. Outside Nathaniel's study. I heard your argument."

My grandmother's face turned stone stiff and emotionless. "I don't know what you're talking about."

"You asked him not to tell your secrets. What secrets, Isabelle?"

She wrenched her wrist away. "That's none of your business. And anything learned from eavesdropping should be forgotten, and fast. No good ever comes of it." This time, when she turned away, I let her go.

I looked up to find Edward watching me, all tales of jellyfish forgotten. But this wasn't the attention of early in the afternoon, when he couldn't keep his eyes – or his hands – off my skin, my curves, my everything. Now his gaze was cool, assessing, as if he were studying me for secrets, for truths, instead of Nathaniel's journals.

I shivered. I hated to think what he'd find.

I didn't linger downstairs for long after dinner. Edward caught my eye as everyone moved from the dining room through to the drawing room and I thought, for a moment, that he was going to suggest that we retire back to his room – until Ellie slipped a hand through his arm saying, "I haven't seen you all day. How is the work on the memoirs going?"

I silently thanked my sister for her unintentional help, then slipped away quietly up the stairs while he was distracted answering her. If I was lucky, he'd be kept occupied for long enough for me to complete my task.

With one last wistful glance at Edward's door as I passed, I hurried on into Nathaniel's study, curled up in my usual chair, and pulled up the next box file in the stack.

At the beginning, I'd sort of assumed that Isabelle was against the memoirs on principle, rather than because of any specific event or occurrence that she didn't want publicised. After all, she'd been married to the same man for fifty years, with no whisper of gossip as far as I was aware. But it was there, somewhere – I knew that for certain now. And it couldn't be Mum's marriage that had her worried, or she wouldn't still be asking what we were looking for. Ellie had already told her we knew everything.

Which meant that there was something else, somewhere in these boxes. It had to be Matthew's death, right? And I was going to have to find out the truth about it before I could make my final decision.

By nine-thirty, I'd given every single one of the boxes at least a cursory going-through, and I couldn't find anything more than a few photos of Nathaniel with his arm around various attractive women who weren't his wife. Which, given my grandfather's reputation for being an enormous flirt, wasn't entirely surprising. There was nothing else – no love letters, no hotel bills, no suspicious presents. Nothing to suggest he'd ever actually been unfaithful. Which, actually, surprised me a little.

"Have you found it yet?" I looked up to see Edward standing in the open doorway, leaning against the frame, his arms folded.

"I just thought I'd get a head start…"

"You thought you'd search for whatever it is that Isabelle doesn't want us to find on your own." The edge in his voice told me he had his suspicions about what I'd do with that information afterwards too.

"There is nothing in any of these boxes that Isabelle could legitimately object to us publishing," I said instead, shoving the last box file off my lap and onto the nearest stack. "We've been through every single one of them." I couldn't even *find* the journal for the year they moved to Rosewood.

Edward shut the door behind him, and came to perch on the edge of Nathaniel's desk. "What do you mean? Nothing?"

"Just what I say," I said, impatiently. "She was quizzing me at dinner. Trying to find out what we'd discovered. But there's nothing here that would justify that sort of concern."

"Then what is it that's missing?" Edward asked, thoughtfully. "I see what you mean."

We contemplated the untidy stack of boxes in silence. In my hurry to find what I was looking for, I hadn't been quite so careful about ordering and dating things as we'd been so far. In fact, I'd go as far as to say I'd just tossed everything on the floor.

"If we ask her directly, you know she won't tell us." After all, she wouldn't have been so desperate to get into the study and hide or burn the evidence if she was going to just give it up to the first person who asked.

"We need someone else," Edward suggested. "Someone else who knows what she's afraid of."

And all of a sudden, Therese's irrational fear that Isabelle would throw her out, that her sister-in-law had never liked her anyway, came back to me.

"I might have an idea," I said. "But I need to do it alone. And not tonight. In the morning." Therese had always been more of a lark than a night owl. If I quizzed her now she might throw me out just for holding up her bedtime.

Edward raised an eyebrow. "And you'll tell me whatever you find out?"

I bit my lip. Would I? Or would it depend on what I found out?

"Saskia…"

"This is my family, Edward," I snapped. "Am I going to tell Edward Hollis, biographer, seeker of truths and uncoverer of scandals, every secret I find out about my family, no matter how damaging? I don't know."

His face froze, slipping into a stiff mask that gave away none of his feelings. "I thought you might tell me. Your friend. Your… whatever we are."

I glanced away. I'd hurt him, and I hadn't even meant to. It seemed I couldn't stop doing that.

"Let me see what I can find out first?" I asked, aiming for a conciliatory tone. "Then we can talk. See if it changes my feelings about going ahead with the project."

"You mean, if you don't like the truth, you won't go ahead with the memoirs?"

"I'll tell you first," I promised, even though I wasn't completely sure if it was the truth or not. "We can talk about it."

"And if whatever secret Isabelle is afraid of getting out is big enough, dangerous enough, what then?" I hesitated, unsure of my answer, until he continued impatiently. "Come on, Saskia. This is my life, my work too. I deserve to know what's happening with it."

"And as soon as I do, you will," I told him. "But right now… I don't even know what she's hiding."

"The truth," Edward said bluntly. "And whatever that is… that's what Nathaniel wanted in his memoirs."

"Even if it hurts everyone?" I shook my head. "He wouldn't do that. But… maybe we can come up with something. A way to publish the memoirs without hurting anyone…"

"You mean, lie." Edward stared down at me, his eyes dark and shadowed. "Spin a nice story that keeps everyone happy. That's not what I'm here to do, Saskia. I'm not going to rewrite history for you."

Of course he wouldn't. It was all black or white, truth or fiction with Edward. "I'm not asking you to." But only because I knew he'd say no.

Edward sighed, and reached out a hand to me. "Come on. If it has to wait until morning, we might as well go to bed. We can't decide anything until we know the truth." One more night, and then I was going to have to face whatever it was that had happened here, forty-eight years ago. The night Matthew Robertson died.

I hesitated for a moment. "Go to bed as in... together, or alone?" There had been too many changes and tides in our relationship for me to be entirely sure.

The corners of Edward's mouth twitched up into a small smile. "Together. If you want."

"I want," I assured him, nodding furiously. "I just wasn't sure..."

"If I was mad at you? Maybe. But for some reason, I'd still rather have you with me than be apart." His grin widened as he tugged me closer. "You've got under my skin, Saskia Ryan."

I kissed him, hoping it covered the surge of relief I felt at his words.

I was already an outcast at Rosewood. I couldn't bear to be an outcast to Edward, too.

Chapter Twelve

And at that moment, the world split in two.
What happened next could have been either
of the following – or neither.

From the journal of Nathaniel Drury, 1968

I'm not sure what woke me. It could have been the breeze from Edward's open window, or the buzz of the insects in the night. It might have been Edward himself, shifting in the bed beside me, an unfamiliar presence. It could just have been sleeping in a new room, one I'd never slept in during all my long summers in Rosewood.

Or maybe it was the sudden realisation of what I'd really seen in the tree house that afternoon.

Either way, at four a.m. the next morning, I was wide awake. And I knew, with an unshakeable certainty, exactly where I had to go and what I'd find when I got there.

It was still dark, as I crept out from under the sheets, careful not to disturb Edward. I dressed quickly, silently, in yesterday's clothes, then opened the bedroom door a millimetre at a time to stop it creaking. It shut behind me with a tiny click, and I waited a moment to listen for any movement inside. Nothing.

Letting out a long breath, I padded barefoot across the landing, down the stairs. Someone had left a light on in the kitchen, and the pale yellow glow echoed the moonlight still illuminating the world through the windows. Rosewood was eerie in the not quite darkness, but I knew my way so well I'd have made it without any light at all.

I paused in the kitchen to grab a torch from the drawer, shoved on some shoes and a jacket from by the back door, and headed out for the woods.

Climbing the ladder to the tree house with a torch in hand wasn't the easiest, but I was motivated, and made it up without too much trouble. Inside, the scent of the wood mingled with the last, lingering traces of Nathaniel's years of smoking up there. I shone the torchlight into the corner where I'd seen the box, relieved to see it exactly as we'd left it the previous afternoon. Caro obviously hadn't had a chance to visit yesterday.

Kneeling, the wooden floor cold and hard through my jeans, I pulled the box into my lap. I'd been distracted yesterday, assuming it was Caroline's, that she'd squirrelled away Nathaniel's pipe along with some of her other treasures. But looking now, it was clear that this treasure trove belonged to Nathaniel himself – the pipe, the tiger's eye that he'd carried as a good luck charm for years, a postcard of Dylan Thomas with a quote from *Under Milk Wood*, a scattering of yellow rose petals… and the notebook.

I lifted the palm-sized black notebook from the box, my heart racing as I opened the cover, hoping I knew what I was going to find. And I was right. There, on the front page, inked in perfect black penmanship, were the numbers I'd been searching for. *1968*.

It was smaller than the other diaries and journals he'd left behind, or I'd have recognised it sooner. Of course, so would Edward, so perhaps it was best it wasn't.

Here, in my hands, was the truth. The answer to all the questions I'd been asking. The secret Isabelle had been fighting so hard to protect.

I was almost too afraid to read it.

But I had to, and quick – before Edward woke and found me gone and started asking questions – or jumping to the right conclusions. So I settled down in the corner of the tree house, turned my torch onto the pages, and started to read.

I skimmed through the earlier months; I knew from the newspaper clipping that the party had happened in August, the same as the Golden Wedding. Still, I kept an eye out for Matthew's name, pausing when it appeared in conjunction with a party in London in the spring – and a visit from Therese.

Therese seemed overly taken with a young nothing from one of the papers. Matthew something. Probably just looking for a new angle on the usual story: me.

It was comforting to see that Nathaniel's narcissistic streak wasn't something that had come later in life, anyway. I skipped forward a few pages, passing over ruminations on the book he'd been writing that, at any other time, would have fascinated me. I'd read them later. Right now, I needed facts.

Another visit from that Robertson fellow. Have made it clear to Therese that I Do Not Approve.

Soon, it was the summer, and the pages were filled with the move to Rosewood, the fresh start, away from London. And then, Isabelle's plans for the party:

As if we haven't had enough of the damn things in London. But if Isabelle wants a party... I imagine we shall be partying.

My hands shook as I turned the page, but even as my eyes scanned over the words, I knew something was wrong. This wasn't the Nathaniel I'd grown used to reading through his diaries. It was as if it were written by another person. I blinked, and started again.

The day of the party arrived, and Isabelle spent all day preparing for it, while I was writing.

Why were those words familiar? Too familiar?

Suddenly, it came to me. Because this was the story Nathaniel had told me, the last time we had sat in this tree house together. This wasn't a journal entry; it was a story. The words sounded wrong because this wasn't Nathaniel, my grandfather, talking. This was Nathaniel Drury, celebrated author. This was fiction, not truth.

Or was it?

He must have been hiding the box up here when I found him, the day of the Golden Wedding. Perhaps he'd even been rereading the entry from the party, before the big announcement. That was why he'd chosen that story to tell me, and why the words were so familiar. I'd heard this story before.

But in the version Nathaniel had told me, Matthew was alone when he died. I had a feeling that might be different in these pages.

I read on, swallowing down my apprehension as he talked about the party, the guests, the booze, the outfits. Until finally, we approached the end, and the tone changed again.

And at that moment, the world split in two. What happened next could have been either of the following – or neither.

I blinked. What on earth did that mean?

It became clear soon enough – and I almost wished it hadn't.

Perhaps I walked in on them: Therese's beau and my wife, kissing. Perhaps the champagne and the fury got the better of me. Perhaps I pushed him, and laughed as

I watched the blood spill from his skull, and the life leave him.

I shuddered at the image. The laughing, I was sure, was Nathaniel overdramatising, making a better story. But what about the first part? Had Isabelle been having an affair with Matthew? Had Nathaniel really discovered them, and pushed him?

I couldn't be sure. Because directly below it was written:

Or...

Perhaps she did it. Perhaps he threatened to tell her husband, her sister-in-law, everyone. Perhaps the fear of scandal, of losing the life she'd grown accustomed to... Perhaps that was motive enough. Perhaps fear made her push him, made her gasp with horror the moment she realised what she'd done.

Either way, Matthew Robertson was still dead.

I sat back, staring blankly ahead at the wall of the tree house as I processed these new stories. Outside, the sun crept up over the woods, sending a shaft of light through the window. Edward would be awake soon. I didn't have long to try and make sense of it all.

I had three versions of the story now: the one Nathaniel had told me himself, and the two in the journal. One with him as the murderer, one with Isabelle. Were any of them true? Was Nathaniel just telling a good story?

There was something about that last version, though. A memory. I'd heard it somewhere before. No, not heard. *Read.*

And suddenly I knew exactly where.

Switching off my torch, and tucking the journal into my pocket, I swung down onto the ladder and raced back to the house. I knew what I was looking for now. And I knew exactly what questions I needed to ask.

*

"Did you really sneak out of my bed this morning to read your grandfather's book?" Edward leant against the door frame of the Yellow Room, and I looked up from the last page of *On A Summer's Night*, tears in my eyes.

"I needed to finish it." And now that I had, I was more sure than ever which version of the story was the truth.

I'd been wrong. The sisters in *On A Summer's Night* weren't ever Ellie and me. They were Therese and Isabelle. And that story – of two women fighting over the same man, until one of them pushed him to his death down a cliff face – *that* was what had made Nathaniel so determined to write his memoirs. Even if I still couldn't be sure if he'd ever intended to include the truth about Matthew Robertson's death in them. He'd never written it down before – except possibly as fiction.

"And now you have?" Edward raised an eyebrow, watching me with a cool gaze, and I knew he suspected already. "Have you suddenly learned the truth about whatever secrets your family are hiding?"

"It's just a story," I said, my mouth dry. If I was right – if Isabelle really had killed Matthew – I couldn't let on. Nathaniel had never said for sure. There wasn't a truth to include in the memoirs – yet. But once I knew… if Edward found out, he'd want to include it. "Just fiction."

"Nathaniel always said there was truth in fiction. If you knew where to look." Edward pulled something from his pocket, and my heart stopped for a moment. "I finally realised that there was one more place the missing information might be hiding," he said, pulling the newspaper clippings I'd hidden so carefully under the floorboard from the envelope in his hand. "I remembered seeing Nathaniel emerge from under his desk with a bottle of whisky one night, when we'd been working late.

No sign of the journal, but I did find these. And this."
He held up the clippings, then tossed the second envelope,
the one with my name on it, onto the dressing table.

"What do they say?" I asked, hoping my nerves weren't
making my voice tremble too badly.

He met my gaze. "I think you know. Don't you?"

I looked away. "Edward. I—"

"You found these clippings and realised that this
could be a huge scandal. So you hid it from me. Right?"

"That's not... Nathaniel told me a story. About a
death here at Rosewood. But it was just a story. And I
wanted to know for sure if it was true before I talked to
you about it. That's all."

"Saskia." Disappointment laced his words. "For once
just be honest, with yourself, if no one else. No more
stories. Just tell me the truth."

"Fine! I knew that there had been a suspicious death
here and I was afraid. Afraid that Nathaniel might know
more about it than he should."

"You were afraid Nathaniel killed the man. Why? Did
Isabelle have an affair with him?"

"I... think so. But I don't know for sure. And... I don't
think Nathaniel did it. Really, I don't." I looked up at
him so he could see I was telling the truth. "I found the
journal. Just this morning. See for yourself." I handed
it to him, open at the page with the two endings, and
watched as his eyes scanned the text.

His mouth tightened as he closed the journal. "You think
it's just another story?"

"I don't know what it is." I took a breath. "But does
it matter? Nathaniel never left any notes about the
death, and he hid this journal somewhere you'd never
find it – in the tree house. So why should we include it
at all?"

"Because the death of Matthew Robertson is public record." He held up the newspaper clipping as evidence. "If we leave it out, we're hiding something. We're not telling the full story. We're lying."

"But we're not! Nobody knows for sure what happened that night! We could just write that. Tell the story Nathaniel told me, where Matthew fell and died alone. Show the police report."

"You're doing it again." Edward crossed the room, staring out of the window at the Rose Garden as he spoke. His words were measured, reasonable – but there was a tightness behind them that told me I'd stepped over some invisible line in his mind. "Rewriting events to suit your story. Ignoring the facts to tell the tale that makes you – or your family – look good."

"That's not fair. Why does everything have to be black or white with you? Truth or lie, and nothing in between?"

"Because it is!" Edward spun round from the window. "Whatever happened that night, it's a fact. A truth. You can't change that just because it doesn't suit the story you want to tell. That's not how biography works. And that's exactly why you should have told me. This isn't just your project – it's ours. I've given up more than a year of my life for it. I deserved your honesty, not another story."

"I would have told you!" I yelled back. Why was he being so unreasonable about this? "You just didn't give me a chance."

He shook his head. "It's not just the memoirs, Saskia. I don't want to live in a novelisation of my own life, written by you, to suit you. I've done that once already – lived with a woman who was the star of her own story, twisting facts and events to make herself the heroine, choosing true love over everything. I won't do that again. My life is my autobiography, the way I'd write it – honest, unflinching, even when it hurts."

"So what are you saying?" My skin felt too tight for my body, hot and uncomfortable. "That there's no place for me in it?"

He met my gaze. "I'm saying that if you want to be a part of my life, you have to stop playing make-believe, Saskia. Especially with people's hearts." He reached into his pocket and pulled out another envelope, handing it to me. "The truth matters, Saskia. But it has to be the whole truth."

I opened the envelope and pulled out another newspaper clipping, this one much newer: LOCAL SCHOOL TEACHER DEAD IN M6 CRASH. *Local teacher, Robert Marks...* I stopped reading and looked up at Edward. "He's dead? Mum's husband?"

"Three years ago," Edward confirmed. "I thought she'd want to know the truth about what happened to him. Thought it might help her stop being afraid."

"It will." I held it close to my heart. He'd gone to find this – not just for the memoirs, I was sure. For my family. For me. "Thank you."

He gave a brief nod of acknowledgement. "Someone knows the truth about what happened that night here at Rosewood, too," Edward said, softly. "And I think finding it, asking those difficult questions, is exactly why Nathaniel wanted you to work on his memoirs, once he was gone. And I think you know that too. Talk to Isabelle, Kia. It's time for the truth. Not another story."

Then he walked out of the room, closing the door quietly behind him, and leaving me alone.

It was almost ten o'clock by the time I'd crawled out of the mental fog Edward's departure had left me in. I knew he was right; I needed to talk to Isabelle. But first,

I needed some more information. Ammunition, perhaps. Truths I could use to discover more truths. Because, just as one lie tended to lead to another, it seemed that truths did the same. I picked up the envelope with the newspaper clippings from where Edward had left it on the dressing table, and paused for a moment to look at the envelope from Ellie again, but in the end I left it where it was. One crisis at a time.

"Have you seen Edward?" Ellie called to me from the kitchen, as I passed. "Only, his car's gone. Did he tell you where he was going?"

"No." The word came out as a croak, and I swallowed to try and find my voice again. "I don't know where he's gone." Except for far away from me. And really, that couldn't be much of a surprise.

I'd worry about Edward, and the future, later. First I had to deal with the past.

I stepped into the kitchen. "He gave me this before he left." I handed her the newspaper clipping about Robert Marks's death, and her face lightened as she read it.

"Oh, thank God." She paused. "I shouldn't say that about someone being dead, should I?"

"I think, under the circumstances, people would understand," I assured her. "Will you tell Mum?"

"Don't you want to?" Ellie asked, curiously.

I shook my head. "I've got something else I need to do first."

Therese had taken to breakfasting alone in her cottage, since the funeral, and I found her taking tea and toast when I arrived.

"How are the memoirs coming?" Therese asked, as she grabbed an extra teacup and saucer for me.

It was the perfect opening, even if I felt a little guilty about shanghaiing her at breakfast. I couldn't let it pass. "There was some amazing stuff in the box files Nathaniel left, as well as his journals."

"Really?" Therese raised her eyebrows. "I never took my brother for the sentimental keepsake type, I must admit."

I shrugged. "Maybe not, but he'd obviously put some time and effort into gathering things together for the memoirs. Photos, letters, newspaper clippings – the works." I looked her in the eye, and prayed she'd finally get the hint. "All the way back to when he first met Isabelle. And when they moved in to Rosewood."

Therese's body went still, her cup raised slightly off its saucer, and I knew I'd got my point across.

"Everything?" she asked, eventually. "You think he really has notes and photos of everything that happened?"

"Everything important. The problem, of course, is that it's all just from his point of view." And some of them were entirely fictional.

"Well, they were his memoirs." Therese had regained some of her composure by then, and placed her teacup and saucer on the table, turning her attention to the toast and jam.

"Of course. But, in the same way that you, quite naturally, want to read the parts he'd written about your childhoods, I'm sure others will want to read the sections about them. See if the stories fit with their memories." I, too, was studying the toast plate, mostly so that Therese couldn't look in my eyes and realise I had no idea what I was fishing for.

"You mean Isabelle," Therese said, bluntly.

"I mean that I want to make sure that what we have is accurate, and to do that we need to ask other people who were there at the time." I figured that was about as vague as it could be without eschewing words altogether.

But Therese wasn't holding with vague. "You want me to confirm what's in Nathaniel's notes, so that Isabelle can't claim it isn't true."

Which was absolutely the case, except for the fact that Nathaniel hadn't given me the truth to work with in the first place. "I just don't want to upset Isabelle any more than we have to."

Therese sighed. "Kia, are you absolutely sure you want to do this? You know that some boxes, once opened, can't be closed again."

"I know," I said. "But I think I have to. I have to know the truth before I can decide whether to publish." I pulled the envelope from my pocket and took out the two newspaper clippings. Therese took them with shaking fingers, touching the photo of her and Isabelle with Matthew. Then she saw the second clipping about the inquest and stilled.

"You want to know how Matthew died."

"I want to know everything. Who was he? Matthew Robertson, I mean? Nathaniel's journals said... he was your, well, suitor, I guess? Before Uncle George?"

My great-aunt sighed again. "Suitor. I suppose he was. But back then... He was... everything to me. Until Isabelle stole him away."

"They had an affair?" I felt cold just saying the words. *Perhaps I walked in on them: Therese's beau and my wife, kissing.*

"Isabelle... she hated that I was younger, prettier, than she was, then. That all the men who'd been dancing attendance on her in London were suddenly lining up to talk to me once I arrived at Rosewood. And that even Nathaniel wanted to talk to me, his sister, about things that mattered."

"She was jealous?"

"She was Isabelle. Same as always. The world had to be about her. So she stole him away."

"Just like in *On A Summer's Night*," I murmured, and Therese gave me an amused smile.

"You noticed that too, then? When that book came out... that was when Isabelle started getting nervous. And when Nathaniel announced that he was publishing his memoirs, well. I think it pushed her over the edge."

"But at the end of the book... Ursula. She pushes Sebastian over the edge of the cliff after they fight. Do you think..." I couldn't say the words. I could hardly think them.

"Do I think Isabelle pushed Matthew?" Therese shook her head. "I think Nathaniel was just telling a good story. As far as I know, the coroner's verdict is correct. He was drunk and he fell. As simple – and as horrible – as that."

"You weren't there?" I'd hoped that Therese might have seen something – even if it was just my grandparents a safe distance away when they heard Matthew's scream.

Therese looked away. "I was young. And there was a lot of champagne at that party. I remember Nathaniel and Isabelle arguing about Matthew, and realising what was going on – that the man I loved had fallen for my sister-in-law. I walked out, grabbed the nearest glass, and got very, very drunk. The next thing I remember is waking up in bed the next morning with a splitting headache. I never even heard him scream." She sniffed at that, and I realised that, for Therese, this wasn't just history. It was her life – her loves, her losses.

Still. My best shot at a witness, and she'd been passed out drunk.

Which only left me with Isabelle.

"Tell your father I don't think I'll join you all for meals today," Therese said, getting shakily to her feet. "I don't feel quite right."

Now I felt *really* guilty. "Do you want me to bring you something? Soup or sandwiches at lunchtime?"

Therese shook her head. "I'll be fine. I have a fully stocked kitchen here, you know. I just... I just feel old, today. A day in bed and I'll be back to myself."

I nodded and watched her make her way slowly to the bedroom, past a mishmash of outfits and accessories from the past hundred years. I thought I knew which decade Therese would be dwelling in today.

Meanwhile, I had to find my way back to the present. By way of 1968.

Isabelle was in the Orangery when I found her, arranging another condolence bouquet into a vase. She didn't look up as I came in.

"So, you've found it then." She dropped the last of the flowers onto the low table between the sofas and stared out of the glass at the woods beyond. "I can't imagine that you would have sought me out, otherwise."

I sat gingerly on the edge of the other sofa. "I spoke to Therese. She told me a little about what happened the summer you moved in here. I wanted to be sure that I had the story straight before..."

"Before you confronted me." Isabelle looked up at me sharply, then. "I know what she will have said. I don't care. I want to know what my husband wrote about me. About me... me and Matthew."

"He didn't." It came out more bluntly than I'd intended. "There was nothing in any of his notes about you having an affair. He hid his journal from that year. And when I found it... He wrote everything that happened at the party where Matthew died as a story. With two possible endings." In fact, I was starting to think that even *he* didn't know what happened that night. Wouldn't it be just like Nathaniel to set us up a murder mystery?

Isabelle's face turned grey under her make-up. "What? Then why…?"

I still wasn't feeling great about this part, so I looked down at my shoes as I replied. "We knew that there was something you were afraid would be in there. I needed to know what it was, before I could make a decision about whether or not to publish the memoirs. When we couldn't find it…"

"You went and asked Therese." My grandmother's mouth twisted into a bitter smile, something I'd never seen on her face before. "And of course she was more than happy to give me up. She's been waiting forty-eight years for the chance to make me pay for what I did. So. What are you going to do now?"

"Was Granddad really never unfaithful to you?" I asked, tangentially. "The diaries say not, but…"

"No." Isabelle sighed. "In fact, I imagine that everything he has written there is the truth. It was messy and ugly enough without any embellishment."

That much I could agree with. "If he wasn't, then…" I trailed off, unable to finish the question. This was, after all, still my grandmother's sex life I was talking about.

"Because I knew he could. Because I worried he might. Because I was twenty-four and insecure and there were all these beautiful girls who wanted my husband." She turned back to look out of the window, then went on. "Because I was jealous. Because even after everything – the grand romance, the book, the elopement, the house – he still spoke to his little sister more than me. I started to think that maybe all it had ever been was a literary pretension – that he loved the story of loving me more than the person I was."

"He didn't." The power with which Nathaniel Drury had fallen in love with his wife was obvious in every scrap of paper he'd left behind, even if it hadn't always been clear by his actions.

"I know that now." Isabelle's voice was sharp. "Fifty years together – don't you think I learned something about the man? But back then…"

"Why Matthew?" Even Therese, who had clearly adored the man, hadn't really said much of substance about him. From Nathaniel's journal, he appeared the sort who showed up for parties, caused trouble and left before anyone had to deal with the fallout.

"If I'm honest, I don't even know any more. Partly because he was making a play for Therese, and I blamed her for the lack of conversation between me and my husband. Partly because he was easy, and I knew it would mean nothing at all to either of us in six months' time. It would only matter to Nathaniel."

"And yet, he left it out of his notes for the memoirs. He barely even mentioned it in his journal." Which still baffled me, a little. Yes, I could understand Nathaniel wanting to spare Isabelle the scandal, or even not wanting his own cuckolding to be common knowledge. But then why wouldn't he tell Isabelle that he wasn't including it? Why wouldn't he set her mind at rest?

"Yes." Isabelle picked up a rose stem and twirled it between her fingers. "I can't quite decide if that was a kindness, or a cruelty. After all, he obviously wanted me to worry, to reflect on my sins, or he would have told me. The fact he'd made plans for what would happen in the event of his death… He obviously suspected it was coming. He must have known how I would react." She touched a thorn with her fingertip. "Perhaps he wanted me to confess."

"I'm starting to think he wanted us all to confess," I admitted. "That he wanted us to get all our secrets out in the open so we could see that we were none of us blameless."

"And then we'd all forgive each other? Have a big group hug?" Isabelle had one incredulous eyebrow raised. "Do you really believe that?"

"I think he wanted Ellie and me to make up."

"He wanted you to stop lying to yourself," Isabelle said bluntly. "Nathaniel always said that fiction could not exist without truth. You have to know yourself first."

"Maybe he's right," I conceded. I'd certainly done a lot of introspection over the last few weeks. But it wasn't something I really wanted to discuss with Isabelle. "Will you tell me what happened? The night Matthew died?"

Isabelle sighed, her gaze still focused somewhere past my head. Somewhere in the past, I suspected. "It was the night that Nathaniel found out about us. He was in a rage, of course. I tried to keep him calm, to keep what was happening from all the guests. And that, at least, I managed. Everyone just assumed it was the drink – and God knows there was plenty of that." She shook her head and looked at me again. "Anyway. He confronted Matthew, tried to throw him out of the house. There was yelling, and Therese overheard us all arguing, realised what had happened."

"She said she walked out and got drunk."

"Yes. And Matthew went back out to the party, and Nathaniel and I went back to arguing. It wasn't until later…" She swallowed, looked away.

"I'd gone outside to get some fresh air. I walked around to the front of the house, and I saw them."

"Them?"

"Matthew. And Therese. He tried to kiss her, and she struggled, pushed him away. He staggered back, then lurched towards her again. I started running, trying to get to them, and the pillars blocked my view, just for a moment. But then there was a scream, followed by the most awful silence."

"*Therese* pushed him? But... she said she was passed out drunk!"

"I don't know. When I reached them... they were both on the ground, Therese on top of Matthew. His head was cracked open; there was blood everywhere. Therese was barely conscious, but I managed to get her up. I dragged her into the shadows before Nathaniel came bounding out the front door, followed by the rest of the party. We escaped round the back of the house, and I got her up to her bedroom, into bed, before I rejoined the party."

"So, Nathaniel really didn't know what happened?"

Isabelle shook her head. "Later, he saw blood on my dress. I'd not noticed it, in the dark and the chaos. But... he saw it. And I think... I think he thought I killed Matthew."

I stared at her. "You never told him the truth?"

"How could I?" Isabelle asked. "When Therese woke up the next morning she remembered none of it. And even if she had... Nathaniel idolised his little sister. If he thought, for a moment, that she might have killed Matthew, it would have broken him. And I don't know that she *did* kill him. They were both drunk. Chances are it was an accident. He slipped and pulled her with him, or vice versa. I don't know. I only know that I didn't kill him."

So nobody knew the truth. I didn't know if that made things better or worse.

For forty-eight years, Isabelle had been protecting Therese, and Nathaniel, and they never even knew.

"Besides," Isabelle went on. "I owed her… something. For what I did to her and Matthew. This was a secret I could keep."

"And one I can, too." I'd have to tell Edward the truth, I knew, but since the truth was that nobody *knew* the truth, and that Nathaniel had known even less than us, I felt on solid ground. As long as Isabelle agreed. "So, what do you want me to do about the memoirs now? Publish or not?"

Nathaniel hadn't known what happened, despite his fictions. There was no story to tell, beyond the one he told me in the tree house, his last day on earth. But Isabelle's affair… That would hurt her, if the world knew.

"Me?" Isabelle raised both eyebrows, this time, perfecting her 'artfully surprised' look. "Darling, I believe the decision was left to you. And to Edward."

"Yes, theoretically. But I'm not going to publish things that make my family unhappy."

That gave her pause, and she studied me for long moments before saying, "No. You should publish. Publish everything. If we are going to do this, then we are going to do it properly. A true history of the family."

"Warts and all," I murmured, with a smile, getting to my feet. Adultery, betrayal, secrets and lies, just like all of Nathaniel's novels. Just as long as it didn't include murder. "Okay."

"Just one thing, darling," Isabelle said, as I headed for the door. I turned back to face her. "What about your own truths?"

"You mean Ellie?" I asked, feeling colour rising to my cheeks. That story would not be pleasant to write. But Isabelle was right, just as Edward had been. If we were telling one truth, we had to tell them all.

"Not necessarily. I was thinking more about Edward, actually."

"Edward?" Now I was very confused. "He's left, I think. Ellie said his car had gone."

"He'll be back," Isabelle said, with more confidence than I had. "So, when are you going to tell him the truth?" And before I could interrupt, tell her that he already knew about me and Greg, she went on. "When are you going to tell him you're in love with him?"

Edward didn't come home at all that night. I skipped dinner and holed up in the Yellow Room, sitting out on the balcony, watching the driveway in case he returned. As I sat, I relived the day over and over in my mind, telling the story a dozen different ways, before settling on the truth. The bare facts of what had happened were more than enough to tell me what I needed to do next. Especially my grandmother's parting words:

When are you going to tell him you're in love with him?

Was I? I considered, stretching my story to encompass everything from our first meeting, up until the moment he'd walked out that afternoon. But even that wasn't enough to give me my answer, so I pushed it further, out into the future, trying to imagine Rosewood without Edward. My life, without him in it.

No. That was unacceptable.

Love isn't roses. Of all people, it was Greg's words that came back to me now. *It's sticking around to fix things, even when it's the hardest thing in the world to do.*

Like he'd done. Like my father had done, sticking with my mum even though it meant giving up everything he'd worked for. Like Isabelle, hiding the truth from Therese and Nathaniel to protect their happiness.

Except Edward had left Rosewood. I frowned. That didn't fit. He'd stayed through everything else. Through my grandfather's quirks and rages, through the Golden Wedding, through Nathaniel's death, through Isabelle's crazies, through my stories and lies... He'd been there for me, every moment, ever since I arrived home. Even though I was the last person he wanted to fall for. After all, I'd already done everything he was afraid of to my own sister. He *had* to know I was capable of betraying him the same way his ex had.

I wouldn't, though. I knew that with a bone-deep certainty that no story could shake. I wasn't that Saskia any more. I was a different me.

And the moment Edward came home to Rosewood, I was going to prove that to him.

When darkness fell, I nipped to the study and grabbed a blank notebook and the orange jumper from Nathanial's chair to keep me warm, and returned to my seat on the balcony. Then, wrapped up in wool and the fading scent of pipe smoke, I started to plan. If I wanted to start again and work out what I really wanted out of my life, there were some discussions I needed to have first – with myself, and with others.

Turning to a clean page, I began to scribble down the most pertinent points.

One. Decisions to make: What do I want to achieve in the next year?

Put like that, it was almost easy. I wanted to write Nathaniel's memoirs, just like he'd asked. I wanted to make up with Edward. And, most of all, I wanted to make things right between me and Ellie.

But Edward's words were sticking with me, no matter how much I wished I could ignore them. Was I just playing make-believe? Pretending that things could ever be okay between me and my sister again? Pretending that I was capable of writing the memoirs the way Nathaniel would have wanted?

He was right about me hiding the truth from him – and myself. Who was to say that he wasn't right about everything else?

I slumped down in my chair, and something on the dressing table caught my eye. Maybe I already had the answer to my questions – the letter from Ellie, addressed to me, that I'd been too cowardly to read until now. I stood, crossed the room, and picked it up, holding the stiff paper between my hands as if I could weigh the contents.

If I really was going to face the future honestly, to try and live in the real world, rather than my own, comfortable, fantasy version, surely this was the place to start?

Closing my eyes, I slit the envelope open with my fingers, and prepared to change my life.

Chapter Thirteen

*Every new story, every blank page, is a
chance to create a whole new self. A new
persona to try on, try out, and discard at the
end of the story.*

*A writer lives more lives than any normal
person can dream of, lives them with more
life – and with more love.*

From the notebooks of Nathaniel Drury

Ellie was in the kitchen, alone, when I found her the next morning. The others must have all already breakfasted, but after an emotional night reading, thinking and desperately trying to plan, I'd slept in. And when I woke up, I realised what I should have known from the start: I needed help.

It was time to break the truce. Time to deal with everything we'd been ignoring and see what happened next. Because something needed to change if we wanted to move on.

And I really, really did.

"Did you hear?" Ellie asked, not looking up from the cookery book in her hands. "Isabelle has decided to throw a proper wake for Nathaniel, here at Rosewood, tonight."

"With guests?" More people. Just what I didn't need right now.

But Ellie shook her head. "Just the family. She says that with it being the first of September tomorrow, it's like we're starting a whole new year. Whatever you said to her about the memoirs, it seems to have worked. She positively bounced down to breakfast this morning, like a huge weight had been lifted. Same with Mum, since she read that clipping."

That was something, at least. Something good that I'd managed while I was home. Isabelle would grieve for Nathaniel for the rest of her life; I knew that. But at least she had let some of the guilt go.

I wondered if I'd ever be able to do the same.

Pulling out a chair, I sat down. "Actually, I was hoping we could talk." Not allowing myself to think through too fully what I was doing, I pushed the envelope and letter towards her, my heart beating too fast, too hard inside me. Ellie stared at the letter, leaving it sitting in the middle of the kitchen table.

"Nathaniel said he destroyed that," Ellie said, her voice very soft. "I only gave it to him because… I knew if I posted it, that would be the end of us, and I couldn't go back on that. Nathaniel read it, then he took it to give me time to think. To decide."

I'd wondered why he'd had it. Whether he'd read it, before it was sealed, or if Ellie had just asked him to keep it safe. I'd hoped he'd remained ignorant to my betrayal. A sharp pain speared through my chest at the realisation that Nathaniel had known everything. Known exactly what I'd done, who I was. And he'd called me home, anyway. Left me to tell his final story.

Loved me, anyway.

And Ellie had never posted the letter. That had to be a reason to hope.

"I think he was keeping it for me to read." I reached out to take the letter back, but Ellie's hand shot out and stopped me, pulling the envelope closer to her. "I think he wanted me to face the truth about what I'd done." To read the bitter, hurt words my sister wrote and never sent. To understand exactly how much pain I'd caused. Because part of loving me was making me face up to my failures.

Ellie's sharp blue eyes flashed up to catch mine. "And you think you've done that now?"

I shook my head, slowly. "No. Not entirely. I think there's a lot more thinking and many more changes to make in my life before I can do that."

"He was everything I had, Saskia. He still is." The words should have sounded accusing, but somehow they came out more hurt.

"He's not, you know," I said, almost absently. "But that's not the point. You have all sorts of wonderful things, not least our family, this house, a job you love. But I know that it's Greg that means the most to you. And I never, ever meant to take that away from you."

"You couldn't." The words were sharper this time. "He loves me."

"I know he does. You're the whole world to him. And I know now that he never really loved me, no matter what I thought at the time. It was a mistake. A hugely regrettable, ruining lives sort of mistake. The sort I never ever wanted to make again once I left here."

"I should think not." Ellie's hands had crumpled around the letter, and her face was pale. It was possible, I realised, that this was just as hard for her as it was for me. Although not the next bit. The idea of saying the words filled me with dread, but I felt like my insides were turning black and dead just keeping the knowledge inside. I had to come clean, let out all my truths, and find my real self again, under all the lies.

I had to remember how to live.

"I realised, finally... I never really loved him either. I thought I did – I was so sure I knew what love was. But I was wrong. I know better now. It's no excuse – there couldn't be an excuse – but... I think we both just loved you so much, and you felt a million miles away. We screwed up hugely, me more than anyone. Because I was your little sister, and you kept my secret from our parents to protect me and that was even worse. So I'll tell. I'll tell the world. You don't have to carry that any more, at least."

Ellie was quiet for a moment, and when she spoke, her words were barely above a whisper. "I was maddest at Greg, you know. For hurting you. For coming between us. Isn't that crazy?"

My heart ached just imagining it. I put my hand out on the table, palm up, just in case she wanted to take it. I could wait. As long as it took. "Not crazy. It just means you're a far better sister than I ever could be. But I want to do better, I promise. Edward... he said I play make-believe with my life, twisting the facts to make them fit the story I'm telling. I think maybe that's what I did with Greg, and that's why I know I have to stop. I have to face life as it is, not as the story I imagine."

Ellie stared at my hand. "In that case... what's going on with you and Edward? The truth, not the story."

"I wish I knew. Things were... They were great. Until yesterday. But...Edward is how I know that I wasn't in love with Greg. Because I know what love feels like now. And that's why... I know I have no right to ask you this. But I need your help. I need to make things right with him."

Ellie considered me, her head tipped to the side. "Playing make-believe," she said. "That's what he said?"

I nodded.

"I can see what he means, I suppose," Ellie said, her tone thoughtful. "You have always preferred your version of reality to anyone else's."

This was not, I felt, particularly helpful. So I said so.

Ellie gave a small laugh, and just for a moment, pressed her fingers against mine. It felt like absolution, like peace, or the rain after the storm, running over my whole body. She pulled away again, but she was still smiling. "Sorry. It's just, I never thought of it that way, before. That the things you did... You didn't always see them the way the rest of us did."

"But I should have." I tucked my hand back in my lap, still tingling.

"It might have made things easier. For you, as well as the rest of us," Ellie conceded. "But that's not the point, now. You're right. We need to figure out how to fix things with you and Edward. Get you a real, bona-fide happy ever after. At least, I'm assuming that's what you want?" She raised a knowing eyebrow and I nodded miserably.

"It would be a start. It's number two on my list of things to do to fix my life."

"What's number one?" Ellie asked, curiously.

I blinked up at her. "Making up with you, of course."

Ellie's cheeks turned a very pretty pink. "You know," she said, watching me carefully, "as furious as I was with you, especially back then, one thing I was never sure about was whether you were mad at me, too."

"At you?" I asked, incredulously. "Why on earth would I be mad at you?"

Ellie shrugged. "Because I won. Because Greg married me anyway. Because you were cast out into the wilderness, so to speak. I'm not sure."

I shook my head. "I wasn't. Honestly. I was only ever mad at myself."

"That helps, I think." Ellie was still watching me closely, and it was starting to get a little bit intimidating. I checked the clock. Gone midday. That was respectable enough, right?

"You know," I said, getting to my feet, "I think that if we're going to fix this, we'll need alcohol."

I had the fridge door already open and my hand was reaching for the white wine when Ellie said, "Actually, I'm not really... drinking, at the moment."

I turned back to face her, the fridge chilling my back as I left the door wide open. My befuddled and confused brain tried to remember if I'd seen Ellie drink at all since I got home. I hadn't really been paying much attention, but I couldn't remember her with a wine glass in her hand. Not that Ellie had ever been much of a drinker, but she liked a glass of wine as much as anyone else I was related to. If she'd stopped drinking...

"Oh my God." I slammed the fridge door closed, leaving the wine where it was, chilling happily in the door. "You're pregnant." Ellie looked down, but her cheeks were even rosier, and she couldn't hide the beaming smile that overtook her face and eyes. "That's why Greg's so ridiculously protective of you at the moment! Ellie, that's wonderful!"

"We're not telling people just yet," she said, glancing up briefly, then back down at her stomach again. "It's still so early... but we think it'll be due in March."

I crouched down in front of her chair, and took hold of her hands. "That's the most fantastic news," I told her, honestly. "And you and Greg..."

"We're finally back where we were when we got engaged," she said, then corrected herself almost immediately. "No. No, it's so much better than that. We're different people now. Better people, I hope. Certainly happier people."

My big sister was going to be a mum. "You'll be wonderful parents," I promised her, thinking of how great Greg had always been with Caroline, and how fantastic Ellie had always been at being the eldest sister.

Ellie looked up, still beaming. "I hope so. But, anyway, that's still a way away yet. First we've got to fix things for her Aunty Kia, haven't we?"

Aunty Kia. I quite liked that. "If we can," I said, sighing. "Any ideas?"

Ellie pulled a notepad from between a stack of cookery books. "Well, first of all I think we need to make a list."

I thought of my own abortive scribblings upstairs and sighed again. "I already tried that."

"Yes, but you didn't have me helping you then, did you?" Ellie smacked my knee. "So, sit back down and help me fix your life."

I jumped to my feet. "Fine. But I'm having a glass of wine, first."

And so, that evening, I found myself surrounded by the bright, golden colours of my room, Ellie's list clutched in my hand, as I tried to get ready for what Isabelle was calling our Celebration of Nathaniel. It should have been pretty straightforward – after all, Ellie and I had spent hours outlining my plan for the next twelve months: what I wanted, what I expected, what I was going to give. I'd then spent a good thirty minutes on the phone to Duncan, handing in my notice and resolving the odd outstanding issue there. I'd spoken with Dad, once he commandeered the kitchen to get on with the cooking, just as Ellie and I were finishing The Plan, and got his smile of approval for my intentions. I'd spoken with Isabelle, Therese and Mum to discuss my plans. And I'd even spent twenty minutes watching a documentary on the mystery of the crystal skulls with Greg and Caroline in the middle room, and slipped in a few words about what was going on to them in the advert break.

The only person left to speak to was Edward. How hard could that be?

I'd asked all the others not to mention my plans to him, as I wanted to tell him myself. To a man, every single one of them had smiled knowingly, which was a bit irritating. Still, now that I was nearly there I was wishing that one of them, any of them, had been able to spill the beans first.

But they couldn't. Because Edward hadn't been there. Since he'd walked out on me the day before, Edward had not been seen by anyone. Glancing out of my window, I could see that his car still wasn't parked on the gravel outside the front door. It was, I realised, entirely possible that he'd decided he was better off without the lot of us, and resolved to spend a couple of days getting bladdered with a bunch of strangers in the local pub. Or that he'd gone back to London. Or hopped on the Eurostar for Paris, for that matter, with no intention of ever coming back to Britain.

All of which would have been kind of understandable, given everything that had happened. And any of which would make my current dilemma easier to solve – after all, my family didn't care what I showed up to dinner in.

"Something that makes you sparkle," Ellie had decided, and written down on my list, explaining, "You shouldn't really need it – after all, you're being open and honest, you're being firm in your decisions, and you're coming to him to make up. That should be enough. But just in case he's feeling awkward, it's probably worth blinding him with something special. And low cut," she added, scribbling a few extra words on the piece of paper. Looking at it, I realised what she'd actually written was 'wear something that will knock his socks off.'

Which was all very well, but I didn't have anything like that. Apart from when I was raiding Therese's wardrobe, I never had. I simply wasn't that sort of person. I was more of a pair of jeans and heels with perhaps a shiny top except I'd get cold and have to wear a cardigan over it kind of girl. Always had been – especially in the freezing cold of Perth's nightlife.

I sighed, and wondered if Ellie would settle for sparkly eyeliner. I had one of those, at least – even if it had come free with a magazine at the station.

I was just searching through my bags for the aforementioned make-up article, when there was a knock at my door.

"I told you she wouldn't have anything suitable to wear," Isabelle said, casting her eyes over my threadbare dressing gown before pushing her way into my room.

Therese, who had obviously known this for much, much longer than my grandmother, having saved me from the sad state of my wardrobe repeatedly over the last couple of weeks, merely rolled her eyes before handing me a familiar-looking dress bag and a heavy leather tote bag, then shutting the door behind her.

"Well, that's why we're here, isn't it," she said, calmly, as Isabelle sat herself down at my dressing table and started fussing with her hair. "So, my dear, who would you like to be tonight? Twenties flapper? Thirties pin-up? Forties siren? I think we've even got a lovely fifties prom dress in here, somewhere…"

Clutching Ellie's list to my side, I said, quite firmly, "I'd like to be myself tonight."

Isabelle raised her eyebrows at her sister-in-law in my mirror. As happy as I was to see them getting along again, I really wished it wasn't my lack of fashion sense that had brought them together.

"I thought the plan was for you to woo Edward in something spectacular?" Isabelle said, turning away from the mirror to face us.

"We bumped into Ellie downstairs," Therese explained. "She mentioned a few more details from your plan."

Leaving the dress bag and holdall strewn across the bed, I dropped down to sit on the window seat and explained my dilemma. "So, you see, the last thing I want to show Edward is me playing dress up as something I'm not. If I'm going to convince him I'm for real this time, I have to show up tonight as myself. Warts and all."

Isabelle was watching me appraisingly. "Maybe not warts…" she said and then, sweeping towards the door, added, "Wait here."

While we waited for Isabelle to return, Therese began hanging out the beautiful vintage dresses she'd brought with her, hooking each coat hanger on the picture rail around the top of the room. The rich colours and fabrics glowed against the warm lemon walls, and I found myself imagining myself as the girl who could wear them, imagining all the different people I could be.

"You know," Therese said, laying out the matching shoes below each outfit, "A little bit of dress up is nothing to be ashamed of. We all need to be someone else, sometimes."

Sighing, I leant forward to rest my elbows on my knees, coveting the range of handbags – from jewelled clutches to sharp-edged crocodile-skin bags. "I know. But tonight…"

"You need to be yourself, I know." Therese hooked a string of glass beads over the flapper dress. "But, you said yourself the other day, you're not so sure who that is right now. Maybe that's because you haven't designed yourself, yet."

Before I could answer, the door flew open again and Isabelle reappeared, her arms full of slippery fabrics, shoes and bags tucked under her elbows and hanging from her fingers. Behind her came my mother, then Caroline, with even more items of clothing, apparently raided from their own wardrobes. Quite what Isabelle thought I was going to do with a nine-year-old's clothes was beyond me, but I sat patiently as they laid them all out on the bed, organised by item of clothing.

"What am I supposed to do with all of these?" I asked, staring at the vast array of silks and satins and cottons and chiffons strewn across my room.

"Well, you said that you wanted to be a new person, the 'real you'," Therese said, folding a tartan sweater across her arm. "And we all know, the first step to becoming somebody new is deciding what they wear."

"But, that's the whole point! I've been doing that. That's what I've got to stop." I sank back down onto the window seat. Maybe I'd just turn up for dinner in my pyjamas.

But Mum was shaking her head. "No. What you were doing before was deciding what other people wanted you to be, and wear. You were dressing for the audience."

"And now?" I asked, still confused.

"Now, you have all these clothes at your disposal, while you figure out exactly who *you* want to be."

I ran my eyes over the clothes again. One thing was for sure, I wasn't a mini-kilt sort of person. "And you're all going to help?"

Therese shook her head. "You need to decide this for yourself."

"We're just here to make sure that it doesn't look awful," Isabelle put in, brightly. Which made me feel *much* better.

It took a while, and there were any number of disagreements about colour, texture and style combinations. But, eventually, I found the outfit that felt right to me – that didn't feel like a costume – and refused to take it off.

"It's a shame," Therese sighed. "I could have sold that skirt for at least fifty quid."

"I'll pay you back," I promised, absently, running my hands over the rose pink circle skirt, with white roses embroidered around the hem. I loved it; it flared out, making my waist look tiny, and it looked perfect with Ellie's white knit bardot top. I had one of Mum's floaty scarves as a belt, and the top fitted snugly across my upper body, showing off my shoulders, which I knew Edward liked. Elbow-length sleeves, and the most beautiful cashmere. And, most importantly, the whole ensemble looked fab with my beloved pink heels, rescued from mouldering in the attic. Finally, I'd get to wear them. I'd grown into the person who was meant to own them, at last.

"No, no," Therese said, not sounding very convincing. "Have it as a gift."

Isabelle, however, was looking at me critically. "Jewellery!" she said, snapping her fingers.

"Ooh!" Caro bounced up and down on the bed with excitement. "I can fix this one!" In one small blur of movement she was out of the door.

Mum, however, was more concerned with something she'd found under a stack of skirts. "Oh, blast. I forgot to give your Dad his new apron." She held up a long, traditionally blue-and-white striped apron – much more sedate than his usual kitchen attire.

"It's nice," I said, trying not to sound too surprised.

"It's to get him into the party spirit." Mum grinned, and held up the attached party hat, and pulled out the party blowers and poppers from the front pocket. Since it was still nicer than usual, I just smiled and nodded my head in agreement as she dashed out the door to deliver it to the chef.

As Mum departed, Caro came running back in, holding a small jewellery box out towards me. "Here you go!"

I took the box and opened it, a familiar tune ringing out as the ballerina started to dance. I hadn't seen my old jewellery box in years, even before I left Rosewood. "Where did you find it?"

"In my room," Caro said. "I mean, your room."

"It's your room, now." I lifted a pair of silver and enamel earrings from the box; delicately wrought roses to match the ones on my skirt. Nathaniel had given them to me for my thirteenth birthday, when I was finally allowed to get my ears pierced.

Isabelle nodded with apparent satisfaction. "They should work. What about her neck, though?"

"There's a matching pendant," Caro said, holding out a slim silver chain with another rose on it.

"Not dramatic enough," Isabelle decided, dropping it back onto the dressing table.

I left them debating that as I took a look in the mirror. I almost felt like myself again.

Therese had draped strands and strands of beads and chains over the edge of my mirror, and I ran them through my fingers, just enjoying the feel of them, until something silver and pink caught my eye. Untangling the necklace from all the others, I slipped it over my head.

The ball-bearing-sized beads alternated between silver, blush-pink-rose quartz and a clear crystal, and they were strung together with a thin silver ribbon that wove in and out between the beads. It sat high on my collarbone, drawing even more attention to my bare shoulders, somehow. "Does this work?"

The others stopped arguing briefly to check.

"You know, your grandfather gave me those beads for my nineteenth birthday. Just after he sold his first novel," Therese said. I went to take them off again, but she stopped me. "They look absolutely perfect on you."

"Besides," Isabelle put in. "The pink always went badly with Therese's complexion." I winced, but Therese was actually nodding in agreement. I wondered if they'd been at the sherry before storming my bedroom.

"Now," Isabelle went on, standing with her hands on her hips as she looked me up and down. "What are we going to do with your hair and make-up?"

I considered. "You know what? I think I can figure that out by myself." I checked my watch. "Besides, you all need to go and get changed if you want to be ready in time for this party."

The room emptied with surprising speed.

I heard Edward's car pull onto the gravel as I put the finishing touches to my make-up, around fifteen minutes later. Considering my hair, I settled for just running a brush through it so it sat tidily tucked behind my ears. Isabelle was bound to complain, but it was comfortable and easy, and that was what I wanted.

If I ran, I realised, I might even be able to catch him before he made it into the house. This could all be sorted out before dinner. Then, maybe the weight that was sitting on my heart would disappear.

But by the time I made it downstairs, Edward was already moving leftover bottles of champagne into the mini-fridge, and Dad, resplendent in his new apron, wanted me to test the food, and then the others arrived, in outfits of various vintages and styles, and the most I got before dinner was a glass of not-quite-chilled champagne and a whispered "You look gorgeous" from Ellie. Which, actually, was worth quite a lot.

Edward, on the other hand, barely glanced my way.

Still, the atmosphere at the dinner table was the most relaxed it had been since I came home. Everyone seemed happy, optimistic, and genuinely pleased to be together. Which was absolutely unprecedented.

Despite some clever manoeuvring on the part of the female members of my family, Edward had managed to score a seat at the far end of the table, as far away from me as possible. From the seat beside him, Mum shrugged a very obvious apology my way, and I had to remind myself that these people were on my side.

Isabelle had, for the first time, taken the seat at the head of the table, and as we all polished off our venison sausage casserole, spitting out the juniper berries, she got to her feet, champagne flute in hand.

"I'd like to make a toast," she said, as we all quietened down around the table. "This has been, in many ways, an astonishing summer. We've celebrated, and we've mourned. We've lost, but we've also gained. For while Nathaniel has gone, he has brought Saskia back to us, and even brought Edward fully into our little family."

There were tears in her voice, but we all pretended not to hear them. "So, whatever the past might have held, the toast I would like to make is to the future. To all the wonderful things still to come. When the clock strikes midnight, our celebration of Nathaniel's life will be over, but I know we'll all keep celebrating in our hearts. And I know he would want us to move on – to live the most wonderful lives we can imagine. So, to the future!"

As I raised my glass and murmured "The future," I realised that Edward was, finally, looking straight at me.

By the time we'd all polished off our apple crumble and sampled Dad's Polish dessert wine, it was almost eleven o'clock. With groaning stomachs we retired to the sitting room for more digestifs and, in Therese's case, her "only on special occasions" cigar, smoked sitting beside the open window, with Isabelle coughing meaningfully every few minutes.

Ellie and Mum, however, were much more concerned with looking meaningfully at me, then glancing over at Edward. Who was, luckily for him, happily engrossed in a conversation with Caroline that appeared to be about children raised by wild animals.

That, I figured, was probably something that could wait until the next day. And, really, wasn't it more important that I speak to Edward before Mum strained an eye muscle?

"Can I borrow you for a second?" I asked, perching myself on the arm of the sofa Edward and Caro were sitting on. Caroline rolled her eyes when Edward looked to her for permission, so he nodded and followed me out.

The collective sighs of relief from my family were audible from outside the door.

On an impulse, I led Edward through the kitchen to the utility room, where I grabbed a soft pink jacket that I assumed belonged to Ellie, and handed him his own black coat.

"We're going outside?" he asked, eyebrows raised.

I shrugged. "We talk better there."

The Rose Garden was in pitch blackness, except for thin slivers of light breaking over the wall from the windows of the house. Wrapping my borrowed coat around my body, more for comfort than for warmth, I settled myself down on our usual bench, then waited for Edward to follow my lead.

"It's getting darker so much earlier already," he said, still standing. "And chillier."

"Well, the faster you sit down, the faster we can sort this out and get back inside. We absolutely have to be back for the midnight countdown."

Edward sat down. "They do know it isn't actually New Year's Eve, right?"

"It is for us," I said with a shrug. More than that, it was a brand-new start. A new year with no secrets in it. "First of September, that's always felt more like a new year than January did. And this year, we're all starting over, beginning tomorrow."

"Really? And what exactly does that mean?"

Taking a deep breath, I tried to plunge into what I needed to say. This was the only part that no one else had been able to help me plan. It was all on me, now.

"I spoke with Isabelle, and Therese. About Matthew's death."

"And? Let me guess. You don't want to write the memoirs. Or you don't want to include it, if you do."

I shook my head. "No. I want to write the memoirs, and we can include all the details that Nathaniel knew."

Edward raised an eyebrow. "That sounds like a clever way of rewriting history."

"No. It's not." I sighed. "Look, I promise I will tell you the whole story, every single detail, before we write it. But I need you to trust me that the truth is… no one knows for sure what happened that night. The chances are, it really was an accident. And I know for a fact that Nathaniel was inside the house when it happened, and saw nothing. If he were writing this book, that's all he'd be able to say."

"The truth? Really?"

"I swear to you. No stories, just facts." I gave him a half-smile. "And a healthy dose of my grandfather's imagination, as usual."

Edward sighed. "Okay. I'll need to know more, but for now, okay. We'll go ahead with the project. Was that everything you wanted?"

"Not even close."

"Oh?" Edward settled back down on to the bench, his arms crossed over his chest. "Go on, then."

"I spoke with Ellie this afternoon," I began, still thinking the words through in my head as I spoke. "For hours, actually. We sorted a lot of things out."

"I'm glad." Edward's voice was neutral, non-committal, and I wondered if I was ever going to be able to swing him back round to the passion we'd had just a few days before.

"I told her a lot of what you said." I smiled ruefully. "She agreed with most of it." I looked up for a reaction from Edward, but his face was still and calm. "We talked a lot about what I want to do in the next year. Who I want to be."

"Another character?" Edward asked, glancing away.

"No." My voice was firm as I reached out and took his hand, even if my fingers were shaking. "I'm going to be me again."

Edward glanced up and raised an eyebrow. "And what is 'you again' going to do with your next twelve months?"

"Well, first I need to get back to Perth…" I started, and Edward pulled his hand away. I grabbed it back. "Because I need to give notice on my flat and tidy up some stuff at my job and pack up all my belongings and say goodbye to my friends. That sort of thing." He didn't look at me, but he didn't pull away either, so I carried on.

"I spoke with Isabelle, and she's happy for the two of us to stay here while we work on the memoirs. Ellie and Greg are, I suspect, going to be moving out soon – but don't tell her I said that. I think Isabelle would like having someone else around."

"Someone other than Therese." Edward gave me a small smile, which I guessed meant he'd caught the hint about the memoirs.

"God yes. I mean, they're getting on okay now, but that's just today… Anyway, I think it will be a big help having them both around to help identify people and places in the notes, and put things in the right order. Especially now neither of them are hiding anything, any more."

"When there are so many secrets, so many lies, it's hard to believe the truth even when it's right in front of you," Edward said, and I knew he wasn't just talking about Nathaniel.

"That's why I need to tell you some truths now," I said. "So that we can start over tomorrow without the secrets and the lies between us."

"What truths?"

I took a breath. "You were right, when you said I twisted the facts to tell my own story. To make things easier for me to forgive myself. But I'm facing the truth now. I know that Greg never loved me – and that I didn't love him either, whatever I thought at the time. I know that my family aren't perfect, any of them, but they all love me every bit as much as I love them. I know that

Ellie is a better person than I'll ever be, but I'm willing to try. And I know that I'm in love with you."

"You're in love with me?"

I guess I couldn't blame him for sounding surprised. "I didn't mean to! I just... fell in love with you. Totally by accident."

"Well, I'd have hated for you to do it on purpose." Edward reached out and wrapped an arm around my shoulder. "After all, it was entirely accidental on my part, too." Which wasn't quite an admission of love and devotion, really, I supposed, but from Edward it was quite good. I let the warm glow flood my face and leant into his shoulder.

I shrugged. "You're the one who told me to start being honest."

"That I did." He pulled me closer again. "I guess I'll have to live with the consequences."

"I think it's only fitting." I lifted my head from Edward's shoulder to look up at him, only to find that he was already looking down at me, his eyes warm and smiling. It felt absolutely and perfectly natural to lean up and kiss him. And then do it again. And again.

I was starting to think I could kiss Edward for days.

When we finally pulled apart I realised that we were no longer alone.

"If you two have quite finished," Ellie said with a smile. "We're having a midnight feast on the South Lawn."

"We just had dinner!" Edward protested.

"Cheese and biscuits," Ellie explained. "And wine, apparently."

"For some of us, anyway," I said, meaningfully, and Ellie laughed as she walked away – a sound I'd started to fear I'd never hear again. That secret would be out in a few weeks, but for now it was nice to keep it with Ellie.

"I suppose we'd better go and see what's happening," Edward murmured, his voice low and warm and full of promises I really wanted to make him live up to right now. "Before Isabelle sends Caro after us next."

I nodded, and let him pull me to my feet. My baby sister finding me making out in the Rose Garden was not in my plan for starting my new life right.

All of a sudden, I was hit with the strangest sense of déjà vu, as if it were the day of Nathaniel's funeral again, and Edward was comforting me. The day I saw the ghost, I realised suddenly.

Blinking, I stared over Edward's shoulder. "Do you see that?" I asked softly, guiding Edward to turn around, very slowly. Clutching hold of my hand, he gave a very slight nod.

Together, we stared out across the Rose Garden, where Caroline's ghost was picking bright yellow roses from the previously flowerless bushes.

Then the ghost looked up at us, cocked her transparent head to one side, and smiled, a slow, sweet smile. A benediction, perhaps.

Edward squeezed my hand, and I smiled. Apparently even truth has its mysteries.

On the South Lawn, looking out towards the woods, Mum and Therese had laid out the picnic blankets from the summer house, a patchwork of different tartans and textures. Dad placed trays of cheese, biscuits, grapes and chocolate truffles in the centre, while Isabelle carried a wobbly tray of champagne flutes out onto the grass, Greg following with two more bottles.

Edward settled onto the blanket and pulled me down in front of him, wrapping his arms around my waist as I leant back against his chest. The night had turned cooler, but there, in Edward's arms, I felt warmer than I had all summer.

More than that, I realised, looking around me at my family. I felt *home* at last.

I smiled up at him, turning slightly in his arms as the honey-bricked exterior of Rosewood caught my eye. From where we were sitting, I could only see the back and east side of the house: the terrace where I'd drunk gin and tonics with Nathaniel, the Orangery, the kitchen windows… Every light in the house seemed to have been left on, and the yellow glow blazed out into the night from every window.

Every window except one.

Nathaniel's study window remained dark, a reminder of his light, gone from the world, and for a moment the grief welled up in me again, too deep to bear.

"Kia? For you." Isabelle handed me a glass of champagne, and I turned back to take it with surprise.

"Do you realise, that's the first time she's done that all summer?" Edward whispered in my ear, as Isabelle moved on to serving the others. "Given you a drink, I mean."

"I know," I murmured back. "I guess I did something right, at last."

"I guess you did." Edward kissed behind my ear. "Several things, that I can think of."

But it wasn't just me, I thought, glancing back up at the one dark window. Nathaniel had given me this. From his first phone call, through all his stories, the Golden Wedding, the memoirs… He'd given me my family back.

He'd helped me find my way home. To Rosewood. To Edward.

And I knew, in that heartbeat, that I would never need to run away again.

I was home for good.

Epilogue

I find, when making new acquaintances, that everyone believes they know the story of how I met my wife, having read, at some point in their life and for pleasure or under instruction, my second novel, Biding Time.

What I have to remind them, again and again, is that the novel is fiction.

Yes, I acknowledge that the book itself is loosely based on real events. However, I would caution any reader against assuming that they can guess which parts really happened, and which did not.

It is all, I assure you, a fiction.

The scene by the fountain in the town square never happened. Neither did the episode in the Winter Garden – you know the one I'm talking about.

The truth, as it so often is, was much more prosaic, but also far more powerful for me.

And that's the core of my reason for writing these memoirs – not so that people in the street stop assuming that the lies they have read about me are true, but to show the importance of truth in fiction. If the real events had not happened, there may never have been a novel. But, conversely, if I hadn't written a novel, the real events may not have happened, either.

So, pay attention to the truth, and listen to what is hidden in the fiction. For one is useless without the other.

From the notebooks of Nathaniel Drury

Acknowledgements

The Last Days of Summer is definitely one of those books that couldn't exist without a whole lot of other people helping to make it possible. Including, but not limited to…

My parents, always (especially for my Dad's cooking, in this case! And the choice of funeral hymns…)

My husband, Simon, who put up with all the usual crazy while I was working on it, and supported me every step of the way, like always

My daughter, Holly, for being Caro brought to life (despite only being a baby when I first wrote the book!) and introducing me to Fairyland, with all its wonders. You make every day magical

My son, Sam, for brightening every day with his gorgeous smile. And keeping me awake in the middle of the night so I ended up rediscovering the original manuscript in the first place!

My extended family, for every Summer Party, Boat Sunday, Easter Egg Hunt, wedding or get-together that inspired Rosewood and the Golden Wedding

My editor, Victoria, for believing in this book when it only half existed, for risking life and limb to read it while negotiating public transport, and for helping me to bring my vision of what the book should be to life

My marketing guru, Jennifer, for loving the book so much she begged to read the edit letter while she was waiting for the full draft, and for dreaming up so many wonderful ways to get people to read it

My agent, Gemma, for her constant support, cheer-leading and general awesomeness

And, above all and always, my grandparents. Because Saskia couldn't love Nathaniel so much if Grandma and Granddad Whitley, and Grandma and Grandpa Cannon, weren't such a huge and beloved part of my life, even now.